ZOMBIE HORDE

ZOMBIE HORDE

AN UNDEAD ANTHOLOGY

ISBN: 978-1-957121-83-3

Text © 2024 by Tim Curran, James Chambers,
Brian G. Berry, Garrett Boatman

All stories are original to this collection

Cover Art © 2024 by K. L. Turner

Interior and cover design by Cyrusfiction Productions

Zombie Horde end sheet by Michael Squid

Editor and Publisher, Joe Morey

Weird House Press
Central Point, OR 97502
www.weirdhousepress.com

CONTENTS

ILLUSTRATIONS

THE SCREAMING

TIM CURRAN

1

Fitz awoke in the gray light of dawn and another day was upon him. Another day to struggle and survive so he could see the sun set and know he had outsmarted them yet again. It was a small victory but the only victory he knew. Nothing else seemed to matter. They weren't clever. They were just brutal and numerous and fused together by one single goal: they wanted to kill him. But he wasn't going to make it easy on them. No sir.

Not yet, he thought. *Not just yet.* A chill had come in the night and he could already feel winter coming, though, realistically, it was many months off. The leaves wouldn't even start to turn for three weeks or so, by his figuring.

He worked the kinks out of his spine and pulled himself free of the sleeping bag. He found his water bottle and pulled off it.

Some coffee would be good, he thought. "And some eggs and bacon, too," he joked with himself. But not here. He took out a can of SPAM and the remains of the cheddar cheese he had stored in a Ziploc bag. That would be breakfast. He pulled on his scuffed cowboy boots and scratched his leg through his greasy jeans. He stood up in the belfry, which was about ten feet square, the bell long gone. He lit a cigarette and leaned against the ledge that looked out over the church roof on one side and

1

the streets below on the other, three stories beneath him. He dragged off his cigarette and watched them moving through the streets. It was like an image from Bosch or Bruegel the Elder, a medieval hell—wrecked cars, shattered windows, buildings gutted by fire, scattered bones and animal hides, garbage and body parts rotting green in fetid heaps. And wandering amongst it all like lost souls across the scarred landscape of hell were the Screamers. He wanted to kill them all almost as much as they wanted to kill him. Had this been a movie or a paperback, he supposed he would be up in the belfry with a sniper rifle picking them off. He chuckled under his breath at the very idea. That would be like waving a flag and saying, *Here I am!* And he had no intention of doing that. As he smoked, he envisioned his life as a movie or a paperback. It gave him pleasure because fantasy life was really all he had by that point.

Imagine, he thought. *Just Imagine.*

Sure, it was easy enough. He was one of these amazingly-prepared survivalist types. He had a bunker stockpiled with food and emergency supplies. He had access to a Humvee, maybe two or three of them. He had a couple hot girls with him. And weapons? Shit, he had machine guns and rocket launchers and grenades and flamethrowers. And … *yeah* … he knew how to use them because he was an ex-Green Beret or Navy SEAL or something—trained to survive, trained to kill, badass to the core. He giggled.

Ah, if only life were a movie or a paperback. What the writers never took into consideration was that the chances of someone like that surviving the plague were infinitesimal. They got infected like everyone else and became something less than human. When you took the population at large and rolled the dice, chances were the guy who survived would be an ordinary schlub like him. A guy with no experience in fighting, surviving, or kicking ass. A guy with no access to military-grade weapons or vehicles. That was the sad fact of the matter. He would have loved to have a machine gun (not that he would have known how to use it) or an assault vehicle, but Fate had decided that its apex survivor would have absolutely no useful skills or equipment. He would not be a comic book hero brandishing an AK-47 in one hand and a samurai sword in the other. No, no, no. Fate had selected a perfectly ordinary guy who drove a pickup and had nothing more deadly at his disposal than a baseball bat.

That's what Fate wanted.

She wanted a guy like him who could carry forth the human race or let it end depending on his cunning, his endurance, and his will to survive. She wanted him to live by his wits as his ancestors had. Because everything he needed was out there, it was just a matter of finding it, stealing it, or making it himself. That's how it was. And if he didn't like that, too fucking bad. No survivalist mentor was going to find him and educate him on the finer points of staying alive in the post-apocalyptic world. It was all on his shoulders.

"Day one," he said under his breath. "Day one. The past no longer exists. There's only the future."

If any of that was meant to encourage him or inspire him, it fell flat. The very idea of survival was grim and overwhelming. There was today. He had enough to get him through today and he had to be satisfied with that.

2

At some point during the night, he had heard a noise which unnerved him. It was sort of a scratching sound and it peeled his eyes open and made him tremble in the darkness. He didn't think it was a Screamer; they weren't known for their stealth. Besides, he was safe in the belfry. The trapdoor had a Master Lock on it and the two doors below that led up were both securely dead-bolted. If it had been a Screamer, they would have had to do a considerable amount of bashing to get through and he would have heard that.

No, this was subtle.

And it wasn't coming from below, it was coming from *outside* the belfry. No Screamer could have climbed two stories of the church and then shimmied another twenty-five feet up to the belfry.

He lay there, absolutely petrified, listening for the scratching that seemed to come and go at irregular intervals. In his fevered imagination, it sounded like a human finger scraping its nail on the clapboarding of the belfry. The very idea of that terrified him in ways he could not completely comprehend. After a time, it stopped. He thought maybe he heard the flapping of wings later, but he couldn't be sure.

It took him nearly an hour to fall back into an uneasy sleep fraught with nightmares of shadowy forms climbing the church spire. Curled up in his sleeping bag, he clutched the .38 Police Special in his hand. He had found many guns in his scavenging, but he liked the .38 best because it was a revolver, which made it simple to use. And simplicity, he knew, was everything when you were in a tight spot.

3

After he finished his breakfast—*mmmm*, SPAM and cheese—Fitz made a mental note that he had to do something about his diet. He had to get more green vegetables in his system. And not the canned stuff he was living on, Del Monte and Green Giant, but *real* greens. There had to be some gardens growing wild about town and he needed to harvest them. Lettuce, cabbage, spinach, snap beans, any of that kind of stuff. Maybe some carrots too. It would be a good idea to save the canned veggies for the winter. Either way, he needed to watch what he was doing because he couldn't afford to get sick. If he got sick, he'd have to stay in one place too long and then the Screamers would get him.

He took his daily vitamins and washed them down with a swig of tepid water. He got to thinking about people who lived in the city and how they used to have rooftop gardens. That was a good idea. Gardening on the ground might be tough with the Screamers around.

He took his little notebook out of his denim coat and wrote:

Veggies—gotta be some gardens around.
Check out greenhouses too.
And rooftops.
Get a book on canning.
Need to learn!!!

With that, he rolled up his sleeping bag and packed his duffel (he called it his "rat sack" because he used it for scavenging). He had the .38 in a holster on his right hip and a knife in a sheath at his left. And his baseball bat. Maybe he didn't have too many practical survival skills, but, man, he sure knew how to swing a bat. That made him smile and he thought about lost summer days playing Little League when he was a kid. Three years running, they'd made the regionals. Never quite got to the Series, but, hey, they did all right. Even after high school, he'd played adult fast-pitch for a couple years and that got him into the minors. Three years in the farm system with the Ironpigs of Allentown. Then he met Dani and she didn't like him playing baseball. All the booze and girls and craziness. He gave it up because he loved her and she was truly and sincerely the only person he'd ever known (besides his mom) that really gave a damn about him. They got married, they settled into uninteresting jobs, but they never had kids. They could have adopted, of course, but it just wasn't the same and as the years passed, they just accepted the fact that some couples were childless and they were one of them. But later, when Dani started screaming, God, he was glad there'd never been any children. Seeing them go like that … *Jesus.*

He policed the belfry area, making sure he'd left nothing behind. He had two more cans of SPAM in his rat sack. He put one of them in a green metal Army footlocker that was bolted to the floor in the corner. It was one of his stash boxes. He currently had eight of them spread across the city. In them were canned and freeze-dried food, airtight containers of purified water, flashlights, waterproof matches, candles, first aid kits, glow sticks, knives, hatchets, tissues, extra clothes, rain ponchos, handguns, extra ammo … In short, just about anything he could conceivably need in a pinch (including bottles of good whiskey in most of them, cartons of cigarettes, and even some weed in case of an emergency).

On his knees, he sorted through the box.

Most items were carefully sealed in Ziploc bags or wrapped in Saran wrap. He checked over everything as he did on a weekly basis. All was dry. Good. He closed the box and secured the hasp, snapping a Master Lock in place. He hid the key behind a loose plank.

It was time to go.

4

He spent many hours worrying.

He was always sure there was something he had overlooked, some insignificant detail that the Screamers could make use of to get at him.

5

They were not especially cunning, but then they were not complete idiots either. They were consumed by the hunt for victims to torment and murder. Once they sighted one, nothing, save death, would stop them. They weren't like zombies on TV. They were fast. They were strong. They were possessed of maniacal, predatory minds that drove them endlessly. They would destroy themselves to get at a victim. They would walk through fire, through bullets, through anything to achieve their ends.

Their strength was not just their numbers but their relentless, cruel hatred of those who were not like them.

5

Fitz made a good day of it. He spent the morning scavenging, avoiding the Screamers, taking chances he had no business taking. He was getting so good at it and they were getting so predictable that he feared he was getting cocky about it. Fate did not favor the cocky soul, he knew. Just when you thought you had everything going your way and you began to exhibit the sin of pride, Fate would throw something at you to teach you humility. It was important to keep that in mind because he and Fate were involved in a contest. He was alone. But Fate had Destiny, Coincidence, and Shit Luck at her disposal, and she could wield them with deadly efficiency any time she saw fit. All he had were his wits, his instinct, and his much-treasured pucker factor which always managed to warn him when the shit was about to fly.

She held the big guns.

Even now in the post-apocalyptic world, he was still swinging in the farm clubs. He had to remember that. If he didn't, he would either become a corpse or a deranged wraith that screamed its mind away.

6

It was funny how he got used to death. How he became desensitized to it to the point that he barely even flinched or raised an eyebrow when he saw it. It was commonplace to find dead Screamers in the streets. Sometimes they were just curled up like dead snakes, hands hooked into claws, mouths open, and eyes staring. He didn't know what killed them; they didn't seem to be damaged.

Other times, he found slimy skeletons baking in the morning light, their flesh scattered in all directions like a blast pattern. He saw it enough to know that, sometimes, the Screamers simply exploded. What the exact mechanics of that was, he couldn't even guess, but it probably had something to do with their rage.

The first corpse he saw was early on. It was on the sidewalk outside his building. This was maybe a week into The Screaming, as it was known. He stepped out, heading to the store at the corner, and there was the body. Some grimy street person who had died during the night. He was lying there, limbs sprawled, eyes wide open, flies all over his face. In his death contortions, he had vomited out some black goo that had dried to a stain on the concrete. The stink wasn't bad yet, but it was there ... a moist and fusty odor that made Fitz's guts climb up the back of his throat like a staircase. He turned away, trying to keep his stomach down. Like any normal, well-adjusted member of society, he looked around, thinking, *Has nobody seen this? There's a corpse here ... There's a dead body here, for God's sake.* But there was hardly anyone out. They were all sick, staying indoors. The light bothered them and the daytime noise caused them agony with their hypersensitive hearing.

Then a voice off to his left said, "I called nine-one-one two hours ago. I'm still waiting for those assholes to show."

Fitz turned and Buff McNeil was standing there. He liked Buff. Buff had played minor league baseball back in the 1950s in Kansas City. He had lots of good stories. He was always smiling, ready to spin a tale or two. But he wasn't smiling that day. In fact, he looked like a doddering, weak-spined old man.

"There's so many bodies now, Fitz, they don't have the people to deal with 'em all. I heard there's corpses over on the South Side that have been rotting for days and days," Buff explained, pulling out his hankie and wiping his eyes, giving his nose a snort. "I never thought I'd see something like this. They say they still don't know what it is. But it's spreading. It's spreading fast."

Fitz just couldn't believe it—bodies in the streets, mysterious plagues/

diseases/outbreaks that could not be identified. What next? Military BioCon units rolling through the streets? It was like something from a movie. He kept telling himself, *It's not happening. It can't really be happening.* But it was. That was the scary part: it *really* was happening. At the age of thirty-three, he watched the world, *his* world, go to hell. More so, he watched it lose its mind, shit its pants, and go completely senile. And in the process, there had been some lunatic intersection of real-world logic and movie logic.

That was the beginning, of course.

After that, corpses went from being some horrible rarity to a grisly everyday occurrence. As the plague spread—and sweet Christ, it spread fast—the machine broke down one gear at a time, one system at a time. City government failed, regional government failed, then down went the state and federal bureaucracy like dominos, one after the other. And in the process, of course, it wasn't just the mail that wasn't delivered or the garbage that wasn't picked up, it was much worse: there were no emergency services. The cops didn't respond when things got crazy and people rioted in the streets. The fire department didn't put out burning buildings. And 911 ceased to exist, as did medical services. Within a matter of months, the world was a dirty, gutted war zone.

A medieval hellhole lit only by fire.

7

Fitz told himself again and again that he was going to take a day off. He had a well-kept 1950s brick ranch (not the apartment on Wessex that he'd shared with Dani. He'd gotten out of there within weeks of her death) that he stayed at now and again. It had bars over the windows (even the basement windows) and sturdy dead-bolted solid oak doors you would have needed a battering ram to breach. He found it while he was out scavenging one day—a tidy, well-stocked house ready and waiting for its owner who never returned. There was even a Ford F-150 pickup in the garage, full tank, good charge to the battery. Whoever owned the house had been preparing for the inevitable. The garage was filled with tools. The house had a good supply of canned and dry goods, bottled water. There was even a root cellar down in the basement you accessed through a carefully-concealed trapdoor. It had a cement floor and concrete block walls and was about eight feet wide by fifteen long. Fitz had put a cot down there with pillows and blankets, as well as a good supply of pickled vegetables in vacuum-sealed jars. There were also lots of books and magazines, which were the only entertainment to be had these days now that there was no power and no internet.

One day soon, he told himself, he was going to spend a lazy day down there eating and reading and taking naps.

It still hadn't happened.

The house was basically his main supply dump. He didn't like to go there a lot because he didn't want to get into any obvious habits that might be noticed. The Screamers weren't smart by any stretch of the imagination, but even they could detect patterns.

And he wasn't about to give them any.

His job was to stay alive. He told himself that if he survived long enough, he might eventually meet some other people, maybe even find a girl who liked him. It was a fantasy but fantasy was more important than ever now. If he had to face stark reality without his dreams, he would have been dead in a week.

And he very much planned on staying alive.

8

Whatever it was, it went fast. Within six weeks of the first news of infection breaking out across Asia, it had traveled the globe and contaminated population after population. The CDC, WHO, every biomedical lab in the world, in fact, went at it tooth and nail but no virus was ever isolated, no bacterium, no strain of fungus, nothing.

People called it The Screaming, which was a pretty good name because when you got it, you screamed your head off. That was late stage, though. At first, people grew tired and listless, as if they had a good bout of the flu. Their temperature spiked. They sweated and thrashed, throwing up anything they tried to eat. They could take water, in fact, just about any liquid, but not solids. Then their hair fell out, not just from their heads but from armpits, pubes, you name it. Even their eyebrows disappeared. Finally, they started mumbling nonsensically. When their eyes changed, going from a serous yellow to a brilliant bloody red and then finally black as marbles, they were gone.

That's when the screaming started.

That's when they went crazy.

That's when they started murdering anyone within arm's reach.

9

That afternoon he got into some shit over on Blanchard Avenue. There had been about 30,000 people in the city before it died and Fitz kept detailed scavenging maps, marking it off block by block in his investigations. He had stockpiled more food than he would ever be able to eat, more supplies than he would probably ever use, but still, he kept searching. There might be something out there he needed and he always hoped he might meet some lone survivor like himself.

Besides, he needed something to do. He had to have a constructive purpose. Without one, he'd probably sit around and drink himself to death. There was plenty of booze around. It was the one thing he found constantly, but getting pissed-up would only make him that much more vulnerable.

And when you were vulnerable, he knew, you were a victim.

On Blanchard, he scoped out a row of two-story clapboard houses that he had not visited yet. He saw very few Screamers and the ones he did see were doing what Screamers did during the daylight hours—wandering about blindly, arms outstretched like stereotypical sleepwalkers, hands fumbling about like those of blind men. At night, they could see very well, but during the day, the light was too bright for them. Most of them stayed hidden, but the braver (or dumber) ones wandered about like B-movie zombies, sightless and disoriented by the light.

If you were careful, you could easily avoid them.

At night, it was a different story.

Fitz checked out the first two houses and found nothing of interest. Oh, there were blankets and clothes, tools and canned food, but nothing he didn't already have. In the third house, he found a treasure trove of glossy porno mags. Hot girls taking it every which way, sometimes with two or three guys, sometimes with other girls.

Fuck books, he thought with some amusement. *Yet another industry that has collapsed.*

He toyed with the idea of taking some of the magazines with him. It was very tempting to look at the girls in them, but that would only make him ache that much harder for a real woman.

As he left the third house, his mind filled with images of full, firm breasts and rounded asses shining with oil, he lit a cigarette and almost walked into a couple Screamers passing by. Two men and a woman. They were naked and filthy, hands reaching out.

He froze in place.

Don't make a sound. Do not make a sound.

They had heard his boots clomping on the porch; they just weren't sure where he was. The two men stumbled out into the street, bumping into each other a couple times and snarling and clawing at each other. The woman waited on the walk.

So get moving, you dumb bitch.

But she was not moving.

She was waiting.

Her head was cocked, her eyes vacant, her hands twitching at her sides. She was breathing in and out, in and out, waiting for her victim because she knew one was near. Fitz figured she had been about forty when the plague got her and she started screaming. She was maybe five feet tall, a Black woman with heavy breasts and muscular thighs, wide hips. She had probably been attractive in life. It was hard to tell now, of course. She was bald like all the other Screamers (whatever took hold of them, they lost all their body hair very quickly). Her teeth were yellow and vicious-looking, her mouth twisted in a canine snarl, her eyes black and glistening. Her ribs were sticking out as if she hadn't eaten in weeks, her skin pocked and split open in places, dried blood and filth smeared over it.

But her breasts.

Her breasts.

They were round and jutting, the nipples very dark and erect. As repulsive as she was, those breasts kindled a fire inside him. He felt himself getting hard staring at them. Some insane, suicidal urge inside him wanted to fondle them. He wondered how they'd feel in his hands, the nipples pressed hard against his palms.

Knock it off, you idiot!

He forced the images from his mind. That was the thinking of a deviant and he was no deviant. The idea of him walking up to her and grabbing her tits was so ludicrous he nearly started giggling. About the time his hands made contact, she would leap on him and tear him apart and then ... and then—

She was still standing there, but she was looking in his direction.

She was not sure he was there.

But she was not sure he wasn't.

Her mouth was opening and closing, lips trembling. That's how they got when they saw you—excited like a cat watching a bird through a window. Drool ran from the corners of her mouth. She was breathing faster now.

Defuse this, dummy, defuse this!

Yes, it was only a matter of time before she walked in his direction and started feeling around for him. He had to distract her. He looked around. There was nothing to throw. Carefully then, he fished a hand into his rat sack and found a bottle of imported olive oil that he had grabbed, thinking the day might come when he could actually do some cooking again.

Screamers had very good hearing.

And this lady had heard him digging in his sack. The olive oil bottle had clinked against the short pry bar he carried in there.

She was breathing fast now. Very fast.

Her mouth was opening and closing rapidly, her body shivering. She was acting like she was hypothermic. She began making sounds, "*Gaah ... gaah ... gaah . . .*" that he knew would soon escalate into a scream if he did not put a stop to it and give her something else to concentrate on.

Hefting the bottle of olive oil, he gave it a good throw and it shattered out in the street.

Her head snapped around and she moved instantly in the direction of the sound, shuddering, limbs quaking.

Fitz took advantage of it and slipped away through the yard, around a shaggy row of box hedges, and into the next yard.

She did not hear him.

He watched her search for the sound she had heard. She walked right through the broken glass. It crunched under her bare feet but she didn't seem to notice. After a time, she wandered off.

He went over to the next house and gathered himself.

Dammit, that was too close.

Watch what you're doing.

10

There was protocol to be observed when entering a house. Going into any enclosed space was dangerous with the Screamers about and houses were particularly bad with all their hiding places. What you had to do was, if the front door was unlocked, open it and kick it wide so it slammed against the wall inside. If the door was locked, you broke a window. Either way, you made a lot of noise. That drew the Screamers right away. If there were any in the house, they would come.

So this is what Fitz did.

The front door was unlocked, so he opened it and gave it a resounding kick. It swung in and smashed against something in there. Lots of noise. Good. Then he waited for a few minutes. He heard nothing. Chances were, the house was Screamer-free.

But there was no guarantee.

Carefully then, his heart beating in his throat, he went in with the .38 in his left hand, the baseball bat in his right. It smelled musty and rotten in there. Most houses had that smell now. It was from food rotting and the occupants decaying. He found one right away in the living room: the corpse of a man in a recliner. He was lounging, feet up, little more than a skeleton in dress pants, a dirty shirt and tie. The rot coming out of him had grown right into the fabric of the chair. His eye sockets were spun with cobwebs. Despite the degree of mummification, he still wore his glasses and had a startling backswept shock of silver hair.

Fitz almost started laughing.

The dead got to him that way sometimes. At first, they had horrified him, but after several dozen cadavers, the fear had lost its edge. Now there was only pity. And sometimes—like now, for instance—there was morbid humor. He had to press a hand to his mouth to suppress the giggles that wanted to explode out of him.

He's like some bad Halloween decoration, Fitz thought. *In fact, he looks like the fucking Cryptkeeper!*

And he did.

The Cryptkeeper made up as a harried businessman kicking back after a long day at the office. The leathery face. The silver hair. The glasses. The yellowed newspaper on his lap that looked as if it had been chewed by mice.

Fitz turned away.

There was something more than a little disturbing about what he was doing. Had he really been desensitized to that degree where he could find a dead man funny? The sad thing was, he knew he had. The realization of this was more than a little disturbing.

But he wasn't there to sort out his fucked-up morals or put what was left of his mind under the microscope. He was there to scavenge. To find things that might come in useful one day. To stockpile them even though he'd probably never use them.

He checked the rooms downstairs and they were all pretty ho-hum. The usual boring canned goods and boxed meals. He didn't need any more Chef Boyardee ravioli or SpaghettiOs. He had plenty of SPAM and Campbell's soup. Too many cases of Kraft Mac & Cheese and Ramen noodles.

He went down to the basement hunting for home-canned vegetables but found none. He did find a nice chainsaw, but he already had two of those and had yet to use either.

Upstairs, there was nothing really worth taking. Secretly, he was glad. Looting peoples' belongings always made him feel like a grave robber or a ghoul. He only took what he really needed or thought he might need.

You've got enough of everything, he thought as he looked out the window of the master bedroom, scanning the street for Screamers. *You're just being a pack rat at this point, a fucking hoarder like one of those weirdos on a reality show.*

14

It was true.

He knew it was true.

But if he stopped scavenging … what else did he have? What else did he really have? Maybe if he got going on the gardening thing, but it was getting late in the year for that. He was planning on whiling away the winter doing intensive horticultural study.

As he stood there before the window, he suddenly became increasingly depressed. He began asking himself what the point of it all was. What he hoped to accomplish. Survival? Yes, but for *what?* Survival just for survival's sake? Alone, always alone, lording over a stockpile of food and goods like a miser? Ten years from now, would he be doing the same thing? Hoarding? Collecting? Stockpiling? Sooner or later, the loneliness would get him, and he knew it. He couldn't conceive of year after year living like a hermit. The idea of it made him picture himself twenty, thirty years in the future, a seriously fucked-up/unbalanced/whacked-out old man picking nits from his beard and coveting all the materials from a vanished culture.

It took the wind out of him.

Feeling hopeless with self-pity over his pointless existence, he sat on the bed, kicking up a cloud of swirling dust. He set the gun down, wondering if the day would come when he would no longer be able to fight against the despair and put the barrel in his mouth.

Shit.

There was a photo album on the bed.

He brushed the dust off it and began to peruse the faded memories of dead people. A man and woman, circa 1960s. He knew neither of them. Photos of them dancing, drinking, and carrying on at parties. The man holding up a steak on a roasting fork at a cookout. Other people raising bottles of beer around him. Wait … now the carefree, fun lifestyle had given way to their marriage and photos of them standing out on the lawn of a house (this house, in fact, before extensive remodeling). Sure enough, there were photos of the remodeling. A new kitchen. The old porch torn off and replaced by a new one. A garage put up in the backyard. And now … yes … the woman was pregnant. And here came the baby pictures. As obsessive as all new parents, they took endless photos of the baby in her crib, on the floor, being held by anyone who came to visit. Time rolled on. The child, a girl, had chocolate on her face as she devoured her first birthday cake. Now Christmas. The family posed before the tree. Fourth of July at a crowded park. Halloween. More birthdays. Lots of pictures of the child being held by middled-aged and elderly people who gradually faded from the book. It just kept rolling and rolling. Girl Scouts and slumber parties and summer camp. Soon enough, the girl was in school and the years swept by. God, now her first prom. High school marching band. Graduation. A shot of her out at the curb, all packed up with suitcases and boxes. Off to college.

Feeling more depressed than ever, he flipped the pages and watched it all repeat itself: photos of the girl with a boyfriend, then a wedding, then children, holidays, her mother and father looking gradually older and more decrepit until they were gone from the pictures and her own children—two boys and a girl—grew up.

That's life, Fitz thought. *That's how it works. The cycle repeats again and again and again. When you're in high school and college, you're still rebellious, thinking, I won't be like my mom and dad. I'll do bigger things, I'll seize the world and make things happen. They'll remember me forever . . .*

Then ... you met a girl and you got married and there were kids and a house and a mortgage and dull jobs that paid the bills and the years mellowed you and before you knew it, you *were* your mom and dad, only it was too late to do anything about it because you were out of time and out of options and you just accepted it, going gray as you tripped steadily to the grave, another fucking cog in the wheel.

Oh Jesus Christ, this is just too much.

He held the photo book in his hands, breathing deeply and feeling increasingly despondent. He slapped it closed ... then opened it again, flipping quickly through the pages in a flutter of motion. There. That's it. Lives lived in a manner of seconds, birth to death, healthy and new to middle age and senility and worm food. That's all lives were. That's all they really were. And as he realized this, as the knowledge cut deep into him like an especially sharp blade, he thought of Dani and the children they never had. He was glad they hadn't had any, given how things turned out, but at the same time, the pain of their loss was denied him and it made him feel worse than ever.

Enough, enough, enough, he told himself. *Get your shit together. Get moving or pack it in and blow your brains out.*

But he wasn't going to do that.

Not until he knew there were no people left. Not until maybe he had some answers on how the Screamers could be in the first place and why he never caught the germ or whatever it was.

There was a reason and he would find that reason.

Resolute now, still feeling depressed and cynical but filled with a slow-simmering anger at the unfairness of it all, he tossed the photo album and it banged against the wall. The noise was loud and echoing in the stillness.

An anxiety began to worm throughout his body.

It rose up and up, filling him, until it became a formless sort of fear that expanded inside him like hot gas. He looked around. His hackles were up, his instincts were alerted. Had it just been the noise of the book hitting the wall or was it something worse? Something threatening? Something real?

The fear was like a ragged fingernail drawn across the nape of his neck. *What? What? What—*

The closet.

The fucking closet.

Oh Jesus H. Christ, I didn't check the closet.

The fear enveloped him now as he saw the closet door slowly swinging open and his trembling hand reached for the gun.

11

Sometimes, like vampires in old movies, they hid in dark places during the day—cellars, drainage pipes, ditches, under beds, and, *yes,* closets—because daylight played havoc with their eyes.

And that's what this one had done.

The door swung open about the time Fitz's hand found the .38. The Screamer was a girl, maybe twelve or thirteen at the time her world most certainly went to hell. She wore the filthy, threadbare remains of a red-and-black plaid hunting shirt and nothing else. It hung on her like a shroud. Her skin was dark with ground-in dirt and

17

dried blood stains, set with scars and pockmarks and what looked to be open pustulating ulcers. She was like a skeleton wrapped in skin, thin, emaciated, but very much alive, breathing in and out with a sort of rasping sound. Like the others, she had lost all her hair, save for an orange-red strand that grew from just behind her ear and hung over her left shoulder blade.

"*Geh, geh,*" she groaned, almost a question: "*Geh? Geh? Geh?*"

This was the prelude, Fitz knew.

She was looking right at him, yet not necessarily seeing him with the sunshine streaming in through the window. She was not certain he was there; she just sensed that he was. He did not move. He did not so much as flinch. Any slight movement and she would be on him. Maybe she looked like a corpse ready for an oblong box, but she would attack in seconds if he made any noise. He had seen it before. They were very fast when they sighted in on a victim.

So he waited, barely breathing.

His heart was pounding painfully in his chest as if it could not suck up enough blood to keep him alive. It was fluttering, missing beats.

The girl stepped out of the closet and the warm, rancid stink of her hit him full-on, making his stomach contract. She stank not so much like rotten flesh but like bile and hot infection.

Easy, easy, easy . . .

She cocked her head, hearing something, perhaps picking up the steady drumming of his heart or the wheeze of his struggling lungs. She was an absolute horror. Beneath the filth, her skin was pallid, nearly gray, with a livid, branching network of veins and arteries that looked almost black. Her face was bulging and tumescent, eyes huge and ebon, the pupils bright red like those of a nocturnal tree frog.

She was making a hissing sound under her breath.

Something was exciting her.

Then, seemingly without provocation, she opened her mouth wide, shriveled lips pulling back from discolored gums and yellowed teeth. She had him. She knew where he was. Her hideous face twisted in a scowl of maniacal hatred.

And she started to scream.

It came out of her like the shriek of a fire whistle, piercing, unearthly, and nearly deafening. "*YAAAAAAAAAAHHHHHHHHHHHHH!*"

Fitz threw himself off the bed as she launched herself at him. From a standing position, she leaped nearly four feet through the air and landed quite near where he had been sitting. As soon as she came down, she began tearing and slashing at the coverlet of the bed, actually seizing it in her jaws and tearing it open with a vicious jerk of her head.

On his ass on the floor, he brought the gun up and fired at her. At that range, it was amazing that he missed her. The bullet came so close to the side of her gleaming white skull that he swore it left a burn mark. From all fours, she jumped up to her feet and he knew he couldn't miss or she'd batten herself onto him with teeth and fingers and never, ever let go.

She let out another wailing scream and it was instantly answered from what seemed like dozens of locations outside.

"SHUT UP!" Fitz heard himself shout. "SHUT THE FUCK UP!"

But that only made her scream that much louder and got the others around the neighborhood worked up into a bestial, howling frenzy. He sighted in on her as she prepared to leap and squeezed the trigger a split second before she moved. The bullet caught her just under the jawline and blew out the top of her head, spraying the ceiling with bone fragments and what looked like red, steaming mud. She went over like a post, hitting the floor headfirst, not two feet from him, shuddering and vomiting out a slimy tangle of black bile.

And by then, outside, they were all screaming.

12

They were all horrible, of course, but it was the little kid Screamers that scared him the most. There was something positively obscene about seeing what they had become, seeing them turned into slavering little monsters with claws for hands and grim appetites, faces pallid and mottled, eyes like black bleeding stones.

About a week after Dani died, Fitz went downstairs to Katherine Pearson's apartment. He knew she had a gun and he wanted it. Katherine was an intellectual, single, a militant feminist who taught art history at the community college. She did not like men. She only tolerated him because she liked Dani. She had a 9mm handgun and she knew how to use it. Everyone in the building was dead or wandering in the streets as a Screamer, so he went to get the gun.

The door was unlocked and he went right in, brandishing a butcher's knife. The stench of decay in there was nasty, but what was even worse were the little kids feeding on Katherine's remains, sucking and slurping at her dissolving flesh, blankets of flies covering their faces.

Fitz ran.

A little girl came after him.

She would not stop.

Outside the door to his apartment, she caught up with him. She dove at him, tripped, and fell. He kicked her in the head. Stunned, she tried to rise, drooling and spitting and screaming. He kicked her again. Then again. But she still kept coming. She slashed at him with her fingers and he stabbed her in the throat. She died on the floor, writhing in her own blood.

Fitz threw up.

Sometimes in his dreams, she still came after him.

13

By the time he got downstairs, he saw five or six of them standing out in the yard screaming their lungs out. Just the sound of it was enough to scrape his nerves raw. Either he charged out there and started shooting or slipped out the back.

One of them, a man with a knife in his hand, saw Fitz dart away from the window. The motion alerted him. He started up the steps. Not walking casually, but charging up them and nearly tearing the screen door off in his wild mania to get inside.

Fitz ran through the living room into the dining room and found himself at a dead end. There was the window, of course, but he could see a couple of kid Screamers out there shrieking at the house.

Fuck.

By the time he made it back through the living room, the man was already through the door. He was a big Farmer Brown type in bib overalls and thudding work boots. A stink of decay, piss, and excrement wafted off of him.

Fitz knew he couldn't play the waiting game, trying to be quiet. Through the picture window, he saw the others making a mad dash for the porch. It was on, it was most definitely on.

The Screamer came at him and he fired.

The slug punched a hole through his shoulder and he let out an enraged squealing. Bleeding but far from done, he knocked a lamp out of the way and came stumbling in Fitz's direction, colliding with the recliner. He tossed the chair out of the way and the Cryptkeeper hit the wall, breaking apart in a cloud of dust and debris.

But that bought Fitz enough time to run past him and down the hall. He saw a bedroom door and went through it, locking it behind him. The door was instantly hit by the Screamer, bashing himself into it again and again, screaming louder and louder with an enraged, cheated fury.

Fitz didn't bother sliding the window open; he fired a round right through it and kicked glass from the frame. He lowered himself out of it just as the door came off its hinges and the huge, porcine Farmer Brown Screamer vaulted into the room, spattered with blood, yellow foam gushing from his mouth.

Out in the grassy yard, Fitz got to his feet.

A little boy Screamer was glaring at him, teeth chattering. He screamed and Fitz shot him squarely between the eyes with a lucky shot. His face exploded off the skull beneath in a meaty spray of gore and he whirled round and round before sinking to the ground.

By then, there were others.

A naked woman with three equally naked children. They ran at Fitz and he popped off his last few rounds, cutting down a little girl with what must have been a lucky heart shot. The others charged forward. The woman had taken a slug that shattered her lower jaw, but that only made her come running that much faster.

Fitz ran, leaping hedges and tripping over a knee-high fence. He needed time to reload the .38. This was where an automatic would have come in handy, he knew, but he didn't trust them not to jam. He had the knife … but to let them get close enough to use it would be suicide.

21

The only weapon he could use was the bat.

Two more Screamers came in his direction.

They weren't sure of his location. They were looking for him, feeling for him, trying to sense his position. Fitz knew he could have fooled them had he the time, but he couldn't play that game. The others were coming. He had to get away. He ran toward the Screamers and they ran at him. At the last moment, he cut to the left and squeezed between a gardening shed and a garage. By the time they figured that they could do the same, he was around the side of a house and into the front yard.

From every direction, it seemed, they were converging. Their screeching was getting louder all the time and coming from every imaginable direction.

You fucked up. God, how you fucked up!

But there was no time for self-recriminations. The situation was desperate and Fitz knew damn well he would be lucky to make it out of this alive. He knew he had to think. That was his edge. They could be cunning, but mostly they were just violent and insane. If he only had the time to think.

A pack of them came running up the street, worked up into a malevolent blood frenzy. They wanted him. They intended on having him. They would jump on him, bury him in their numbers, rip him open, and swim in his blood.

Well, fucking do something!

He had only seconds and he knew it.

He took off across the street and they zeroed in on him instantly, frothing at the mouth and screaming. He dashed through a yard, around the side, and saw a couple more coming down the alley. He was cut off from just about every direction. Sweating, shaking, almost mindless with terror, he looked around.

The pack of Screamers was in the front yard now.

Their howling summoned the others down the alley and three, then four more appeared two yards away.

Shit!

One of them cut off his advance and he cracked its skull with the bat, dropping him. Another appeared and yanked the bat right out of his hand as he swung at her. He stomped her kneecap and kicked her in the face when she went down.

So much for his bat.

Then Fitz saw his opening. It was a stupid idea. More so, it was probably suicidal, but it was his only way out. There was a big maple not ten feet away. Throwing the rat sack over his shoulder, he jumped up and grabbed a stout limb, swinging himself up there. Like a monkey, he climbed higher and higher, making no attempt at stealth. By the time he was twenty feet off the ground, the Screamers filled the backyard.

They screamed and hissed and gibbered and whooped, sounding like apes in the jungle thrown into some psychotic feeding frenzy.

He kept climbing and now the Screamers were trying to do the same. But such was their greed and gluttony, a dozen tried to do it at once, smashing into one another. By then, Fitz spied what he had seen from the ground: an overhang that shaded a small sunporch at the back of the house.

He pawed branches out of his way and shimmied along a limb that was not as sturdy as he would have liked. Halfway out, it began to bend precariously downward. If it broke, there were a few smaller branches beneath it, but he could just about imagine himself falling and breaking through them, landing right in the arms of the Screamers below.

He didn't have a choice; already, several were beginning to climb up toward him.

The limb continued to bend. He was maybe four feet from the overhang. Just a little farther and he'd have it. The entire tree was shaking as the Screamers climbed, more jumping up to join in on the hunt every moment. Fitz's heart was hammering in a steady drumroll, his body greasy with sweat. He had never been this close before. He'd gotten so good at avoiding them, playing on their weaknesses during the day and keeping under cover by night, that it had never been this dicey.

Two feet from the overhang, the bent-down limb made a cracking noise. It was giving. Had it been dead wood, he would have already been on the ground, but healthy green wood had incredible elasticity.

He shimmied farther.

It cracked and dropped down another foot.

Oh shit, oh fuck, oh shit . . .

The overhang was nearly close enough to touch now. Just a foot or so. The Screamers were shrieking and slavering not five feet beneath him. The branch let out another crack and he jumped for the overhang, landing on his belly. He lost his grip momentarily and almost slid right off, but he dug his fingers in, pulling himself up.

Snapping branches off as it came, the first Screamer was at the limb now.

Fitz had seconds, but he was counting on it to give way.

He had two choices: either he kicked in the window and tried to hide out in the house, which would leave him vulnerable and boxed-in, or—

He climbed atop the dormer and used it to get up onto the roof. Just as he made it up there, the Screamer, using no caution whatsoever, scrambled out on the limb and as he reached for the overhang, it snapped from the tree and down he went, hitting two others on the way down and spilling them into the yard.

Fitz sighed.

Now there was no way onto the roof.

He moved carefully about up there, checking it from all angles. No, there was no way up unless one of them came through the dormer window (something which would take some planning but was not beyond some of them). Sitting up on the ridgeline at the highest point, legs straddling the roof incline to either side, he dug out his water bottle and took a good long swig. Then he pulled out a speedloader and recharged the .38. There. He began to feel better. He looked around, seeing nothing but trees and roofs in either direction. Interesting. He'd never thought of living above them like this. Maybe it was worth considering.

Okay, now what?

That was the question. He lit a stale cigarette and listened to the blood-maddened packs below screaming and shrilling. If it hadn't been for them, it might have been nice up there. At least they couldn't get to him. Then again, he couldn't get down.

He shimmied backward and rested against the chimney.

Just relax.

Just wait it out.

In an hour, at most, they'll have moved on.

He had about three hours until sunset. By then, he had better be off the roof or on his way. If he had to spend the night up here . . .

No, that wasn't an option.

He hadn't been out at night since this began.

And he wasn't about to start now.

14

Thirty minutes later, it was quiet.

By then, despite having a sore ass from straddling the ridgeline, he was feeling sleepy. He desperately needed to close his eyes. Not that he would. He couldn't trust himself not to fall off the roof or to let his guard down for even a ten-minute catnap.

He waited another fifteen.

Okay. Let's get to it.

He scaled the incline down into the valley where the two roofs of the house met at right angles to one another. He crept carefully and cautiously until he reached the eaves and could look out across the back and side yards. He saw no Screamers. He moved around the roof until he had scrutinized his surroundings from every vantage point. It looked safe. He saw nothing that concerned him. Just to be on the safe side, he went back up to the ridgeline and, using the chimney, stood up and peered around the neighborhood like a sailor in a crow's nest.

Nothing.

He saw his pickup truck parked two streets away, right by the little park. Damn. If he could just get to it.

Time to go, then.

He saw only one way down. He climbed onto the dormer and lowered himself onto the overhang. He needed to get inside the house. But if he had to shatter one of the windows, it might bring the Screamers running again. That was his fear, of course. The sun was already drifting far into the western sky and the shadows were beginning to make themselves known. He didn't like that at all; he was never out this late.

But there was time, there was time.

The first window was locked, but the other was open. That was the first break he'd gotten since he got to the roof. He slid it open all the way and dropped onto a bed. God, but it was soft. Dusty and cobwebbed, but damn soft. He could have stretched out. It would have felt so good.

Sure, then you'd wake long after dark and where would you be then? A mouse in a fucking snake pit, that's where.

The dust he had stirred up on the bed filled the air and as much as he tried to stop it, he sneezed. Of all things. He sneezed two more times into his sleeve. There was no avoiding it. Even pinching his nostrils didn't help.

After that, he spent a few precious minutes listening and listening. Were they out there? He should have heard them if they were. The .38 in hand, he opened the bedroom door. He saw nothing but a corridor with some cobwebs strewn from the ceiling. A cross-stitched print on the wall read *GOD BLESS OUR HOME.*

Sure, that worked out pretty good, didn't it?

He bit his tongue against the flurry of raw cynicism that filled his mind. He didn't need that now. He had to be positive. There was no place for negativity if he really wanted to survive.

He moved down the corridor to the stairs and started down at a leisurely pace like a guy who was going to get the mail or a snack. Inside, he was tense, his belly filled with tacks, but he refused to let it take control of him.

In the foyer, he waited, peering out the window in the door and seeing nothing that concerned him.

"Do it," he said under his breath.

So he did, stepping out into the world.

15

Fitz didn't know what he really expected, but not this. Not such silence. There was no breeze in the trees. No insects. No bird calls. Absolutely nothing. It was so quiet, it wasn't just silent but like some void where noise could not exist naturally. It was uncanny. It was like ground zero at an old A-bomb test site.

He stood pensively at the bottom of the steps, feeling for something, knowing and not knowing, aware and completely unaware. He moved down the walk, painfully cognizant of his footfalls, which, in the exaggeration of his imagination, were like hammers striking forges.

He shook it from his head.

He had the gun. He would be okay. He moved down to the sidewalk and then out into the middle of the street. If they came for him, he would see them, hear them. They wouldn't be able to get the drop on him. He would walk to the intersection, cross down the avenue and then he should be able to see the truck. Once he was in it and rolling, they wouldn't be able to stop him.

At least, that's what he told himself.

16

He had a recurring dream that he was lost in the city and no matter which way he turned, he could not find his bearings. It wasn't the city he knew, not exactly, but another that had been devastated by war—buildings collapsed, neighborhoods gutted, trees and telephone poles fallen over, houses lying in ruins. Everything was gray and bleak and sort of misty. He wandered and wandered, paranoid and scared of something that followed him, only (in the dream) he did not know what it was.

As it closed in on him, he turned this way and that, but every path and street and alleyway just led to more steaming wreckage.

He saw no Screamers.

But there was something worse and it was after him. He had something it wanted and whether that was his flesh and blood, his soul, or something equally as indefinable, he didn't know. Only that it wouldn't stop until it got it.

He had a gun, but it was not the little snub-nosed .38 he carried, but a huge black metal piece of killing hardware like Dirty Harry's .44. Every time he stopped in his flight, he could hear the thing that trailed him breathing with a guttural, ragged sort of sound like a grizzly bear.

He knew it would show itself and when it did, it was like a writhing black shadow made of dozens of other shadows that flowed along the ground like spilled oil or against the charred still-standing walls of houses. He could not be sure what threw it or what it was meant to represent.

He only knew it was deadly.

That they would meet because it was destined.

In the dream, he would tell himself again and again at this point that he must wake up. He must come out of it because it wasn't real. None of it was real. This technique had worked with other nightmares through the years, but it was powerless against this one.

No spell could break it.

Then, as always, as he moved faster and faster away from the stalking shadow, he realized, to his horror, that he was not moving away from it … but toward it.

In a grassy lot with crumbling, almost gothic-looking walls of buildings hemming them in which looked rather like medieval battlements, the shadow waited for him. In the bright moonlight, he saw that the shape was a very large wolf—its fur was black and glossy, its body rippling with muscle, its eyes huge and green like glimmering emeralds. It looked less like a wolf than a woman wearing the skin of a wolf.

It grinned at him and its teeth were long, sharp, and white as ivory. "*We're both hungry,*" it said in the voice of a young woman. "*And you know what has to happen next.*"

That was where the dream ended every time. There was never any more to it. Sometimes he screamed and sometimes he fell to his knees as the wolf prepared to lunge at him and drown him in its drool, but that was it.

The only constant beyond that was every time he woke from it, his skin was crawling and he felt disturbed deep inside, as if he had witnessed something terrible in the dream that he just could not remember.

17

He had the worst premonition of his own oncoming death all the way to the truck, but he made it there in one piece. It was a stroke of good luck; the second was that he did not see a single Screamer. *Maybe I tired them out.* Which almost made him laugh. He dug the keys for the Chevy out of his pocket, feeling pretty good despite what he had been through. Tired, yes, but certainly intact.

As he inserted the key into the lock, he realized he wasn't alone. He swung around and there was a Screamer. It was the big, burly Farmer Brown guy. He was breathing hard, blood still leaking from the hole in his shoulder, black and red slime gurgling from his mouth and dripping down his overalls.

He was on the other side of the truck.

He must have been hiding behind the bushes.

Fitz just stood there. He didn't think Farmer Brown knew exactly where he was, but as soon as he turned the key, it would draw him right in. Even the subtlest of sounds was enough sometimes.

Fitz thought about the gun.

He could have it out in seconds and waste this son of a bitch once and for all. Then again, the noise would draw others in. He felt the old terror fill his blood and make his heart pound. His mouth was dry. His hand on the key shook. The Screamers were absolute horrors and the fear they inspired could be debilitating, he knew. But he'd been through so much by that point that fear was suddenly eclipsed by anger.

Go ahead, come for me. It can only end one way.

Still, even as the rage boiled in him, fed by frustration and fatigue, he made no sound. Screamers, in general, had the attention span of toddlers.

Farmer Brown stood there breathing with a sound like water gurgling in old pipes. He cocked his head, listening, then he opened his mouth and gnashed his teeth. He did not scream. He simply started shambling away in the other direction.

Fitz turned the key, opened the door, and jumped behind the wheel, throwing the locks. Farmer Brown heard it, turned around, and came right back. He stepped out into the street and it looked for a moment as if he might just go on his way, then he turned and faced the truck, opening his mouth and letting out a roaring sound. His black eyes shined like pools of ink … and he charged.

Screaming now at full volume, he ran at the truck and smashed right into the front end with enough force to rock it on its springs. Had it been a normal person, Fitz knew, they would have knocked themselves flat and been very slow in getting up.

Not Farmer Brown.

He was back on his feet in seconds.

As Fitz started the truck, Farmer Brown came loping around the front end and slammed himself into the door again and again, leaving a spatter of blood over the glass. By then, Fitz had the truck in drive. He stomped on the accelerator, steering away from the curb. He looked behind him, expecting to see old Farmer Brown trying to chase him on foot, as Screamers were wont to do.

But no, he wasn't there at all.

18

Shit.

He was hanging off the box. Since battering the driver's side door hadn't gotten him any closer to his victim, he decided to climb into the back of the truck at the same time Fitz laid some rubber. Now he was raging and screeching and spraying a mist of blood and goo from his mouth. It was almost comical the way he ran with everything he had to match the speed of the Chevy while he hung on with one arm.

Bullshit.

Fitz pressed down on the gas pedal, pushing the truck up to fifty and then sixty. He was going way too fast for the narrow and crowded city streets, but he was bound and determined to throw his rider one way or another.

In the rearview, he saw Farmer Brown was still hanging on. He was very tenacious—he had sighted his prey and nothing, save death, was going to deter him now. Fitz was dragging the bastard, but still, he clung. In fact, he was doing more than clinging now; he was climbing right up into the bed of the truck.

Fitz did some fancy (and dangerous) stunt driving trying to throw the Screamer, but he had swung himself up into the bed now. He was crawling toward the cab window, rising up to get at his prey.

Fitz stomped on the brakes and Farmer Brown was slammed against the cab, then tossed flat in the bed. He rose up right away, ribbons of yellow foam hanging from his black-red gored mouth. He was snarling now, showing his teeth. He dove at the cab, his nails clicking on the window. He threw himself at it again and again, smashing his face into the glass, painting it a horrific scarlet.

Fitz stomped on the accelerator and tossed the Screamer.

When Farmer Brown found his feet, he swayed unsteadily, and Fitz slammed on the brakes, sideswiping a row of parked cars. The Screamer bounced off the cab but this time, the impact created a long, jagged crack in the rear window of the cab.

It wasn't working.

It just wasn't working.

If he slammed the Screamer off the cab a few more times, the glass was going to give way, and then that drooling, insane bastard was going to be right inside the cab with him.

He thought about shooting him, but if he did that, the window would shatter. Then he'd have to find a new vehicle.

"YOU FUCKING COCKSUCKER!" he shouted. "GET AWAY FROM ME! GET THE FUCK AWAY FROM ME!"

Fitz knew he was rapidly losing control of not only the situation but himself. He was raging. He was scared. He was pissed-off. That wouldn't do. He was letting the Screamer dictate the rules of engagement and that was a big taboo and he knew it. He was intelligent; they were psychotic animals driven by some warped, basically fucked-up instinctive drive to kill. Such a thing made them not only dangerous and unpredictable but also rash and stupid.

Play it, play it, he told himself. *Turn this around.*

Yes, that's what he had to do.

He passed by some other Screamers wandering about out in the streets. They got enraged when they saw him pass, but he outdistanced them quickly enough. Then he slowed down. *Okay. Come and get me.* The Screamer grabbed hold of the side of the box and pulled himself up. By that time, Fitz had the truck nearly stopped in the middle of the street. When the Screamer stood up, bare inches from the tailgate, he jammed his foot down on the accelerator and the Screamer was thrown backward. He struck the tailgate with the back of his knees and was flipped right out of the box.

So much for you, bitch.

But as he stared into the rearview, enjoying the sight of Farmer Brown trying to climb to his feet, he made a tactical error. He cut across an avenue and saw it was crowded with wrecked vehicles. He slammed on the brakes, missing a bus, sideswiping a minivan, then rear-ending a little Fiat. The impact threw him forward, bouncing him off the steering wheel.

"Shit," he said under his breath.

Thank God, the truck was still running.

He backed out of the cul-de-sac, bringing the Chevy around, and saw six or seven Screamers running in his direction, squealing with delight. This time, he put on his safety belt. Then he opened up the truck and hit them dead-on, pitching three of them aside and rolling right over a fourth.

Ha!

Except they were everywhere now. They were running out of alleys and coming out of doorways and crawling out from beneath rusting cars at the curb. They cast evil eyes at him, screeching and gesturing and clawing at the air with their hands.

He was in a fucking colony of them.

19

They charged from every direction, shrieking and hissing, converging and filling the streets. To his shock and horror, he saw what he thought must be at least a hundred of them massing like army ants, charging relentlessly forward, baring their teeth and slobbering.

He spun the wheel, wiping out four or five kid Screamers, rolling right over them, the sound of their splintering bones like green twigs snapping. He floored it and more of them massed before him, launching themselves suicidally at the truck. In their reckless fervor, dozens bounced off it but others leaped onto the hood. Two women scrambled up into the box. A half dozen others were clinging to it like Farmer Brown.

More came and still more.

He was in a fucking hive. The Screaming was so loud it was like being in a stadium of shrilling lunatics. They screamed and screamed, beating at the windows and clawing at the doors. For every two that fell off the truck, five more took their place. Several were standing on the hood and kicking at the windshield.

Fitz couldn't see where he was going.

In fact, he couldn't see a damn thing. Their leering, lewd faces filled every window, drooling and spitting and grinding their teeth, splashing the glass with blood and body fluids as they tried to pound and claw their way through. He'd never been in anything like this before. Not so many. Not so damn many.

Even though he couldn't see, he began accelerating the truck because he really didn't know what else to do. If he kept driving slowly, they'd bury the truck in their numbers. So he edged the Chevy faster and faster, sideswiping cars and freeing Screamers, popping the curb once and throwing a few others. Still, their constant maniacal screeching seemed to get louder and louder until he wanted to scream himself.

The battered Chevy bowled over street signs and glanced off fire hydrants, rolling over fallen Screamers and plowing others out of the way. But the riders still clung.

Fitz activated the wipers and squirted wiper fluid over the cracked windshield and finally he could see something. He'd lost the Screamers on the hood, but there were still three or four in the back and one particularly tenacious lunatic on the roof that kept beating at the passenger side window. The driver's side glass was already spiderwebbed with cracks and the rear window was in the same condition.

They were going to get through.

It was only a matter of time now.

His heart pounding, eyes bugging out of his head with sheer terror, sweat running down his face, Fitz took advantage of the situation as he had done before: he stomped on the gas and the truck vaulted forward. He took a corner squealing on two wheels, throwing the rider on the roof who landed on the pavement behind him. Then he hit the brakes, bashing the riders in the back off the cab. When they climbed to their feet, he stomped on the accelerator, tossing two of them out of the box.

But there were others.

All he could really see through the bloody, mucus-grimed, spiderwebbed glass were vague shapes back there. Right away they started beating at the rear window and to Fitz's horror, it came apart and fell into the cab, and then their scaly claw-hands were tearing at him, laying open the back of his neck and tearing bunches of hair from his scalp.

He fought and cried out, trying to get his gun and accidentally stomping the gas. The truck jerked, jumping the curb, and tossed the Screamers back into the box. But as it did so, the wheel spun from his hands.

Shit! Shit! Shit!

The Chevy, doing an easy and precarious forty miles an hour, bounced off a building, struck a bus in a scraping explosion of sparks, and clipped the back end of a bakery truck as it veered off the sidewalk. Then it plunged through a barrier of sawhorses and into an open ditch, flipping over and then over again. The windshield shattered. In fact, it seemed to explode inward in a loose gray sheet. The truck, laying on its side, trembled like it might right itself, then came to a stop.

And for a time, there was silence.

20

Unlike every movie Fitz had ever seen where the driver in a crash routinely was knocked cold, he did not go out. In fact, wired by terror, which was nature's own amphetamine, he remained quite lucid. He was jarred and crushed in the embrace of the seat belt and it felt like his spine wanted to spear out of his asshole, but other than that, he was relatively unharmed.

He had to get out.

He had to get somewhere safe.

But he waited. He wasn't going to charge into another clusterfuck blindly. *Just wait a moment or two, then quietly climb out.* The cab was filled with suspended dust. There was dirt and glass everywhere. The situation was bad, very bad … yet he knew it could have been worse. As far as he could tell, other than being sore, he was uninjured.

That was a plus.

The world was still quiet. Quietly, he popped the catch on his safety belt and squirmed his way free of the harness. The truck was laying on its

34

driver's side, so he had to climb up the seat and knock out what remained of the passenger side window. Something which was easy enough.

He fished his rat sack off the floor. Halfway out the window, he peered around. He was in a ditch that was about twelve feet deep, give or take. The truck sat atop a section of cracked pipe that must have been being replaced when The Screaming got going. Another unfinished project of mankind.

Okay.

He lowered himself off the truck, scrambling away from it on all fours in case it decided to tip over. The ditch was crawling with shadows. Above, the world was looking dim. Sunset was coming. That wasn't good. In fact, it was the worst possible thing. If he got caught out in the streets after dark, he wouldn't stand a chance.

One step at a time.

Looking around, he could see that one of the Screamers was crushed beneath the truck. His or her hand—it looked like a gray, seamed claw—was still trembling slightly. He had a nasty urge to go stomp on it.

But there was no time for foolishness.

He moved across the ditch, finding the smell of cold subterranean earth somehow calming. He began climbing up the dirt wall to the world above.

And behind him, there was a groaning sound.

21

He turned quickly and saw a Screamer crawling through the dirt toward him. He figured it was a rider from the back of the truck. It was a woman covered in soil like a ghoul rising from a grave. She hissed, reaching out for him with a gray hand that was desperate to flense the flesh from his bones.

He had the gun in his hand by then.

She wormed in his direction, her bloodied, shattered mouth opening and closing like that of a dying carp on a river bank. The breath whistled from her lungs. Her back was twisted, her left leg bent at an unnatural angle. It looked as if her neck was broken as well.

But it did not stop her.

She would keep coming until the last drop of malignant life was drained from her.

She grinned, offering him a view of her splintered teeth, the gushing blood socket of her mouth. Her scabrous eyes lusted for his death.

He raised the gun and fired when she was only five feet away.

The echo of the .38 was like cannon fire in the ditch. The bullet was right on target. For a guy who had never shot a pistol in his life, he was getting pretty good at it now. The slug drilled her right between the eyes, blowing out the back of her head in a scarlet eruption of gore and brain matter. She rolled violently for a moment or two, then slid back down deeper into the ditch until she hit the pipe.

Fitz crawled up the dirt wall until he was looking over the edge of the excavation into the dead world of the city: abandoned cars, grimy storefronts, weeds sprouting from the pavement in clusters.

He saw no Screamers, but they were near.

He could hear them screaming.

Night was coming and they were excited.

22

Once he realized the human population was crashing and there was no reversing it, he came up with a simple strategy. He figured if he just kept off the streets, scavenging food and other necessities only when absolutely crucial, he could stay alive for a long time. He reasoned that the Screamers had a limited shelf life. By their very nature, they were burning themselves out. Every morning—after their wild nights of shrieking and violence— he would find a few more dead in the streets. Some had obviously been attacked by the others and their corpses showed evidence of this, but others were simply dead. He was certain if he could hold out a year or possibly two, the problem would take care of itself.

So, at first, he only went out when he had to.

Then he started getting bored.

Sitting around, holed up, staring at the walls … he just couldn't take it. That's when he started getting more aggressive in his daytime sojourns.

And, of course, once he saw how it could be done, he did it regularly and got reckless. It was only a matter of time before he got himself in a real mess like this.

23

As the sun set and a fear took hold that was literally larger than any he had known since The Screaming had begun, Fitz ran. He ran like a rabbit, a terror-filled, bright-eyed, soft, weak, hunted thing. He searched for hidey-holes but in his paranoia, he only saw nests that would be crawling with Screamers.

They'll get you.
You know they'll get you.
Tonight is the night you die.
And you've got no one to blame but yourself.

These were the sorts of things that went through his mind as he crept across the city. Darkness had come and it was blacker than anything he could have imagined. The moon was up but the heavy, leaden clouds blocked its light. Now *he* was the one with the disadvantage.

They could see good in the dark.

But he couldn't see shit.

He was nearly as helpless as they were when the sun was out. At any moment, he knew, one of them would spot him and cold, graveyard hands would seize him. Once he was spotted, they would have him. He knew they would have him.

He moved silently past grimy plate glass windows and ducked behind rusting cars and hid behind bushes. They were everywhere. He could just make out their shadowy forms prowling around him. Sometimes they hissed and clawed at one another. Sometimes they screeched like fighting cats. Regardless, they were not quiet. The night was an eerie place of screams and shrilling cries. The city was a mass grave that had opened and let its dead wander its streets and avenues.

The big problem was the darkness itself.

He'd grown up in the city and he knew it pretty well. Or at least, he thought he did. But his knowledge was of the city in the bright sunshine or lit by streetlights. Now, in the utter darkness, it was an alien, unfamiliar place. He moved down streets slowly and cautiously, but he always saw Screamers or heard them and then he had to dart into an alley or hide in a doorway. When the danger had passed, he would start out again but he had gotten turned around so many times he could not be sure if he was going the right way or simply turning in circles. He had a flashlight in his bag, but he didn't dare turn it on.

The moon, he thought. *If that fucking moon would just come out.*

Then, to his amazement, it did.

It came out and the streets were silvered with its light. Oh Jesus, it was the difference between night and day. He saw that he was not at all where he thought he was. In fact, he was many blocks away. His plan was to sneak over to the house on Ridgemore which was a well-stocked fortress. Once he locked himself in, he knew he had enough stuff to last for weeks or months. But he was much farther away from it than he thought.

Change of plan.

His closest hideout was the church on Brighton and Willard Avenue. It was about three blocks from his present location. If he could just get there and up into the belfry, he'd be safe. The stash box there was well-supplied.

Three blocks were nothing in the old days, but now (and especially at night), it was like running a gauntlet. He would have to be quiet, sneaky, and wily to make it.

After all, he was one man.

And there were thousands of Screamers.

And every one of them wanted to kill him.

24

The first block was easy.

So easy, in fact, that he was afraid he had used up all his good luck in one fell swoop. Something he was almost certain of when he slipped around a corner and saw dozens of them in the street. Not moving. Not doing anything. Just standing there as if they'd been waiting for him. The idea terrified him that they knew he was on the run and they were waiting in ambush. That would mean they had unity, organization. And if they had that, it was only a matter of time before they got him.

Crouched down, he watched them.

No, they were not waiting for him; they were staring up at the moon. Like primitive savages, they were in awe of the glowing sphere in the sky. They seemed so enrapt, he considered sneaking past them. Then he heard one of them growling like a dog and he knew that wasn't a good idea.

He backtracked.

He found an alley and cut down it. He saw several putrefying bodies. The stench was horrible. He passed them and saw an empty street ahead, but at the very end where he needed to go, there were several shuffling shapes.

Shit!

He had to backtrack again, hiking in the opposite direction. Even though he knew he had to keep his paranoia to a minimum, he couldn't help feeling that he was being carefully herded by them. But the idea was ridiculous—it *had* to be ridiculous—because they were nothing but lunatics, warped and mutated from The Screaming; hideous animals but not truly sentient things capable of reasoning.

At least, he hoped not.

He kept moving, putting down one foot after the other carefully and quietly. He was certain they were watching him, that he could feel their eyes crawling along the nape of his neck.

He still had the .38 and knife, but he felt the loss of his baseball bat. Somehow, carrying it as he had in the good old days calmed him, centered him. He supposed, in a way it was like a pacifier to him (one you could split somebody's head open with or smash the teeth right out of their jaws with). He felt oddly naked without it.

The moon decided to hide behind a bank of ebon clouds and he was plunged into an unnerving, seamless blackness. He was completely blind. To make matters worse, it began to rain. The sky grew darker and thunder rumbled and he had no place to hide. At least, no place he was comfortable with that wasn't possibly crawling with Screamers.

Rain running down his face and dripping down the back of his neck, he groped blindly forward, seeing a vague shape before him. A truck.

Well, that was something. It had high clearance so he crawled under it, feeling vulnerable, but at least he was out of the rain.

Now what?

That was a question he had no answer for. Best case scenario, he could spend the night hidden there; worst case, one of them would find him and crawl under there with him. If that happened, he'd have to shoot him or her and the noise would bring every Screamer in a two-block radius down on him.

The thing was, he didn't know how the Screamers would react to a storm. Would they stand out in the rain and stare up at it, transfixed as they had been by the moon, or were they smart enough to get out of it?

There was a peal of thunder that shook the streets, followed by a flash of lightning that seemed very close. The rain came down harder than ever and it was all he could hear as it pounded on the roof of the truck. Streams of water ran beneath it, soaking him and making him more miserable than ever.

Of all nights to get caught out here, you pick this one, he chided himself.

If he survived this, he was taking three or four days off and resting. *If,* that was. *If, if, if.* He thought of Dani and how much he missed her, wishing he could have died with her and avoided all this. All those years he bemoaned his existence, complaining to himself about his shit job and shit prospects for a better life, but Dani had been there. Sweet, pretty, salt-of-the-earth, ultrapractical Dani. He'd bitch about things and she'd say, *Oh, we don't have it so bad, Fitz. We have a pretty nice place, a roof over our heads, plenty to eat, nice clothes to wear. We go out to dinner or to the movies on the weekends. And we've got each other. We've got more than a lot of people will ever have. Look at it that way.* And he tried. Sometimes he was successful, but other times, it didn't seem like enough.

But it was enough, he told himself now as water dripped on him and he feared every passing moment. *God knows, it was more than enough. And I was happy. Even if I didn't admit it to myself enough, I really was happy.*

"Oh, Dani," he said under his breath. "Oh, what in the hell am I going to do?"

And he could hear her voice in his head. *You're going to survive, because you'll disappoint me if you don't. So get to it.* He sighed; she was right. He crawled on his belly toward the passenger side tire. The rain was really coming down. It made a lot of noise. The Screamers wouldn't hear him in it. They wouldn't be able to.

Now you're thinking, bright boy, Dani said.

Yes, there was a chance now and he was going to take it.

25

Fitz waited for the lightning to flash again. Then it did, following a loud, resounding *crack!* And he saw the streets in detail. No Screamers. Acting purely on instinct, he rolled out from under the truck and ran down the street. He put on the speed like never before in his life. He created a scenario that he could understand: he was playing ball again and had just cracked a moon shot—a long, high home run—and he was rounding the bases for the glory of home plate, a real four-bagger, as it was known. He made first and now he was running for second, which was the next street over.

Push it, push it, he told himself as the rain hammered down and the lightning flashed, strobing wildly now.

He made second base, panting, but feeling better than he had in a long time. Now to the next street, that was third base. He kept pushing, running like he hadn't in years. In the flashing light he saw nothing but emptiness and pooling water, abandoned cars rusting at the curb.

Come on, come on, you can do this!

He made third, which was Willard Avenue. Home was just ahead now: the intersection of Brighton and the church belfry where he could spend the night in safety and relative comfort.

Do it, do it!

There was Brighton. He was going to do this. He was really going to do this. Though his lungs were aching and his limbs were sore, he poured it on. Nothing could stop him now. Then, as he rounded the corner, he saw two Screamers waiting for him in the lightning flash. The gun was in his hand and as the lightning flashed again, he zipped right past them and they weren't even aware of it.

Home base.

He jogged through the courtyard of the church, unlocked the front door with the keys from his rat sack, doing it completely by feel, then he was inside and the door was locked behind him. On his knees, gasping for breath, he rested for a minute that became two and three and finally five. Then he slipped quietly through the doors to the belfry, locking them carefully as he went. Then, he was through the trapdoor and it was closed, Master Lock in place.

"Not so bad," he said. "Not so bad at all."

The belfry was dry because of its overhanging roof. That was a plus. He unlocked the stash box, drank some water, and got out of his wet things and into some dry clothes. That was better. At least he wasn't shivering now. He ate some cold food, took a belt of Jim Beam, and had a cigarette. He unrolled the spare sleeping bag and crawled inside with the .38 still in his hand.

It was some time before he closed his eyes.

But it was the best sleep he could remember having for a long time.

26

He kept his word: for three days, he did nothing. He hid out in his fully-stocked ranch house with its heavy doors and bars over the windows and he lay around reading his favorite books—Uecker's *Catcher in the Wry* and Kahn's *The Boys of Summer*—and doing little more than eating, drinking good booze, and taking a lot of naps. And, of course, spending more than a little time feeling sorry for himself.

Once again, he got bored.

The four walls seemed to be pressing in on him and all he could think of was what had been and would never be again: Dani, his old life before the Screamers, his boyhood, baseball games, wild times with the Ironpigs, on and on and on, reminiscing and living in the dusty past like an old man in a nursing home. He began having imaginary conversations with people who were long dead and fantasizing that Dani had never died and what their life would be like now. He spent an inordinate amount of time trying to remember the lyrics to songs he had not heard in years and the plots of old TV shows he had not seen since he was a kid, and attempted to recall in detail chats he'd had with his mom and dad and friends until he just couldn't take it anymore.

There's not necessarily peace or contentment in being safe and snug, he told himself. *If you don't have something to challenge yourself with, you're going to go senile long before your time and get lost in your memories and never get out of them. You'll drink yourself silly every day and your brain will go to mush until you actually start believing that Dani and everyone else are still with you. Mental deterioration will set in and you'll be as crazy as a loon until the day comes when you blow your brains out.*

Is that what you want?

Is that really what you want?

And, no, it wasn't. He wanted to live, to thrive. He wasn't so far gone that those things held no attraction for him. The problem was, he just wasn't sure what he was living *for.* There was no light at the end of the tunnel, no carrot at the end of the stick.

He needed something.

He needed someone.

He needed interaction with another human being and all that entailed. He needed someone to care about besides himself, someone to protect and live for, the welcome distraction of an ordinary friendship or relationship.

So, get out there then.

Get back at it.

Don't let those fucking Screamers, those goddamn muck heads, force you into hiding like a scared little rabbit. Get out there and do what you've been doing—scavenge, look for signs of other people, find them if they exist, but don't give up. Not yet.

With that in mind, he knew it was time to get out into the world. He was going to go out again, only this time he was going better armed and he was going to be smarter.

There was no choice in the matter.

27

He went at it with a vengeance, day after day after day, investigating one house after another, searching, sniffing around, looking for something he could use or signs of recent occupation by normal men and women. He found nothing and his despair not only increased, it escalated.

He found the waterlogged corpses of a woman and a little girl floating in the flooded basement of a house. They were in such a state of decomposition that it was hard to know if they had been Screamers or not. But it did look like they still had hair, which was a good sign that they might have been normal.

He went through the rest of the house, searching for anything that might give him a clue, but there was nothing. The house had been gradually falling apart for some time, the walls soft with wood rot, green mildew slicked over everything. He found magazines that were bleached and swollen, books that were soggy and moldering. Water dripped from the bowed ceiling, there were holes rotted into the floor.

Although it wasn't remotely safe in there, the entire house appearing to be on the verge of collapsing, he stayed for some time, studying the darkness and smelling the decay, feeling trapped in a black vacuum of nothingness, a mold-encrusted casket that threatened to bury him alive at any moment.

After a while, he forced himself to leave, still wondering about things.

Depressed but undeterred, he explored more houses and found nothing of any interest. Most appeared to have been abandoned since The Screaming began or, at least, shortly afterward. He found a nice Cape Cod behind a wrought iron fence that was well-supplied—clothing, canned food and dry goods, guns and ammunition, green metal footlockers of survival gear and medical supplies. Somebody had stockpiled a lot of stuff there. That gave him hope. The only problem was that everything was covered in a layer of undisturbed dust. Even the floors were dusty and there was not a single track in any of it, save for the ones he made.

He went upstairs and it was the same. Apparently, even the Screamers hadn't bothered visiting this place in many, many months. He found a big telescope in a room that must have been some type of office at one time. He dragged it over to the window and looked around the city.

He could see houses and streets four and five blocks away in great detail. Screamers blinded by the daylight wandered about helplessly, guiding themselves by feel along the walls of buildings. At that distance, they didn't look so much dangerous as pathetic.

Wrecked cars. Refuse and corpses in the streets. Rubble. More Screamers. Half-burned houses. Storm-blasted trees blocking intersections. Flocks of birds pecking away at dead Screamers.

It was hopeless thinking he'd find someone out there, some sign of orderly human life.

He zeroed in on a street three blocks over. He could see a little outdoor mall that Dani used to love. The windows were all dirty and plastered with leaves. A Screamer came out from behind a minivan and slowly approached it.

Wait.

It was a woman, but she wasn't stumbling about blindly; she was looking around carefully.

He swallowed.

She was normal.

Screamers didn't move around like that in the daytime. They didn't look around because they couldn't see a damn thing and they moved like sleepwalkers, not with a precise destination in mind.

Fitz raced downstairs. The Ford F-150 was parked up the block. He took a quick look around for Screamers, saw none, and ran for the truck. In a few minutes, he was at the mall. He jumped out, looking in every direction.

The woman was nowhere to be seen.

Litter blew up the streets and a few Screamers at the end of the block wandered about. They'd heard the sound of the pickup, but they were unable to pinpoint it. Fitz studied the storefronts—Apple and Sephora, Bluemercury and Fannie May, L.L.Bean and Starbucks and Shake Shack … relics from a vanished consumer-driven civilization.

He knew he was inviting trouble, but he shouted out, "PLEASE COME BACK! I'M NORMAL LIKE YOU! I'M NOT DANGEROUS! PLEASE COME BACK!"

His words echoed off the storefronts and a gang of Screamers started up the street in his direction. But there was nothing else. No woman. No signs of life. Nothing but the wind and standing puddles, a crow cawing from atop a streetlight. Nothing.

He couldn't wait.

He jumped back in the truck and got away. He could only hope she heard him. It was understandable that she would be hesitant to make contact. She was a lone woman and as far as she knew, he was some violent deviant.

But he would be back.

He'd keep coming back until he found her.

28

Although he knew nothing about the mystery woman, save that she had long brown hair, Fitz dreamed about her. He spent some two weeks doing an intensive search but came up with nothing. He began to wonder if he hadn't imagined the entire episode. Night after night, he had dreams about catching up to her, but at the last moment, she always faded from sight. In one disturbing instance, he dreamed it was Dani.

And when he wasn't dreaming about her, the nightmares of the she-wolf (as he referred to her) tormented him.

The latest one started much the same as all the others: the ruined city, the mist, the collapsed buildings, everything broken and crumbling, a surreal cityscape.

The wolf was again tracking him and something in the dream told him that if he would just open his eyes, he would understand exactly what it was all about.

It was at that point, that the nightmare changed. Still trying to get away from her, he stumbled into a field of yellow grasses. The wind blew waves through them. In a soft blue flickering light that made everything look starkly black and white, he realized he was in a field of the dead, a killing ground. Body after body after body, impaled on stakes and in various states of decomposition. Though he was terrified and the piss-yellow smell of his fear was in his nose, he did not run. He stood his ground even though he knew everyone there had been offered as a blood sacrifice and collected as trophies of the hunt.

Turning this way and that, looking into the agonized faces of death all around him, he heard his voice say, *I don't want to be here. Please, God, let me be anywhere but in this awful place. I don't want this. I don't want any of this.*

In response to this, there was a low, evil chuckling, definitely female in tone.

This is exactly where you want to be.

The she-wolf waited ten feet from him. She grinned with a blood-dripping mouth from the corpse of a little boy she was chewing on, pulling strings of meat from his throat and gobbling them down. She licked her thin black lips and laughed again, her bloodstained muzzle pulling into the sardonic grin of a cadaver.

You've been looking for me a long time and I've been looking for you, the wolf said. *Now we've found each other and can be joined. Separately, I'm just a beast and you're just a frightened man, but together we are something bigger than the sum of our parts. The time has come for you to sit at my table and satisfy your desires.*

No! No! I don't want that! I never wanted that! I'll run from you! I'll get away and you can't catch me!

The wolf kept grinning, its huge green eyes luminous and hypnotic in their intensity. Its black pelt was lustrous with blue highlights. There was something darkly beautiful about the she-wolf and his hands begged to touch her as she moved in closer, mouth open, ivory-white teeth glistening like pink-stained icicles. Her breath smelled of blood and meat and hot slaughter.

I don't have to catch you, Fitz, because you've offered yourself to me. All I have to do is reach out and take you. You want to put your hands on me and I want to sink my teeth into you. We're both hungry, but only together can we feast.

That's when he woke, shaking and slicked with sweat. To his horror and disgust, he was sexually aroused. It took him a long time to get the nightmare out of his head.

29

Although he couldn't find the woman, he spotted her again using the telescope a couple days after the she-wolf nightmare. When he saw her not two streets over, his heart began to hammer in his chest. He raced out to the pickup and drove there, but like a ghost, she had once again vanished.

He started to think that driving over in the truck was a mistake—maybe she heard it and ran away.

His heart plummeting, he sat behind the wheel and smoked a stale cigarette. It was hopeless. Absolutely hopeless.

Then he looked at a park across the way and he saw her running through a baseball field. He went after her on foot, but again, she was gone. He searched neighborhood after neighborhood, barely escaping the clutches of several daylight-blind Screamers, but she was nowhere to be found.

But she's here, he thought. *I know she is and I bet she's watching me right now.*

Not that it really mattered. She would not be found unless she wanted to be found and it was pretty obvious she did not want that. At least, not yet.

There was little else to do but keep scavenging and searching.

Inside a trim little ranch house with wild roses growing in the yard, he discovered what he assumed were the skeletons of a man and woman. They were both dusty and cobwebbed beneath the moldering sheets, one on top of the other as if they had died making love. He initially found it sad, then he began to laugh with his twisted sense of humor, mostly because he felt jealous that Daddy Bones was getting some and he wasn't.

That's a sick little statement on the nature of your new reality and your seriously skewed mindset, he thought.

And right away, that dried up the laughter in his throat and made him feel diseased inside where it really counted. He wondered, and not for the first time, if he was really starting to lose it. Who was he to judge himself accurately? What might someone else make of his behavior? Like maybe a lone woman with long brown hair. Is that why she had run? Did he come off as some sort of madman chasing her down? Was that it?

He refused to consider it, mostly because he feared it might be true.

House to house again.

He found more corpses, more destruction, and in one house, a plethora of human bones scattered about from the living room to the kitchen, bedrooms to the dining room. They seemed to belong to at least six or seven individuals, several of whom were children. And they had obviously been gnawed upon: femurs and ulnas and ribs riddled with bite marks.

As he stood there, looking at them, a sinking feeling in his chest, he thought, *Maybe dogs were at them. That could explain it.*

But what kind of dog shut the front and back doors after they were finished? Screamers fed on the dead routinely, but they weren't exactly house-proud and responsible enough to shut doors when they were done.

All of which brought a seriously unpleasant scenario to his mind. One in which some poor family or group of survivors were trapped in the house, surrounded and besieged by Screamers so they could not escape. One by one, they died, and the others, starving to death like sailors on a lifeboat, had no choice but to eat them.

He told himself this scenario was pure fantasy, a dark turn of his imagination, yet it was certainly within the realm of possibility. And thinking that, his imagination took one last dark turn and showed him the final survivor—an insane, skulking ratlike thing with eyes like glass balls, pushed into a corner and gnawing on a child's leg bone.

But the Screamers would have lost interest and wandered off.

Maybe. Maybe not. If they knew there were people to be had, they could be very determined. The survivors would have been starving, but the Screamers would have had other things to eat—corpses and the carcasses of dogs, anything they could find. And they could go without food for a very long time. Fitz had seen plenty of them walking around, emaciated, sticklike things that should have dropped but didn't. They had an almost supernatural ability to survive. He'd capped one of them with two rounds in the chest one time and saw her go down, leaking blood like a watering can, only to see her walking around the next day with two bullet holes in her, vicious and lively as ever.

He finally left. Too much thinking and speculating. It wasn't good for his state of mind.

In a house over on Freemont Way, he found a badly damaged door leading into sort of a large family room. It had taken such abuse, he could barely get it open. He had to use the short pry bar he kept in his rat sack. The other side was cracked and splintered, encrusted with dry gore. That wasn't a surprise, exactly—in their manic delirium, sometimes Screamers seemed to forget that some doors opened in and some opened out. They'd ram themselves against them in their frustration, regardless of the damage they'd incur.

The thing that *did* surprise him was that the Screamer that had been trapped inside had quite literally exploded as if it had swallowed a hand grenade. Tissue and blood were sprayed over the walls, strings of flesh hanging from the ceiling, bones and anatomy spread over the floor.

He kicked its bald, rotting head aside, thinking, *Goddamn thing erupted like a volcano.*

Despite the stench and the buzzing swarms of flies, he made a thorough investigation, seeking evidence that a tremendous amount of firepower had been turned on the Screamer. But he found nothing. No shrapnel or spent casings or bullet holes in the walls.

Another exploder.

Trapped in there, frustrated, raging, the Screamer had blown up. That was a good indication of the wrath and frenzy bottled up inside them.

30

The next day, he stepped directly into the shit.

He was out cruising in the Ford, paying special attention to the area in which he'd seen the woman, when he saw a group of at least a dozen Screamers gathered outside a house. Nothing unique about that, really; they often moved about in packs, day or night. What drew his attention was that they were all fighting and clawing each other in their sun blindness for the chance to get up on the porch. A bunch of them had already succeeded and were violently battering the front door. There was something inside they wanted. They had its scent and they weren't going to stop until they got it.

He drove by twice, wondering.

On his second pass, he noticed that all the windows on the ground floor were boarded up.

To keep the fucking Screamers out!

There were people hiding in that house. Had to be. Only the scent or sound of normal human beings could drive Screamers into such a frenzy, particularly in the daytime when they had the tendency to be sluggish.

He came around a third time, and now he was on a mission.

He floored the pickup and the Screamers heard him coming. Five of them disengaged themselves from the battle on the porch steps and came right at him, arms held out stiffly before them, again, like sleepwalkers.

He bowled them right over.

With sadistic glee stemming from long months of bitterness and frustration, he drove over their bodies, then backed over them, finding the sound of their breaking bones more than a little satisfying.

As a throng of them left the porch to join in, he threw the Ford in reverse again, gunning it and knocking them down. One of them he pinned against a concrete pillar of the porch and smashed to a pulp.

Then he pulled back into the street and hopped out, this time loaded for bear. He carried not only his .38 with two spare speedloaders in the pockets of his frayed denim jacket, but a riot gun he had taken from a State Police car.

More Screamers came for him.

He dropped them with the riot gun, working the pump as fast as he could. He emptied the gun into the broken ones crawling through the grass. He finished the job with the .38 until none of them were moving and the lawn was red with blood, pools of gore glistening in the sunlight like oil spills.

Breathing hard, he emptied the spent casings from the .38 and recharged it with a fresh speedloader. Then he stepped through Screamer blood and guts up to the front door.

He rapped on it with his knuckles. "YOU, IN THERE! OPEN UP! THEY'RE ALL DEAD! I KILLED THEM!" he shouted. "I'M NORMAL! I'M LIKE YOU!"

There were a few moments of uneasy silence when he wondered if there actually were people inside, then he heard voices and the door opened. An old man with a Santa Claus beard stuck his head out.

"Jesus Christ," he said, pulling Fitz inside. "I didn't think there was anyone left! I thought we were it!"

It took Fitz a moment to find his voice. He realized he hadn't spoken above a whisper (and only to himself) in many, many months. "I might be the last. I don't know."

He expected to see the woman with the long brown hair in there, but she wasn't. There was an old woman with blatantly accusing gray eyes and two women in their twenties with the same brilliant red manes. They all looked not only frightened but stark, even shell-shocked. He saw it in their eyes as he'd seen it in his own reflected in mirrors. This was the look all survivors had in common, that there were unimaginable horrors locked inside them.

The man introduced himself as Hector. The old woman, his wife, was Pauline. The redheads were sisters, Celeste and Mira. They both flinched when Fitz reached out to shake their hands. He didn't even want to imagine what they'd been through.

While Pauline eyed Fitz suspiciously, Hector brought whiskey and asked countless questions: "Where'd you come from? Where you been hiding? What did you do before The Screaming? Have you found any other survivors?" And the big one: "Why the hell are the five of us immune to it all?"

Fitz was in the process of answering each one in turn when he heard a sound out on the porch. They all went suddenly rigid.

And Fitz thought, *The door ... Oh Christ, Hector forgot to lock the door after I came in.*

He and Hector both ran for it, but it was too late—they saw the knob turn. Then the door flew open with a bang, knocking Hector on his ass. Three Screamers vaulted into the room in an insane killing frenzy, overturning tables and knocking furniture aside.

Celeste and Mira both screamed, but the sound they made might as well have been the coo of doves in comparison to the shrill, nonstop screeching of the Screamers themselves, which seemed to have the same biting, jarring quality of air raid sirens.

Fitz shot one of them in the head, but another stiff-armed him and knocked him to the floor. Before it could leap on him, he fired a round under its jaw that exploded out the top of its head in a perfect fountain of blood that painted the ceiling red.

By then, it was sheer pandemonium as more Screamers rushed in, shrieking and clawing out for flesh to mangle. Hector tried to get away, but a woman Screamer jumped on him, burying her mouth in his soft throat.

Fitz shot two more, turned to help Hector but the Screamer had already torn out his throat in a brilliant sanguine expulsion. She looked right at Fitz, blood dripping from her mouth like red ink, a flap of meat dangling from her jaws. Beneath her pallid complexion, the branching purple-black veins of her face and bald head seemed to be throbbing, her bulging ebon orbs with their juicy red pupils leaked serous tears.

Fitz shot her between the eyes.

He killed another that was bearing down on Pauline, then he was out of shot. Two of them took hold of her and smashed her repeatedly against the wall until her bones snapped and she left a bright scarlet smear on the wallpaper.

By then, Celeste and Mira were menaced by four other Screamers, valiantly fending them off with fireplace pokers. One of the Screamers was a huge, naked man with black vomit bubbling from his mouth.

Fitz ducked away from another one, grabbed the empty riot gun, and cracked heads with it like he was trying to knock them out of the park in the good old days.

He jumped away from two more, leaped over the overturned couch, and quickly recharged the .38 with the last speedloader. There were Screamers everywhere by then, seeming to come from every direction, wild with the smell of blood and killing. Their constant screaming only added to the chaos.

He killed another one, was knocked down, kicked and stomped and bloodied.

He rolled away as they tried to seize him and a woman clawed at his face, tearing open his cheeks. He wasted her, then a third and fourth and fifth.

He was fighting for survival by then.

He had no idea where Celeste and Mira were.

He kicked out, punched, elbowed, and used his body as a battering ram, finally breaking free. He was splattered with gore, abused and hurting, a savage fighting thing, half out of his mind in a killing frenzy. So when hands grabbed him from behind, he reacted instinctively. He whirled around and fired his final round.

He didn't even realize it was Celeste until she hit the floor, trying to stem the flow of blood from the hole in her neck.

It was too late to do anything; she was buried in Screamers.

Mira shouted something unintelligible to him in the cacophony, death boiling in her eyes that was directed solely at him. Then she was gone.

Fitz raced from the house using the back door that Mira must have left open and swinging. He knocked blind Screamers out of his path with a vengeance. When a little girl Screamer leaped onto his back, he flipped her to the ground and kicked her brutally in the head with his heavy boot again and again until her white skull cracked open and brains spurted into the grass.

He somehow made it to the truck and laid rubber, squealing down the street, hysterical and blood-drenched.

31

He had no idea how long he drove or what state of mind he was in. When he came out of it, he was parked before the house with the telescope. His hands gripped the wheel white-knuckled and he lowered his head until his nose touched them and then he began to cry. There was no way to staunch it. The tears spilled hotly from his eyes, running down his cheeks, and his body shook with the whimpering.

Finally, it ended.

With badly shaking hands, he dug another speedloader from his rat sack and recharged the .38. Then he just sat there, empty inside, completely hollowed out and trembling with despair.

You found people today, then watched them die one by one, a voice tormented him. *You didn't follow basic protocol in your excitement and make sure that fucking door was locked. And that cost them their lives. And if that wasn't enough, you killed Celeste. You murdered a normal human being.*

Another voice tried to offer him a dozen reasons why none of it was his *fault—the old man knew better than to leave the door unlocked, you did everything you could to save them, Celeste was killed by friendly fire in the heat of battle, et cetera, et* cetera—but he wouldn't accept any of it. He couldn't bring himself to. The guilt and remorse he felt were crushing, squeezing not only the wind from him but the life.

He kept thinking about Celeste. He had known her only a few minutes,

54

really, yet he felt it went much deeper because she was a survivor, one of the few. And he had killed her. He could see her face. Her beautiful red hair. Her eyes. Then he saw her on the floor, writhing and bleeding out.

Fitz opened the door of the truck and vomited into the street. He sat there for some time, barren as a desert inside, unable to feel even the most basic emotions. He was a blackboard scrubbed clean.

After a time, he went to the house and stumbled upstairs to the office. He looked through the telescope, focusing it many streets away in the direction of Hector's house. With the trees and rooftops, he could see very little, but he did see an unusual number of Screamers wandering about.

He focused the telescope over toward the outdoor mall. He did not see anything there, particularly the woman with long brown hair. And he knew that's why he had come here, to catch a glimpse of her, to know that there was still someone real who was alive, someone whose life he had not ruined.

And today, tomorrow, next week, if you see her, you're going to leave her alone, he told himself. *The best way you can protect her is by staying away from her and not dragging death in her direction.*

He remembered the way Mira had looked at him after he killed her sister. The absolute hatred in her eyes. She was still out there, still raging and hurting over it all, as she would be for a long time to come. Maybe one day, she wouldn't be able to take it anymore and she'd hunt him down and kill him.

And maybe that will be for the best.

Dejected, beside himself with anguish, feeling like something dead sculpted from wax or wood, he went downstairs and left the house.

32

By the time Dani got sick, everything was crashing—bureaucracies, the country, world culture. Everything was in ruins. The city administration was failing fast, following suit with centralized state and federal government, which had either gone belly-up or was on its deathbed. Medical services were extinct and there was no point in taking anyone to those hospitals that were still running because none of them had a cure for The Screaming. They didn't even know what caused it. No germ of any sort had ever been isolated.

And civilization as such ground to a halt.

When Dani exhibited the initial flu-like symptoms, Fitz—who'd pretty much been living on a diet of raw stress and anxiety with what was happening to the world—went into complete denial.

Sure, Dani was sick, but it wasn't The Screaming.

It wasn't that mysterious, horrendous germ of horror that many people were calling *Virus 666* by that point. No, it couldn't be. It couldn't possibly be happening to Dani. She was his heartbeat and lifeblood, the air in his lungs and the anchor that kept his feet on the ground. She was his very reason for living and fighting on despite the fact that the world was dying one wheezing breath at a time.

She would come out of it.

She *had* to come out of it.

But she didn't, of course.

In fact, she got progressively worse. At first, she alternated between bouts of sweating and shivering. When she was awake, the things she said made very little sense. She was feverish and disoriented. Mostly, she slept, moaning and groaning as the infection advanced, grinding her teeth and quite often crying out.

The Screaming was hard to fathom. Sometimes it was a gradual illness like what was going on with Dani, but other times, it happened very quickly with little recognizable symptomology other than a lot of sleeping and an aversion to bright light. He'd heard that people sometimes shifted into Screamers within twenty-four hours. Maybe that was true, or maybe it was an urban legend, because there had been lots of those making the rounds toward the end.

Fitz was at Dani's side constantly.

When she was burning up, he gave her alcohol rubs to bring her temperature down. And when she was freezing, cold to the touch, he wrapped her in blankets that he heated in the dryer while the power was still on. He cleaned her and tried to feed her thin broths. He talked to her and held her hand and told her all about what they were going to do when she was better. He had an uncle who had a fishing lodge up north, many miles from any population center, and that's where they were going to go.

When she was well enough to travel, that was.

He knew he was talking to give himself comfort; he doubted she even heard him as the days passed. Her expression was blank, her face bloodless. Her eyelids fluttered from time to time and she had violent seizures that came and went with disturbing rapidity. Now and again, she would let out a doglike guttural cry. Several times, she had terrible episodes where she writhed like a snake and he had to hold her down so she didn't hurt herself.

He kept hoping for the best, even as her symptoms grew worse— teeth chattering, eyes rolling, body jerking with clonic spasms, her mouth pulled into an evil grimace, her tongue flicking snakelike from between her graying lips.

It was at this time that she began to thrash so violently that it took all the strength he had to hold her down. Her body was a hot, squirming sack of muscles and the hot breath that blew from her mouth smelled like tombs. She began making hoarse, croaking sounds that were terrible to hear.

About the time he noticed how white her face had become and how the veins beneath the skin looked almost black, she began tearing her hair out in clumps. Her eyebrow hairs fell out and her eyes—dear God— became black and glistening, the pupils the color of blood.

At this point, she became uncontrollable.

She was violent to the extreme, slashing at him with her nails, trying to bite him, kicking and punching and battering him with her smooth pale skull.

And then, even this accelerated until she attacked him again and again. She was a Screamer and there was no doubting the fact—she was wild, savage, a fierce animal wearing human skin. She would try to hit him with anything at hand and the only way to stop her was to open the shades and let the sunlight strike her, then she fell over and screamed.

The final stage came when he was sleeping out of exhaustion in the rocking chair across the room and she leaped on him, punching and clawing his face, muttering some hissing language as black slime dripped from her mouth. She would have killed him, but the door burst open and there was Katherine Pearson from downstairs, standing in firing position with her 9mm Glock in her hands.

"DANI!" she shouted. "OVER HERE!"

Dani hissed at her and abandoned Fitz, and Katherine put a round into her forehead that blew out the back of her skull in an eruption of blood, skull fragments, and pink brain matter.

Fitz screamed and when he launched himself at Katherine, she put the gun on him. "Don't make me use it, Fitz, because I will."

He sank to the floor, beaten and bloody and helpless.

"Wrap her in a blanket," Katherine told him, "and bury her in the yard. It's the only thing you can do."

An hour later, he did just that. He buried Dani and most of himself in a shallow grave. That was the end of it.

33

For days, he couldn't sleep and he couldn't eat. All he could think about were the Screamers and how much he hated them, how he wanted to kill each and every one of them in the bloodiest and most painful ways imaginable. Maybe he had no right to hate them any more than someone had a right to hate all sharks because one of them bit off their foot. Yet, he did. They were sick, diseased things, both physically and mentally. Maybe he should have pitied them because they had been normal human beings once with lives and families. Through no fault of their own, they had become psychotic monsters.

So he told himself, *They're no more to blame than victims of the black death or cholera or shingles, for God's sake. They did not want to be this way.*

That was solid, rational, humane thinking. But the more he tried to apply it, the less sense it seemed to make. It got so nothing seemed to make sense, not the way it once had. His thinking was off, it was skewed. Maybe he was on the verge of a breakdown, something devastating and colossal that would strip his mental wiring bare right before it shorted out completely.

One afternoon, he sat concealed on a rooftop and studied the

Screamers in the streets. With the sunlight, of course, there were mostly just a few strays. Regardless, he plotted their deaths in detail. He saw two Screamer children, a boy and a girl. They were horrors with their bald, mottled skulls, pallid faces set with gaping sores and cadaverous hollows, eyes gleaming like black marbles. Yet, near-blind in the sunshine they stumbled along, holding hands, of all things, like sweet, innocent children who feared they might lose each other.

And that incensed him.

How can they act like that? he thought. *Like ordinary children? How can they dare pretend to be something they're not? They're not fucking kids! They're monsters, horrible monsters! Murdering, violent monsters!*

Generally, he gave kid Screamers a wide berth because they not only creeped him out but offended him at some primary level. Ever since he'd killed that monstrous little girl from Katherine Pearson's apartment, they made his skin crawl.

But watching these two, it was suddenly different. He *wanted* to kill them, to exterminate them like rats. And not with a gun, no, that was too impersonal. He wanted to use his hands on them or maybe a hatchet. He needed to hear them cry out as he chopped them into pieces, to feel their hot, diseased blood spraying in his face and staining his hands—

Oh Christ, he thought then, his heart pumping and his limbs shaking uncontrollably, *what the hell is wrong with you? They're victims, nothing but pathetic victims.*

The rational part of his brain kept telling him this, but his raging emotions wouldn't hear of it. He kept thinking of Hector and Pauline, Mira and Celeste (particularly Celeste), and the guilt weighed so heavy on him that he thought about slitting his wrists more than once. Instead, it was rechanneled into juvenile revenge fantasies where he killed Screamers by the hundreds.

You're like a stupid kid who got thrashed by the playground bully. Now all you can do is fantasize that you're John fucking Rambo taking out the bad guys.

His insomnia went on for three days straight, regardless of how much whiskey he poured down his throat. And when his eyes did manage to close for a couple minutes, he jerked awake out of nightmares of being stalked by the demonic she-wolf or of Celeste dying in his arms and drowning him in her blood.

On the fourth day, he finally passed out. He slept for seven hours, but when he woke—though his mind was refreshed, his thinking was certainly no clearer—he went out hunting. He killed sixteen Screamers that day. A dozen more the next. After a time, he lost count. They were monsters that wanted to kill him and he was certain they were of some communal hive mind and he could almost feel them thinking about him all the time. Hating him. Despising him. Revolted by his very existence, as he was by theirs.

He kept going out and he kept killing them.

There was nothing else but hatred to keep him going. He didn't scavenge or stockpile or do anything constructive. He emptied his weapons, cleaned them, reloaded them for more killing, and plotted out his attacks and reprisals, and at the end of each day, he got roaring drunk so his brain would stop tormenting him with images of Dani and Celeste.

He was not in a right state of mind and he knew it.

But there was nothing to be done.

Nothing left but to kill.

And he would keep killing them, he knew, until the time came when they caught him and tore him apart. He grew bolder and bolder in his raids until part of him was certain he wanted them to get him, to end his suffering already. But one suicidal banzai charge after another, he escaped, literally by the skin of his teeth.

His mania was complete and irresistible.

He thought about nothing but wasting Screamers and delighting in their deaths. *Walking pestilence, all they are is walking pestilence.* The world beyond them no longer existed. He rarely ate. He dropped weight. He never bathed. He didn't even change his clothes anymore.

One day, out on the hunt, he caught a reflection of himself in a dusty store window and he barely recognized what he saw. In fact, he flinched and his heart raced, thinking some savage feral human or Screamer was coming at him. But, dear God, it was him, *it was him*—clothes filthy and ragged, his long, matted hair streaked with gray, his unshaven face shaggy with beard growth, his mouth twisted into a grimace, his skin pale and streaked with grime. He looked violent and unpredictable, a dangerous man with fixed, deranged eyes.

Was this why the woman with the long brown hair had run from him? Is this how he presented himself to strangers?

The reflection offended (and frightened) him so much, he shot out the window and ran shrieking up the sidewalk.

And it all steadily got worse and worse until his mind no longer seemed capable of rational thought or action. He moved through the streets by day, talking to himself, sometimes humming nonsensically beneath his breath, and the city he'd known so well his entire life became an alien, grotesque place of crumbling buildings and rotting houses eroding like sea cliffs. It was an ominous, evil place that was wholly strange to him, its physics distorted and out of sync, a nightmare geometry that pushed in from all sides to crush him, to bury him alive in concrete and steel. He did not belong there. It was as if he was seeing it, truly seeing the graveyard it was for the first time in his life. And it made him feel small and inconsequential, like a fly waiting for a swatter to crush it to paste.

And when the days grew late and the shadows grew long, his terror amplified because the city was waking up; he could hear it rustling around him, breathing and filling itself with dark, sinister life.

The nights hiding away from it all were even worse because he could feel the Screamers out there, hundreds of them, thousands of them seeking him out, watching and listening. And he could hear their thoughts, the continual buzzing of the hive mind, that sterile thrumming machine, and how his very existence revolted them. How they wanted to kill him, to smash him and skin him and scatter his guts in the street and write their names in his blood on dirty brick walls.

Through the weeks, the rising paranoia got worse and worse. His sleep, what there was of it, was a booze-addled cauldron of fevers in which he sweated and shook with chills and woke in abject terror that they had found him at last.

After a time, he barely had the strength to get out of bed.

He huddled in the corner and peered around the shades at the desolate streets beyond, knowing that day by day and hour by hour, they were creeping in, getting closer and closer.

34

And then one day, they found him.

It had to happen and he'd been expecting it for some time. He had gotten too weak to move around like he used to, so he squatted in the ranch house and waited for them to come. They *had* to come. And when they did, he had decided in his delirium, he was going to destroy them like never before because that's what men did: they destroyed monsters and nothing less was acceptable.

He heard the front door creak open and a wild thought raced through his head. *Why didn't I lock it? Why didn't I lock that fucking door?* But on another, unbalanced level of his mind he knew he hadn't because he wanted them to come here, to track him to his lair, his cave, his kingdom.

It was a woman.

A Screamer—a monster that wore the skin of a woman, but not a real woman. He watched her from his hide behind the recliner as she stepped into the living room and then she tried to trick him in a way they had never tricked him before: she spoke.

She said, "Hello? Is anyone here?"

The words were a shrill buzzing that his brain could not decipher because Screamers were monsters and monsters could not speak the way normal humans did, not the way he could.

He jumped out to face her, a rawboned, stick-thin predator, and he called out to her, but his throat didn't seem to work right and the words were thick and ungainly in his mouth; his swollen tongue could not get out of the way to set them free. He cried out in a series of guttural barks and the woman screamed at him as their kind always screamed.

The amazing thing was, she actually tried to get away, but Fitz wouldn't have it—he launched himself, taking hold of her and throwing her to the floor. She was wild and violent, scratching his face, kicking and biting him, but he punched her in the face again and again until his fists were red with her blood. And that only excited him more because he'd long wanted it to be this way: intimate and ugly.

And it was that, all right.

Oh yes, it most certainly was that.

Because as he held her down, fist cocked to deliver another blow, her gored face seemed to liquify and change, mutating into a dozen ever-changing faces—Celeste and Dani, Katherine Pearson and Mira, and the woman with the long brown hair. It shifted from one to the other and back again with a sliding, pulping sound of realigning bones and gristle, tissue and sheaths of muscle, and then it seemed to cave in, bubble and ooze until it became the face of the thing he feared most: the she-wolf. The eyes went green and a snout jutted free, snapping at him with long yellow fangs.

Yes, the she-wolf.

The very thing his dreams had warned him about.

But as horrified as he was, he would not let her go. She was not going to get away. She was going to die.

To the bitter end she fought, God, how she fought, but Fitz did not waver or weaken in his horror. He hit her again and again and again until her face was shattered and smashed, swollen and disfigured.

And at some point during the process, a voice screeched in his head, *She's not a monster, she's not a monster, can't you see that? Can't you see who and what she is?* But those words were lost in his hysteria and the shouting voices in his mind as he gripped her by her long, bloodied brown hair and slammed her face onto the hardwood floor until something in there broke and hot, red liquid gushed over his knuckles and pooled around her shattered skull in a puddle.

Exhausted and delusional, he fell away from her carcass, running shaking hands over his bald head, unable to remember tearing out his hair, and then, and only then, did he start to scream.

NECROPOLITAN

JAMES CHAMBERS

Elle sniffed and dabbed a tear from her eye as the star-crossed lovers onscreen *finally* kissed to the accompaniment of romantic flutes and violins mingled with the moans of the dead and the screams of the dying. A choir of horrified shrieks applauded the perfectly coifed passion simmering at a Hawaiian beachfront dance party, all happy smiles and jiggling bathing-suit bodies, while a muffled voice shouted, "God, no, no, it's horrible! Please, no, don't!" Nick lost his composure and laughed. Elle flashed him a disapproving side-eye and elbowed his ribs.

"Sorry, babe," he whispered. "These walls are paper-thin. It's kind of hilarious."

"Shush, don't ruin this," Elle whispered back.

She slurped cola from their shared cup, then refocused on the screen. Nick admired her ability to lose herself in a silly movie and unfetter her emotions for people who didn't exist. He preferred action and special effects flicks, where the visuals mattered more than the story. He sighed and tried to ignore the soundtrack leaking through from the neighboring theater screening *Necropolitan*, advertised for months as the most gruesome horror film of the century. Just his luck, Elle's turn to pick for movie night coincided with its opening weekend. Not that he minded romantic comedies. If they took Elle's mind off their troubles for a couple of hours, he would sit through them all. He even half liked the stars of this one despite their surgically augmented looks, but, man, he wished he were seated on the other side of that acoustically inferior wall. The gasps, howls, and screams filtering through confirmed that *Necropolitan* more than delivered on its promises.

Their big kiss complete, the movie stars held hands and strolled along the beach under a CGI full moon. Surf washed their bare feet. Leis dangled from their necks. A dolphin nosed up from the breakers, walked on its tail, and squeaked. The male lead, all chin, teeth, and gelid brown eyes, stopped short, listening. The woman, all wind-resistant hair, limpid blue eyes, and a road-reflector smile, gazed lovingly at him while magically coherent dolphin squeals revealed the secret of who'd been working to keep them apart.

Screams of the realest terror Nick had ever heard accompanied the brief montage of the couple running back to their hotel to confront the male lead's rich cousin who'd thwarted him so many times since childhood. Elle squeezed his hand, warning him to keep quiet, and he squeezed back, his way of saying, *Anything for you, babe.* That had been his mantra from the day he fell head over heels for her two years ago, the pledge that had set them both on the run from Elle's dangerous and disapproving father. They had lived life looking over their shoulders and jumping at shadows ever since. At the movies, in the cool, anonymous dark, they could catch their breath and feel like regular people.

A rectangle of gloomy light appeared below the dim, red EXIT sign at the lower right of the screen as an emergency door opened. A silhouette filled the space. It wavered in the low light from an evacuation corridor behind the auditoriums. A high school kid sneaking in for free, Nick figured, except when the man entered the movie glow, he didn't look like a kid. Mussed hair, his clothes disheveled, torn, and stained, he looked like a street person. A woman bumped into him from behind, nudging him farther into the theater on his unsteady feet. She looked even worse. The front of her blouse hung loose, ripped from her left shoulder, exposing her bra. A bruise as large as a dinner plate marred her pale chest. As they drifted into the projector beam, their eyes glinted like possum's eyes reflecting headlights at night. They swayed on their feet and stared at the audience as if lost.

Several rows ahead of Elle and Nick, a man wearing a baseball cap shouted, "Hey, close the door!"

The woman jolted into the theater, shoving the man. The door swung closed, and the gloom swallowed them. Nick forgot about the movie, wondering how drunk or high the pair were as they shuffled along the first row of seats looking confused, maybe seeking a place to sleep it off. A little knot of tension tied itself in his gut. He shifted in his seat, relaxation fading as bodyguard training took over, preparing him for action should the intrusion become a threat.

Screams from the next-door auditorium peaked with shrill resonance. The theater vibrated from sound effects pumped through high-end surround sound speakers. Even the floor quaked in hyperrealistic waves, the rumbling of a phantom army marching on the other side of the wall.

The door opened again. Dusty light washed out the lower corner of the movie. Another disheveled man entered. He coughed loudly then gurgled something wet from his mouth that dribbled down to his neck.

"Hey, chuckleheads, enough with the damn door!" Broad-shouldered and over six feet tall, Baseball Cap stood, ignoring his date, who tried to hold him back, and stormed down the row. "Go buy tickets, you cheapskates." He rushed to the front of the auditorium to pull the door closed, but several hands gripped its edge from the other side and tugged it wide. Three people ambled through, as ragged and disoriented as the others. A woman stared at the screen, head lolling back, arms raised as if to embrace the whole, happy world playing out on the pearlescent vinyl. Her eyes glittered like stars shining through smog.

"You fuckers!" Baseball Cap said. "I'm gonna bust your heads."

"Should we do something?" Elle asked, her attention finally bounced out of the movie.

Nick's anger flared at these morons robbing Elle of her enjoyment. He craned around to survey the rest of the audience. Incredibly, a handful still gazed at the screen, transfixed by the hypnotic rectangle, although most now watched the conflict unfolding beneath the feature. Nick swiveled forward to watch Baseball Cap swing at the nearest intruder. His fist connected with the man's chin, snapping his target's head back with a dull crack and staggering him several steps.

"Fucking *freak*!" shouted Baseball Cap.

Before he could reposition himself to throw another blow, the intruders seized his arm, and half a dozen hands yanked Baseball Cap off-balance.

"Hey! Get offa me! Don't fucking touch me!"

They reeled him in against his dug-in feet, fingertips tearing into the sleeve of his shirt. Nick wondered what they intended to do—then a wave of shock filled him as one of the women leaned in close and bit Baseball Cap on the throat. Blood welled around her lips and soaked into his shirt. Another pawed the cap from the man's head, bared his teeth, then chomped into the back of his bald skull. Blood spurted into the attacker's face. Baseball Cap screamed, a high-pitched wail of pain and shock far removed from his gruff threats. The commotion drew several more intruders who converged until they buried him with their bodies, the mass of them sinking out of sight as Baseball Cap's cries faded to wet, spitting squeals, then died. The intruders' quiet, relentless assault on the man chilled Nick to his core, and the knot at his center doubled itself, tensing his every muscle for action.

"Henry?" Baseball Cap's date stood from her seat, spilling a bucket of popcorn. "Henry! Oh my God! Leave him alone! Somebody help! Please! Help Henry!"

"Let's split," Elle said to Nick.

Nick put his arm around her. "No, keep cool. This has to be a stunt for *Necropolitan*. Idiots cosplaying for opening weekend. They just went too far. That guy was a plant rigged with blood squibs."

"Are you sure? The way he screamed . . ." Elle shivered.

Nick didn't answer. More screaming filtered through the wall, drowning out cornball rom-com dialogue. Everyone in the audience teetered in the same moment of uncertainty, the same state of frightened disbelief. Some stood in front of their seats, recording the attack on their phones. Others called 911, which meant cops, and questions, and uncomfortable answers for Elle and Nick. You could never tell which cops to trust. Elle's father kept so many on his payroll.

A voice from a back row said, "We damn well better get a refund after this bullshit."

In response, two of the intruders detached from the gang. They cut shadows against the movie screen. Scraps of soft material flapped between their grinding teeth. They clambered over the first row of seats, stiff and clumsy, then the second row, then the third. A melon-sized object arced above them and smacked against the screen, where it deposited dark, dripping smears. The two seat-climbers reached Baseball Cap's date, clutched her, and sank their teeth into her throat from both sides. Her screams joined those still coming from beyond the wall. It dawned on Nick that not all the sounds from the adjacent theater were part of the soundtrack.

The exit door jolted open again, inviting a slow parade of intruders in torn, bloodstained clothing, their eyes shimmering like smoky glass in the projector beam.

All uncertainty erased, the audience erupted into panic.

The intruders added grunts, groans, and malformed words to the riot of exclamations and shouts from the hysterical moviegoers. People dropped soda cups, popcorn tubs, and candy boxes as they dashed up the aisles, some even climbing over seats, all rushing for the rear doors. Nick threw a protective arm around Elle, pulled her into a crouch on the floor, and flipped their seats up to create a hiding space. Joining the crowd would only increase their risk, especially when it bottlenecked at the theater's main exits.

"Nick?"

Elle's voice cut him to the heart, her fear held at bay by her confidence he would answer and that his answer would keep them safe. More intruders shuffled into the theater and moved up the side aisle, attracted by the melee. Hunkered in front of their seats, Nick and Elle escaped their notice.

"Nick, we have to go," Elle whispered. "Why aren't we getting out of here?"

"Because both exits are cut off. There's nowhere *to* go," said Nick.

"You still think it's a publicity stunt?" Elle took several deep breaths, then poked her head up to survey the theater. "Who the hell are these people? Some kind of cult? Terrorists? Is this a gang attack? What the hell do they want?"

"I can't even guess," said Nick. "They look like meth heads cosplaying zombies."

Nick raised his head to see still more intruders shamble into the auditorium through the door near the bottom of the screen. Baseball Cap's date now walked among them, wounded and bloody, somehow still on her feet with her throat torn to shreds. A swell in the volume of screams snapped his attention to the rear of the theater.

The audience, attempting to escape, now retreated, a shrieking, trampling tangle of bodies flowing back into the auditorium. Nick couldn't see why. The gloom rendered everything murky. Tight-packed bodies rippled like tall grass in the wind until the mob butted the back row of seats and squeezed itself into two groups, right and left. A third formed as people fell over seat backs into the last row. A crowd of the ragged intruders pushed into the theater from the main doors, forcing the reversal. Nick felt grateful he'd trusted his instincts to take cover rather than run.

"These freaks are coming in from the lobby now, too," he said. "We're surrounded."

Elle popped up, looked to the back of the theater and then the front, noted intruders flowing in from both sides, the audience corralled between them, then slumped down beside her raised seat.

"Fuck," she said. "I knew I should've kept my .38 in my purse tonight."

"Didn't we agree? No weapons on date night?" Nick asked. "Anyway, they don't seem interested in us as long as we stay quiet and keep out of sight."

"How long can that last?"

A high-pitched wail of agony answered on Nick's behalf. He stifled an inappropriate, unexpected burst of laughter. The absurdity of the situation made his skin itch. Bright, happy scenes still flickered on the blood-smeared movie screen, a beach wedding against a Hawaiian sunrise with dolphins dancing in the breakers, while in the last row of seats, intruders pinned a woman in a halter top to a seat back—then wrenched her arms from her shoulders. Her joints cracked audibly as tendons snapped and blood sprayed. Another intruder grabbed her head with both hands, then bit down on her face, grinding his teeth on her cheekbones.

"These freaks are *cannibals*," Nick said.

Elle popped up to peek over her seat back. "Eww, gross. Sick. Fuck."

Nick tugged her down, out of sight. "We've got two exits, both blocked. Right now the creeps are all in on everyone running around making noise—but eventually, they're going to find us. We need an exit before that happens."

"What about behind the screen? Like, backstage?" asked Elle.

Nick gave an exasperated sigh. "This isn't a playhouse, babe, it's a multiplex. There's no backstage, only a wall of speakers and a frame to mount the screen. And we're in the last theater, which means the exit door down there is a dead end because it leads wherever these freaks are coming from."

"There has to be some space back there for maintenance and whatever."

"Not enough to hide in. The screen won't provide any protection if they see us scurry back there. We'd have nowhere else to run. Besides, hiding isn't good enough. We need to get out." Nick leaned his head back, thinking. His gaze fell on the dust-filled projector beam still flashing sappy rom-com hilarity through the dark, the dancing light oddly happy with scintillant shafts of blue and pink reflecting off dust motes. He crept up for a glimpse over his seat back. Light streamed from a square window high on a wall that overhung the last seat rows.

"There." Nick pointed at it. "We go out there, through the projection booth."

Elle inched up beside him. "*That* window? There's glass."

Nick squinted at the block of light, catching a faint reflection. He slid a hand into his jeans then pulled out a pocketknife and presented it to Elle.

"What happened to no weapons on date night?" she asked.

"It's a tool, not a weapon," Nick said. "That pointed tip on the handle is a glass breaker, in case we ever got jammed up in a car. We'll vault the seat backs to the last row. I'll hoist you up. You need to flick the tip hard at the corner of the window. Got that? The *corner*, not the middle. Shield your eyes when you do it. The glass is probably coated, so if it shatters but doesn't fall, push it in and climb up. Then you can reach back through the window. I'll jump and grab onto your arms. You pull me up until I can grip the window frame. Then we're out."

"This is going to break that window?" Elle studied the sharp, conical protrusion on the knife handle. "How am I going to hit it hard enough while I'm standing on your shoulders?"

"Don't hit it hard. Hit it fast, like a punch, at the corner." Nick met Elle's wide-eyed stare with his own and mustered a grim smile. "What do you think, babe? We can do it. Right? We've gotten out of worse scrapes."

Elle's expression froze, then tightened with determination. "No, we haven't. This is, fuck, I don't know what this is, but it's way worse than my dad's knee-breakers catching up with us or those assholes who tripped us up in Pittsburgh. But, okay, yeah, we can do anything when we stick together."

She kissed Nick on the lips. He kissed her back, grasping onto her warmth even as his blood ran cold at the thought of what would happen if his plan failed. Then they surged into motion.

Nick stood first, jumped over his seat, then launched into the clumsy process of vaulting one row after another. Elle kept pace. After three rows, they found a sort of rhythm. Nick silently thanked Elle for never letting them drop their guard or stop training. Nearly two years since any sign or word from her father or his goons, they still lived in a state of heightened awareness, ready for fight or flight. Leaving her .38 at home on date night was a now-failed experiment in trying on a sense of security that Nick regretted encouraging. All he wanted was a life with Elle. It seemed there would never be an end to fighting for it.

They kept as quiet as possible to avoid drawing attention to themselves, but each time they surmounted a row, they rose into the projector beam like frogs hopping past a rising full moon. Intruders scuffing up the aisles noticed them and turned into the rows toward the center seats. Some of those attacking the audience shifted in their direction.

Nick hit the third to last row, leaped onto a pair of seat backs directly beneath the projector window, and found precarious footing. He wedged a foot into the crevasse between two adjacent seats and prayed he kept his balance.

"Don't stop, babe, just keep moving. Jump right onto me, use your momentum," he said.

He spread his arms, watching Elle frog-leap a seat row, then spring upward in front of him. He gripped her waist at the apex of her leap, put all his strength into it, and thrust her upward. Shifting his grip to her feet, he formed his palms into a step and steadied her. Elle screamed, not from fear but determination, a martial arts cry to focus body and mind. She snapped the knife handle at the glass, which deflected it with a dull thump. The rebound rippled down their bodies. Nick's right foot slipped, wedging deeper into the space between seat backs. Spikes of pain launched up his ankle and calf. With another furious cry, Elle thrust again. This time the glass cracked and shattered across its plane. It did not scatter, held intact by a safety coating. Elle pushed it into the booth, and then her weight lifted from Nick's hands, filling him with a blast of triumph as she broke contact.

He dropped his tiring arms to his side, then lost his footing as more pain lanced up his leg, and he toppled backward into the seat row. His world became a tumult of light and shadow, of metal and hard plastic cracking into his ribs, his back, his skull, of eyes staring in the dark all around him. His tumble terminated on the floor, compressing his body against a seat. Lightning bolts of pain ran up and down his spine; thunderclaps burst in his head from the whiplash cracks against seats and floor.

"Nick!" Elle shouted. "Oh God, Nick! Move! They're coming! Hurry!"

Nick's head spun as he scrambled upright. Overhead, Elle poked out through the smashed window. Her mouth moved, but her words sounded out of sync with her lips: "Hurry, move, jump, get up here, move, jump, please, go, go, go." And Nick went. Concentrating to compensate for his dizziness, forcing himself to ignore rising nausea, he clambered over the seats, then climbed onto their backs. Electric rings of pain radiated from his right ankle. It buckled and he almost fell. He peered upward at Elle safely framed in the projector window. Part of him wanted to urge her to flee, to leave him and get to safety, but as she extended her arms for him to grab, he knew she'd refuse. Like the last two years of their lives, they would escape together or not at all. In spite of his fogginess, he believed he could manage to leap the few feet between them, but every muscle in his body wobbled, and his head spun. The intruders neared, crawling over each other to reach him. Screams and cries ripped the air, so many, so loud, a sonic bombardment that worsened his disorientation.

Only three, maybe four feet to safety.

Nick jumped, arms stretching, fingers grasping for Elle's—falling short.

He landed on the seat backs and kept himself upright by jamming one foot against an armrest despite the pain crackling in his ankle. If he fell now, he wouldn't get another try.

Again, he jumped. His fingertips brushed Elle's.

"For fuck's sake, Nick, jump like you mean it, you lazy son of a bitch!" Elle screamed.

A groping hand touched Nick's leg, sparking a terrible shiver through his body. He bent his knees, poised himself to put all he had left into one furious jolt, then jumped, thrusting hard with his left leg, springing off the toes of his right foot. Elle's wrists filled his hands. He seized them. She grabbed onto his wrists and pulled. Bracing herself against the wall beneath the projection window, she exerted all her strength and dragged him up bit by bit, while half a dozen intruders attempted to grab his feet. They clambered awkwardly onto the seats to extend their reach. Fingers scraped the soles of Nick's boots, until his hands reached the window frame.

He found a solid grip, then hoisted himself up, silently patting himself on the back for his devotion to the pull-up bar, then tumbled headlong into the projection room. He knocked over Elle, and they wound up in a jumble on the floor, glass crunching under them, bodies wedged against the heavy mount of a digital projector. Nick wrestled himself to his knees then looked out the window. More intruders than he could count in the chaotic shadows now swarmed the seat from which he'd launched himself. All the nausea he'd contained during their escape surged through him, and he vomited out the opening. A vile cascade rained on the heads of those who wished to eat his skin.

Drained and exhausted, he crumpled back into the projection room and slumped against the wall.

"Thank you for not doing that in here," Elle said.

Heaving to catch his breath, Nick offered her a weak thumbs-up.

"Hey!" a voice shouted. "Who the fuck are you two? What the hell are you doing in here?"

Across the room stood a man in blue jeans, a threadbare, black Dokken T-shirt, and a beat-up leather motorcycle jacket. Lines of gray streaked his long hair, an unkempt stormfront around his weathered, wrinkled face. In one hand, he clutched a utility knife, its blade glinting in the projector light. Blood dripped from its edge. Behind him, a man dressed all in white lay still on the floor in a deep crimson pool slowly spreading around the base of the projector for the neighboring auditorium.

Nick met Elle's rueful stare and said, "I know, I know, you should've left your .38 in your purse. I'm sorry. How the hell was I supposed to know this crazy shit would go down at the movie theater?"

"Hey!" Dokken said. "I asked you a question."

He stood between them and the door in a room that spanned the length of the multiplex. A row of digital projectors aimed like pirate cannons into dark squares, spitting flickering light and color into theaters. Fans whirred, pumping heat out of exhaust ducts snaked to the ceiling. An old recliner occupied a space by the door. A man in a polo shirt with the theater's logo embroidered on the breast reclined in it. Nick would've thought him asleep except for the clear, plastic bag pulled over his head and zip-tied tight around his neck and his open eyes staring at nothing.

Dokken brandished the short knife.

"Did you come to stop me? You're too late," he said. "Not that it fucking matters. I tried, man, I really tried, but I just couldn't catch up to him soon enough. Shit, it's all over now, isn't it? I failed. Maybe some of the others didn't, though. Maybe there's still a chance." The anger and threat that had steeled him dissipated. He lowered the bloody knife and rubbed his eyes with his other hand. "If you're here to kill me, fuck, just do it already. We're all as good as dead anyway." He gazed at Nick and Elle. His expression spoke volumes of fatigue, sorrow, and despair.

"Whoa, slow down, chief." Nick struggled against lingering vertigo to stand. The room whirled. "We're not here to kill anyone. We climbed up here to escape the murder-crazies. Are you with them?"

"Me? With the dead people? I'm *alive*, man. Are you too stupid to tell the difference?"

"Why do you call them dead people?" asked Elle.

Dokken snorted. "Are you fucking blind?"

"Hey, it's dark down there. We don't know what the hell is happening, except a bunch of freaks rolled in, went cannibal, and ruined a lot of date nights." Spying a broom propped against the wall, the only potential weapon in sight, Nick inched toward it. "Who's that on the floor? You kill him?"

"I hope so, the fucking weasel. Just wish I'd done it before he killed the projectionist. That poor guy didn't deserve that. I could've taken him out two weeks ago, but, no, I had to be a smart guy and try using him to reach the distributor. Figured maybe I could disrupt a whole region and really screw up their plans." Dokken shifted his weight then kicked the body onto its back, revealing the sallow face of a man in his thirties, dressed in a long-sleeved white T-shirt, white jeans, and white sneakers, all stained with Rorschach blots of congealing blood. His glassy eyes, ringed in dark circles, stared without seeing. Sunken cheeks. Scabby lips. Makeup smeared on his forehead. "Bastard was cagier than I figured. I was on his heels until two days ago, then I lost him. Took too long to relocate him. He got here before me and killed the projectionist and loaded the movie. Now a whole lot of other people are dead and more will die soon."

"Was this guy part of a cult?" asked Nick.

"That's what I think, has to be some kind of cult," Elle said.

Dokken regarded them as if he'd forgotten their presence for a moment. In a smooth, swift motion that reignited the turbulence in his gut, Nick snatched the broom in a fighting grip, ready to defend himself and Elle. Dokken's eyes narrowed, reading the challenge, then he gave a long, sorrowful sigh and dropped his knife. It clattered on the floor.

"Aw, shit, you folks are just trying to survive. I'm sorry you had to see any of this. Sorry you lived through the chaos down there. Better, maybe, if you died fast. I got no problem with you. I have other work now, for all the good it will do anymore. Good luck."

Dokken stepped toward the door of the projection room. Nick slid forward and snapped the broom down to block his path. Ignoring a pulse of fresh nausea, he tapped the man's chest to stop him.

"Oh hell no, buddy, you don't walk out of here just like that. First, we have no idea what's on the other side of that door. You open it, you might let in those freaks to take a bite out of us all. Second, you know what's happening? Good. It's story time. We need to know everything we can to stay alive."

"Let's start easy," said Elle. "What's your name?"

Screams of agony and fear intermingled with the wet, gnashing growls of the intruders and rose from the theater to fill the lingering quiet as Dokken weighed his response. Only the hum of the fans cooling the projectors, soothing in their steady normalcy, provided any rebuttal to the animalistic noises. Nick braced the broomstick, solid like a security gate, despite the room still penduluming around him like the cloying whirlpool of a bad hangover.

"Michael. My name's Michael Sterling," the man said. He placed two fingertips on the broomstick and pushed down, lowering it with Nick's acquiescence. His shoulders slumped, and he shivered. "You won't believe anything I tell you, but, sure, I'm game. What do you want to know?"

Nick wavered as his head throbbed. "Why'd you say you're alive when I asked you if you're with those freaks?"

"Those freaks are dead. I know, I know, but they're walking around attacking people, how can that be, right?" Michael said. "They're the *living* dead."

"Like in the movies. Like in *Necropolitan*. You expect us to believe that?" asked Nick.

Michael laughed. "Hell no, man. I said you won't believe anything I tell you, but I won't lie to you either. You want answers, I'll give them. What you believe isn't my fucking concern. I don't even know what I believe most days."

"Why are they attacking people? Why are they eating them?" Elle asked.

"That's what the living dead do," said Michael. "Haven't you seen the movies? There's like, half a fucking century of movies and TV shows about it."

"Movies are only movies," Nick said.

"Not anymore, man. *Necropolitan* changed everything. The distributor, the producers, and the Director changed the world. They've been planning this for decades. We tried to stop them. I *tried* so fucking hard, but I failed. Maybe we all failed. I don't know yet. They're so strong. They've got influence and power. It's hard enough to go up against them without the fact that no one—not one *single soul* outside of it, not even *you* after seeing it with your own eyes—ever really believes they can bring the dead to life and turn them into flesh-crazed monsters. The gore fest of the year, *Necropolitan* ... lines around the block opening night, parent-group protests, outraged reviews—all part of the ritual conjuring. It's magic, man, *real* movie magic, onscreen sorcery, digitally cast *necromancy*, an orchestrated memetic contagion, and in every theater, all it takes is one unhealthy, brain-dead fucker to fall under the spell and kick it all off. Then you wind up with what's down there in who knows how many other theaters around the world tonight."

"You're saying *Necropolitan* drove those people nuts and made them think they're ghouls? I've heard of people losing their minds over a movie but not literally," Nick said.

Michael shook his head. "That's *not* what I'm saying. See? You hear the truth, but you don't want to believe it, so you rewrite it. Everyone puts their own spin on it, makes it all about themselves. I say *Necropolitan* killed people and reanimated their corpses driven by hunger for living flesh. You twist it around to say they lost their minds. They're brainwashed. Hypnotized. Temporary insanity, right? Well, you need some temporary *sanity*, man. Open your eyes."

The words drifted through Nick's muddled brain, a lifeline. He focused on them, on what he and Elle had witnessed, what the horrible soundtrack of death and pain rising from the theater represented. Still his mind resisted. The dead didn't come back to life. Walking corpses didn't eat living people. No matter how he tried to buy into Michael's story, his consciousness diverted to alternatives. Mass hysteria. Sodas spiked with hallucinogens. A flash mob gone wrong. Even a stunt by students at the local art college to raise awareness for some hopeless cause or other. Because the world simply didn't work this way. None of the options fit the puzzle pieces together like Michael's—except Michael's was impossible—and Michael was a murderer, maybe as bad as the freaks. Grunts and screams drummed Nick's ears, pounding at his already throbbing head. He didn't know what made sense anymore.

Elle gripped his arm, startling him out of his daze. She pointed to the broken projector room window. "Nick, company."

A pair of bloody hands gripped the window ledge. A blood-smeared face rose into view. Nick reacted without thought, wielding the broom in a swift, smooth swing that jammed the end of the stick into the man's throat, jarring him loose. He fell from sight. Nick peeked out to see a body pile of the freaks, clawing and climbing atop each other in a slow-motion frenzy to reach the projector window. The theater soundscape had changed. No more screams. No more pleas for help. Only their attackers' inarticulate vocalizations remained. No more victims, only killers. A woman crested the top of the body mound, groped upward. Nick swiped down with the broom and banished her to the bottom of the pile.

"They're coming for us, and we can't stop them all. We need to leave," he said. "Elle, pick up that knife. Michael, you open the door, *slowly*, and let's hope no one's waiting on the other side."

Outside the projector booth, a gloomy corridor greeted them.

Empty.

To their right, a dead end. To their left, a stairway. The trio crept from the projector room, footsteps soft on the carpeted floor. Nick looked back to catch sight of a feral man, the left side of his face chewed away, groping through the broken window. He shut the door and then set the broom head against the floor at a sharp angle. A swift thrust of his foot snapped it off, and he wedged it under the door and kicked hard to jam it in tight.

"That won't hold long if a bunch of them push on it, but it might buy us time," he said.

"Hey, man," said Michael. "What's *your* story? The two of you are a couple of cool cucumbers. Why aren't you losing your shit over all this?"

"Losing your shit is how you get dead," Elle said.

"Who we are is a long story," said Nick. "Maybe we'll tell you sometime. Right now, we need the quickest way out of here that doesn't cross paths with the freaks."

"Right, right. There's a service entrance. It's how I came in." Michael pointed to the stairs. "The first flight goes to a landing. There, it splits. One way leads to the lobby. The other goes to a back door that opens onto an alley behind the theater."

"You go first," Nick said. "So Elle and I don't have to watch our backs."

"I got no problem with you two." Michael shook his head wearily. "Long as we're alive we're in this together, because we might be the last living people in here."

Michael slow-footed down the hall, controlling his breath to preserve the bubble of stillness around them. Nick hoped that if they stayed out of the chaos and the fury, they would remain safe. The attackers didn't appear to think or plan, only to react. If he and Elle hadn't shown them the projector room window, they never would've thought to go there.

They descended the first flight of stairs to the landing. It offered two options, as Michael had said, easing Nick's anxiety about their impromptu alliance. One way reached down into the brightness of the lobby, from where savage moans echoed. The other led to a long, windowless corridor that terminated at a steel fire door. It looked like an exit, but Nick feared winding up trapped in that narrow passage if they couldn't open the door or go through it. He weighed the notion of taking the other route and bum-rushing their way through the lobby, which offered multiple exits, until a surge of ragged growls telegraphed excitement among the freaks, and a shaggy object thumped the floor at the bottom of the lobby stairs. It rolled a few seconds before stopping against the lowest step—a woman's severed head, hair and scalp torn from the right side of her skull. The freaks had cracked it open like a jelly jar. Brain remnants coated the jagged bone edges of the hole. Nick abandoned all thoughts of going out the front doors.

He turned to find that Michael had already descended to the service corridor, Elle halfway down the stairs, and he followed them. They hurried, then halted at the door to listen. Michael pressed his ear to the steel.

"It's solid. Can't hear a thing." He pulled his head back. "Maybe they're out there, maybe not."

"They're not hunting us. They only chase what's in front of them," Nick said. "If they've even left the theater, what reason would they have to go into the alley?"

"None, I guess," said Michael.

"Then it's probably empty."

"We know what's waiting for us if we go the other way," Elle said.

Nick nodded and tightened his grip on the broomstick. "Yeah, just … everyone be ready."

Michael clutched the door handle, eased it until it clicked, then pushed open the door to the alley. He growled as he surged out across the space, then slammed against the wall of the neighboring building. He rolled until his back butted flat, ready to fight. No one attacked. Nick and Elle edged outside. Only the three of them occupied the littered alley. Dumpster stink tainted the air. Nick stared at the full moon hanging in the blank night sky, staring down at them with lunar shimmer like a projector too weak to transmit its images all the way to Earth.

"Now what?" asked Elle.

Michael lifted a finger to his lips to shush her. He scurried to the mouth of the alley, where light from the theater marquee illuminated the street and blue-and-red lights flashed and flickered. Pressing himself against the wall of the theater building, he peered around the corner, then gestured for Nick and Elle to join him. Sirens wailed from every part of the city, echoing down the alley in fever-pitched protestations against an outbreak of urban madness. Police vehicles swarmed the multiplex.

"The dead haven't left the theater yet," Michael said.

"Good, the cops can contain them there," said Nick.

"Naw, man, the cops don't know what they're facing. They're going to open those doors and rush in to bust heads. They'll die in minutes, then all the dead folks fish-bowled up inside will rage onto the street."

"We need to warn them," Elle said.

Michael shook his head. "No way."

"We can't let them walk in there and die," said Elle, voice rising.

"We *can't* help them." Michael struggled to keep his composure. "You think I don't want to warn them? You think I want them to die? The only way it plays out if we step out there and squawk is they refuse to listen to our crazy story, take us into custody until they sort this shit out for themselves, then when the dead come outside looking for food, we're trapped in the back of police cars with our hands cuffed and no way to run or fight. Then we die too. But either way, those cops die."

"He's right," Nick said. "We avoid the cops. Even if they did listen and didn't arrest us, they'd hold us for questioning. We'd be sitting ducks. We need our car."

"Where is it?" Michael asked.

Elle gestured. "The theater parking lot."

"Forget it. The lot is already blocked off by a patrol cruiser. I saw it," said Michael. "My car's parked on the next block. If we can reach it, there's time to get out of the city before this really blows up and things get worse."

Elle snorted. "We're running from crazy people and ducking the cops. How can things get worse?"

Michael pushed his messy hair back from his face with both hands, smoothing it against his skull as he inhaled several deep breaths. He rolled his shoulders, releasing tension, then exhaled a long sigh.

"I know you haven't wrapped your heads around what's happening here, but hasn't it occurred to you that this isn't the only theater in the city premiering *Necropolitan* tonight? Not the only theater in the city where the shit is now hitting the fan? Listen to those sirens. That's all hands on deck, the city's entire police and emergency response departments in action. And these *aren't* crazy people. They're corpses. Walking corpses. Our city isn't the only one where they're attacking the living. Unless others made out better than I did trying to stop this shit, soon almost nowhere will be safe. Those monsters aren't criminals or a cult, they're a necromantic, memetic contagion. The movie kills them. They kill others. They kill the cops, the cops come back to life and join them. Anyone the cops kill joins them too. In hours, this city will be a necropolis."

Tears welled in Elle's eyes. Her lips quivered as she absorbed the horror of Michael's words. Nick placed a hand on her shoulder, offering comfort.

"Enough, you made your point," he said. "When the police move on the multiplex, they'll be focused on what's going on inside. That's when we run. We use the confusion for cover. Even if we're seen, they'll be too busy to bother with us."

Michael's gaze flickered from Nick's face to Elle's as if assessing how likely they were to get him killed, then he gave a sharp nod. "Let's keep thinking like that and stay alive."

The police were out of their cars now, armored in bulletproof vests, some wearing riot helmets, carrying shields and clubs. Several wielded shotguns. Voices crackled from radios in their cars and clipped to their belts and shoulders. A handful positioned themselves behind their vehicles, parked in an arc to contain anyone who exited the multiplex. They looked wired and rattled. Nick wondered what kind of reports were coming across their radios, what they expected to encounter inside the theater. Someone shouted an order. Everyone fell into formation.

Nick clung to a moment that felt like it might never end. Voices in his head urged him to ditch Michael and his bullshit. They shrilled about the impossibility of the dead coming back to life, of a movie that killed its viewers. They pleaded with him to lie down and rest, to soothe the pile-driver aching in his skull, close his eyes and stop the world spinning, but the only voice he listened to was Elle's.

We can do anything when we stick together.

One of the cops shouted an order. They rushed the doors like a football team. The moment they opened them, the freaks poured out, and the two groups clashed, the swift cops overwhelmed by the awkward mass of slow bodies that didn't register blows from their clubs, that ignored bullets and shots that ripped through their bodies, that kept coming regardless of what the cops threw at them. Frantic hands seized riot shields by the edges and pulled cops to the ground. Shotgun blasts thundered, forcing small pockets in the crowd that quickly filled with oncoming attackers.

"Run, now!" Michael shouted.

He dashed into the street. Nick took Elle's hand and led her on his heels until the pain in his ankle flared too hot, and he fell behind. The world tilted around him, and he shoved Elle on ahead. He focused on her sneakered feet as he took one limping step after another, propping himself with the broomstick remnant when he felt he might tip to the side. Police voices shouted at them. Gunfire cracked. Something sizzled the air as it passed Nick, then bricks on the building across the street exploded into dust.

Ahead of him, Michael and Elle vanished into another alley. He moved against pain running buzzsaws up his leg and knocking down walls in his head, terrified he wouldn't get going again if he stopped. A bullet chewed pavement at his feet, and then he chased Elle and Michael into the alley shadows. The gunshots stopped, but the screams continued. They sickened Nick. He had put himself through so much without a moment to breathe, stood resolute for Elle when he wanted to lie down and sleep until his head stopped whirling. The world spun and tilted and spun and tilted, and light gnawed on his eyes. He braced himself against a wall, doubled over, and vomited.

He lifted his head in time to see Michael and Elle exit the other end of the alley. They stopped dead in their tracks. Skull throbbing, he wiped his lips on his shirt sleeve, then steadied himself with the broomstick and stumbled to them.

"I'm sorry, man. I'm really sorry," Michael said as Nick emerged from the alley.

An SUV that Nick guessed belonged to Michael sat parked at an expired meter. A man, dressed all in white clothes like the dead man in the projection booth, stood atop the hood. He held a black, three-foot wooden rod in one hand. Silver carvings marked its surface in serpentine lines that formed signs and letters incomprehensible to Nick, like cave paintings and writing on stone tablets too ancient for translation. The man regarded the three of them with a wicked grin.

Another man and two women dressed in identical attire stood on the sidewalk. Gray pistols hung in white holsters on their hips. Four freaks advanced ahead of them, a wall of seeping wounds, arms raised, fingers already grasping, mouths opened slackly to bare cracked teeth jutting from vermiform gums. Their decayed clothes clung to their flesh like a second skin, like tattoos of a business suit, yoga pants, a Hawaiian shirt, and a sundress. These freaks hadn't come from the theater.

"Hello, Michael," the man atop the car said. "Things not go how you hoped? You know what I said the night you ran. You were a loser when you joined us, you will always be a loser, and you were destined to fail. Loser, loser, loser. You sorry, pathetic failure."

The man jumped down from the car, then took a phone from his pocket. He snapped pictures of Nick and Elle, then tapped on the screen, texting them into the ether, awaiting a reply. When his phone pinged, he tilted his head as though surprised by the answer.

"Well, okay then, Michael … you're coming with us, and so are your friends. Apparently they're on the list. And you—you long-haired, pretentious loser—you're going to help make up for all the trouble you caused."

Nick wondered if he hadn't hit his head harder than he thought and slipped into a hallucination. Only the fierce resolve in Elle's eyes anchored him now. He had seen it the night she betrayed her father, the night they'd fled his estate, her hometown, that entire region of the country. He had seen it every time her father's goons caught up to them, and they'd had to fight and flee again. Her resolve had carried them both through months of running until they built new identities for themselves, new lives, off the radar, using cash and disposable credit cards, no cell phones that could be tracked, blending into the ordinary world, striving for an ordinary life—a hope that now seemed naïve and risible.

He had long feared the day a handful of Elle's father's thugs showed up at their door, but he knew how to face that threat. He and Elle had trained and planned for it. He had protected her as a bodyguard before they ran and never stopped shielding her. They had been inseparable ever since—except for one night in Pittsburgh when they'd blundered into the wrong diner and run afoul of her father's local attack dogs. He'd rescued Elle that night, tracked and found her before the assholes could hand her over, and killed three of them in the process. But the six hours apart from her had been the longest of his life. This, though, this unreal chaos and madness erased the world he knew. He never could've predicted such a threat. Whenever he tried to accept it for how it looked, how Michael insisted it was, his mind rejected the possibility that the dead walked.

Even as he boarded a luxury minibus onto which the people in white herded them as prisoners, he stole glances at their "corpse" escorts. *Makeup*, one part of his brain said. *Drugs and hard living,* said another. *Malnutrition. They're only ugly, not dead. Ugly motherfuckers with phobias about bathing.* Their stench, masked poorly by aerosol air freshener, pushed through artificial lavender and lemon scents. It burned in his nostrils and made his eyes water. He read the same disgust on Elle's face. *Good. Better than fear. We still have a chance as long as we don't give in to fear.*

Nick stumbled up the steps of the bus. One of the women in white laughed at him.

At the head of the aisle, he stopped in his tracks. Freaks occupied every seat in the back half of the bus. A dozen pairs of glassy eyes glared at him. He gagged on the choking cloud of rotten flesh odor mixed with artificial lemon and lavender scents. He couldn't imagine how the men and women in white tolerated it—unless longtime exposure had acclimated them to it. How long did that take? How long had this been going on?

"Keep moving. Take a seat," the man with the rod said.

Nick braced himself against the seat back as he moved to the first opening he saw and fell into it, his body unexpectedly relieved by the comfort of plush cushions and the chance to stop moving. Elle came next, but when she tried to sit next to Nick, one of their captors pointed her across the aisle. She and Nick exchanged glances before she settled into the aisle seat. They sent Michael to sit beside Nick. The freaks and the others in white boarded. One of the women seated herself behind the wheel. The man with the rod stood in the aisle as the doors whooshed shut and the bus rolled into motion.

"Who are these people, Michael?" Nick whispered.

Michael only closed his eyes and shook his head.

"No need to whisper," said the man with the rod. "My name is Langston Wood. I'm an associate producer. See this?" He raised the rod to display it. "It's a necromancer's rod. It gives me control over the common dead. Think of it as my clipboard, a sign that I'm official. What I say goes when the producers and the Director aren't on set. You'll meet them soon enough. How do you think they'll take to your new friends, Michael?"

"Fuck you, Langston."

Langston laughed. The bus turned and slowed as it passed the street where the multiplex stood. Through tinted windows, Nick watched freaks wander from the theater into the flashing blue-and-red lights of the police cruisers. A crowd of the freaks clustered around one of the cars. They beat on the window glass with clumsy hands. They pushed the car, rocked it, tried to lift it, craving the lone cop trapped in the driver's seat. *Trapped.* Like Michael had warned they would be if the police took them into custody. Like they were now as the bus cruised along streets full of city lights and panic. Hundreds of people were out, all running, rushing, crying, screaming as gangs of murderous freaks hunted them. Four more blocks, and they passed another chaotic mob. Nick knew the cinemaplex on that street. He and Elle went there for midnight movies.

"Such a beautiful sight, isn't it?" Langston said. The man and the woman in white seated in the front row twisted around to face the bus occupants. Warped smiles disfigured their faces, smiles not of enjoyment but of practiced habit. Mechanical smiles to hide emotion. Their eyes gleamed with anticipation. "After so many years in 'development hell,' it's hard to express how gratifying it is to see everything come together. Years and years untangling all the rites, perfecting the casting, scripting just the right sigils. Michael knows. He was with us a long time. The Director had high hopes for him. Such a disappointment. A little of Michael's soul is still in *Necropolitan*, though. Rewrites didn't erase all his contributions even if he didn't get onscreen credit."

They entered a tourist district where three multiplexes stood within six blocks of each other. Freaks filled the streets, stalking, feeding, killing, slicking the pavement with gore. Blood looked black and lurid by the light of streetlamps and neon signs. The bus windows muted the screams of the victims, the wordless growls of the killers. Langston held the rod and whispered words too softly for Nick to make out. The crowd parted, forming an opening in the street for the bus to continue its journey. It motored on through a city awash in death and violence. Witnessing the scale of the mayhem, the relentless onslaught of the freaks, Nick doubted they would've escaped the city in Michael's car. Wherever Langston and his team took them, for now at least, they had saved their lives.

The bus turned downtown. Nick felt Elle's eyes on him, encouraged by the resolve that still filled them. He had no escape route to offer her now, no plan other than to ride things out and wait for an opportunity. He hoped, somehow, she understood and would wait with him.

The driver pushed buttons on the dashboard. Screens descended from the ceiling.

"The three of you are so fortunate the producers want to take a meeting with you," he said. "They've wanted Michael for a long time, but I don't know what they have in mind for the cutesy couple. Here's a little preview to help you set the mood."

Light filled each screen. A rumble of surprised gasps and moans rose from the freaks in the back seats.

"Close your eyes. It's best if you don't watch," Michael said. "They need you to buy the hype. It's about getting inside your head, flipping your lid, and making you one of them."

"One of who?" asked Nick.

"The common dead, if your mind breaks that way. Or one of *them*, the premium dead, if you're special enough, or if you're really A-list material, something else altogether." Michael indicated Langston and the others in white. "Some went along because they wanted to. Most needed to be persuaded to believe in the production's greatness. Not hard given the alternatives and the potential power to be gained. Necromancers have ways of keeping people in line. There are different forms of death. You can die inside. Your mind, soul, or spirit all can die, while your body carries on. They can murder your ego, every part of you that makes you truly alive. They control every type of death. Still, it takes conviction and commitment to produce a blockbuster that can change the world. They're trying to soften up you and Elle to buy into their vision."

A scene coalesced on the screens. Audio pumped crowd murmurs through speakers above each window. A view into a vast auditorium took focus. Frightened people filled it, clinging to each other, herded by the dead. *No, by freaks.* Nick's brain still fought the narrative. *People made to look dead. Drug addicts. Street people. Sick people. Violent people. It's not real. Nothing in movies is. Nothing on a screen is ever real. It's all false, a fiction, a phantasm, only electricity, light, and pixels.*

"It's a special screening," Langston said. "We could wait for word of mouth to spread, let things take their course, but opening night returns are so crucial. We've brought people in off the streets so they can watch *Necropolitan* for free. We're even live-streaming this for folks who skip the theater. The 'wait-for-streaming' crowd is so important. Sad, really. Watching movies from the comfort of home is nice, but there's nothing like a theater experience. I'm sure you agree."

The camera angle widened. On massive screens suspended above the audience, credits rolled. During sports events, the screens might show advertisements and instant replays. For concerts, they provided people in the nosebleed seats a close-up look at the band. Tonight, they rolled *Necropolitan*.

The opening credits ended. The film title seared itself into view. Nick struggled to focus on the screen within a screen, to understand the images, their details, and meanings. The film launched into action without hesitation. A series of sequences from a world filled with walking corpses more monstrous and decayed than any freak he'd seen tonight. The movie gore, limbs ripped from bodies, spilled blood, heads cracked open, faces torn to shreds, torsos raked and split to divulge organs—it all looked more real than any actual violence Nick had ever witnessed. Hyperreal. Elevated. Archetypal. Exaggerated for ultimate clarity and emphasis of terror.

He couldn't follow the story, but the images worked their way into his head, seeking a place to nest, quieting the voices in his brain. Until the lights needled too much at his photosensitive eyes, reigniting the awful, throbbing ache in his skull. His stomach turned. Bile rose in his throat. As the onscreen dead closed in on a stranded school bus full of middle schoolers, he clamped his eyes shut and waited for it to subside.

"Don't watch, Elle," he said despite the pounding in his head, but she didn't answer. He slit open his eyes, ignored the wave of pain even the dim light in the bus sent through them, and saw Elle staring squarely, solidly, at the little screen suspended from the ceiling. Fascination replaced her resolve as *Necropolitan* cast its spell upon her. "Elle! No, don't watch."

"It's okay, Nick. I understand it now," she said.

Nick twisted in his seat, pushing against Michael, and shoved across the aisle, knocking Elle sideways and breaking her gaze at the screen. She yelped as she bumped against the side of the bus. When she righted herself, her anger and rage returned. She beamed it hard at Langston, seething for the first chance to erupt into a fury Nick swore long ago he'd do everything possible to avoid ever having targeted at him.

"Oh my God, what was that?" Elle asked. "It was inside my head. I wanted to watch it all and keep watching."

"Don't look again. Please, Elle, don't watch anymore," Nick said.

"You can't deny it's kind of beautiful," Michael said.

Nick dared a quick glimpse at Michael, who watched the screen with avid, wide eyes.

"Look away, don't watch," Nick said, closing his eyes again to soothe his churning head.

The screams from the auditorium swelled over the bus speakers. Nick guessed people in the crowd had begun to turn, to die and rise. *Not dead, only broken-minded: something violent and feral inside them unlocked, a hypnotic command to savagery implanted.* He didn't know how a movie could affect those who watched it, how it could change them. He had read about experiments in subliminal messaging, but he didn't think that really worked. Part of him wanted to look at the screen again, try to decode it, but the pain behind his eyes helped him resist. He refused to disappoint Elle. Screaming, crying, and moaning drowned out the soundtrack and film score. Nick imagined the absolute riot filling the auditorium. The dead—*no, freaks, just freaks,* a voice insisted from the back of his head—slaughtering the others, feeding on them, turning them into more mindless killers.

"It's like a vaccine," Michael said. "The movie creates antibodies, the antibodies create more antibodies. Soon the pathogen is eliminated."

"What the fuck, Michael? The 'pathogen' is people," Nick said.

"People? No, it's … it's . . ." Michael slammed his forehead against the back of the seat in front of him several times, grunting. "What the hell am I doing?" he cried. "Turn it off, Langston, switch it the fuck off. I don't want to see this. I don't want to hear it."

"No can do, Mikey." Langston dialed up the volume until the speakers crackled with distortion, filling the bus with what sounded like all the screams in Hell rising to the surface. The movie soundtrack played tinnily but steady. The freaks in the rear seats growled with excitement. "You don't want to miss the best parts of the story. I know how much you love *story*. You never appreciated the value of sheer spectacle."

The bus rolled on through the city for a while longer until it jolted over a pothole as it turned down an avenue toward one of the city's tallest skyscrapers, a tower of glass, light, and steel that rose into the night, a grounded lighthouse beaming solace and safety amidst a sea of chaos. The driver parked at the curb outside the main entrance. Langston killed the video feed. The bus doors opened behind him. He clapped his hands.

"Time to meet the producers," he said. "I hope you're ready to pitch for your life."

The people in white exited the bus. A few of the freaks followed, but Langston pointed the black rod at the ones in the rear seats and ordered them to stay. They complied, but every one of them tickled the back of Nick's neck with their stares. He felt like a lobster in a tank being considered for a meal. Off the bus, he stuck by Elle. Shading his eyes, he leaned back to gaze at the full sweep of silver and reflected light prodding into the hazy night sky where the moon shed its brightness into diluting light pollution. They were deep in the city now.

"What is this place?" Nick asked.

"The producers' office," Michael said. "Fuck, man, I can't tell you how sorry I am you got caught up in this with me. You might've had a better chance if we split up before we left the theater."

Elle frowned. "What will they do to us?"

"Do *to* you? Nothing. At least, nothing you won't agree to," Langston said. "You're getting a meeting with the producers. You should be thinking about what they can do *for* you, what deal you can make. Give them your best pitch. Not everyone gets an opportunity like this. If they like your vision, who knows how far you can go? Someone high up has their eye on you two. Sky's the limit."

"Michael, what the hell is he talking about?" Nick asked.

"I rarely met with the producers," said Michael. "I usually dealt with associates like this douchebag."

"Shut up, Mike, Mikey, Michael," Langston said. "You enjoy living in your car? No one gives a shit about Shakespeare and character development and thematic integrity. No one has for four hundred years. Loser. William Goldman farted better than he wrote."

He gestured with the rod. One of the freaks shoved Michael from behind with a blotchy hand. A yellow fingernail snapped loose with the contact and fluttered to the ground. The group advanced. Dead—*no, freak*—doormen in bloodstained uniforms opened the glass doors and directed them into a vast lobby with marble flooring and polished granite walls. A waterfall trickled down from three stories high, spilling into a pool half-hidden by large-leafed plants. Cold seeped into Nick's flesh and bones. Elle shivered. Air-conditioned breezes poured out of overhead vents, turning patches of sweat to ice.

"It's so cold in here," she said.

"Cold preserves the flesh," Langston said. He leaned on the security desk, behind which sat a man in a navy blue suit, a badge with his picture clipped to the lapel. Lipstick brightened his lips, flaking powder covered his cheeks. "We're here for a meeting, Sam. The big guy wants to see these three."

The security officer stood and grinned that forced grin that made Nick's skin crawl. "Michael, that you? I thought you swore you'd never come back here. You fucking loser. I told you if you ran, you better run to the other side of the world. Look at this guy. He flips us the bird, now he's meeting with the producers. Good for you, but hey, Hitchcock and Truffaut still suck, and I can shoot better pictures out of my ass with an iPhone than Kubrick ever could. Fuck you. Loser." Sam read a computer monitor then handed Langston a key card. "Elevator four. You, your guests, and Annie. Everyone else waits here."

Langston poked Nick in the shoulder with his rod. "Move."

Nick shuddered. The bus ride had allowed him to recover some strength, and the spinning sensation had subsided. He positioned himself between Elle and Langston. While they waited for the elevator, the others in white took seats in the lobby. Their freak escort loitered by them, mindless. The elevator chimed, and the doors slid open. The five entered. Langston pressed the key card to a reader above the keypad, then pushed the button for the second-to-top floor. The gentle pressure of ascent stirred the unease in Nick's stomach.

"Like old home week for you, Michael," he said.

"It's not like it looks, man," said Michael. "Langston and that security jackoff, they only know what the execs tell them. The truth is another story altogether. I never wanted any of this to happen. Whatever else I've done, I was always working to stop this, but sometimes they change what we write, you know? They want it different, force your hand, or get a script doctor to revise it how they want. Too much of that, you don't know what ideas are your own anymore. You almost forget how to think for yourself."

"You tried to subvert the Director's vision." Langston rapped the back of Michael's head with his rod. "Shut up, asshole. You think anyone but you remembers Robert Towne today?"

Michael groaned then glared at Langston. "Okay, enjoy it while you can, ass-kisser. Time will come when I pay you back for it all."

Langston chuckled, unconcerned. The elevator stopped. The doors opened onto a bright lobby filled with high-end leather business furniture and abstract art gallery paintings. Beyond the front desk, a sprawling cubicle farm buzzed with white-garbed people. A few wore similar outfits in dollar bill green. Some of them worked phones. Others hurried around with files and tablets in their hands. Small groups clustered intently in urgent discussions. A sound cloud of voices, cellphone pings, and the soundtrack of *Necropolitan* piping from unseen speakers hung over it all. Nick squinted and recoiled from the light and noise.

"Hello, Langston," the receptionist said. "Leave these three with me. Archie wants to see you and Annie in his office."

"We have to get them to their meeting, Sally," Langston said, annoyed.

"I'll make sure they get there. Give them the VIP treatment." Sally came out from behind her desk. She wore a snug, professional, emerald dress and a pearl necklace and looked like she could've been a movie star. "Go on. You know how Archie hates to be kept waiting."

Langston and Annie glanced back once as they walked away down a corridor to the right, then moved out of sight.

"You're all going to behave, aren't you? You can't go anywhere without permission. You need a key card to operate the elevator, even going down.

Can't be too careful about security. Can I get you anything? Espresso? A vitamin water? Do you need the restroom to freshen up for your big meeting?" Sally stepped back, looked them up and down. "I can't even say how excited the producers are to hear what you can bring to the franchise. Especially you, Michael. They're so thrilled to have you back."

"Hardly sounds like you were working against them, Michael. You must have been pretty important around here," Nick said.

"Yes, Michael was one of our rising stars." Sally squeezed Michael's arm and smiled. "The producers haven't found the right person to fill his shoes. The Director himself has been trying to contact him for months."

"I've been busy with my own projects," said Michael.

"What the fuck is all this?" Elle asked. "Everything is going to hell outside, and you're all in here working like it's no big deal."

Sally laughed. "It's a very big deal, especially to us. Opening night always is. You never know for sure how a movie's going to hit with the public until the box office rolls in."

"So what's the verdict? Hit or flop?" Nick asked. "How can you even tell with half the city off their rockers in a murder frenzy?"

"A frenzy?" Sally frowned, then raised one eyebrow. "That's an ... interesting perspective. I'm sure the producers will be eager to hear your take. Now, please, follow me."

Sally led them down a corridor lined with glass-walled offices, each one occupied by a man or a woman in an expensive-looking, tailored power suit—dark gray, navy blue, or black, a few in pinstripes. All of them with some flair that distinguished them from the kind of suits that might fill a Wall Street office or a law firm. Loud ties. Sleek sunglasses hanging from the breast pocket. Orchid boutonnieres. Silk blouses with distractingly deep décolletage. Everyone worked their phones or keyboards, intent, anxious, and hyperfocused on whatever task occupied them.

The *Necropolitan* soundtrack didn't play here, and the corridor seemed to go on and on, office after office, until they passed the last glass panel and arrived at a pair of mahogany doors. Sally guided them through into a conference room dominated by an extended, black lacquer table lined with leather chairs. One wall comprised of floor-to-ceiling windows letterboxed a stunning view of the city. Constellations of illuminated windows burned against a slate-black sky that looked paper-thin and fake. Flickering light and smoke gyred up from brick-and-concrete canyons. Helicopters flitted around, spitting brightness from high-lumen spotlights. No sound penetrated the glass. The chaos played in silence, an action movie on mute. Nick felt the urge to reach for a remote and raise the volume.

"Make yourselves comfortable," Sally said. "The producers will be with you soon."

She withdrew from the room, shutting the door behind her. Michael gravitated to a countertop against the interior wall and fixed himself a cup of coffee at a station of paper cups and carafes. Elle stood at the window, staring out, one hand raised, fingertips pressing the glass as if testing its solidity. Nick placed his hands on her shoulders. She gripped them with hers and settled against his chest. Body language and contact communicated everything between them. How they'd wound up here and what might happen next didn't matter as long as they remained together. They'd made that choice the night they fled Elle's father and never questioned it. Elle had made *her* choice that night—had chosen Nick over the life she'd lived since birth. Nick found himself incapable of imagining life without her. Even death held little fear for him if they died together, and he believed Elle felt likewise, a conviction he'd reached after many nights of soul-baring talk and honest acceptance of the high probability they had both shortened their lifespans by crossing Elle's father. They only wanted to spend whatever life they lived together.

A door clicked. Nick watched it open, reflected in the window. Half a dozen people in suits even more expensive and fashionable than those on the office workers entered the room and spread out to seats around the far end of the conference room table.

"Michael!" one said. "We're so happy to have one of our best writers back."

The last man to enter paused in the doorway. A broad smile beamed on his face. He made eye contact with Elle, then with Nick—and the bottom dropped out of Nick's world. He fell inside himself. His mind plummeted toward an abyss of bewilderment and fear. He knew that face, had seen its fierce blue eyes and close-cropped gray hair in his nightmares, had long wondered how it came by the rough scar above its left eye—and hoped to never see it again.

"Nick, Elle! There are no words for my joy at our reunion," said Elle's father, Devlin Branniff. He strode to the empty seat at the head of the table, then gestured to three open chairs to his right. "Come. Sit. Let's talk. I knew I picked the right man for the job, Nick. I owe you much for returning Elle to me safe and sound. There'll be a bonus in your account. Consider it hazard pay for what you handled tonight. Consider your contract fulfilled."

"Nick?" Elle stood rooted to the floor. Her face turned pale. In a quivering, half-whisper voice, she asked, "What the hell is he saying? What contract?"

Nick's head swirled, struggling to bring his thoughts into coherence. The room dipped to the left, then the right, then dipped again, and again, a boat riding on shrugging waves. He reeled at Branniff's smug expression, repulsed by his family resemblance to Elle.

"Nick!" Elle gripped his chin and directed him to face her. Tears welled in her eyes. Her fingertips pinched him and trembled against his jaw. "*What* contract? *What* the hell is he saying? *Tell me.*"

"I have no idea," Nick said. "There's no contract."

"Don't *lie* to me." Elle exposed her heart in her widening, pleading eyes, bared her soul, opened herself entirely, as vulnerable as an infant. A single wrong word from Nick would stab to the core of her entire being, then the Elle he knew—the Elle he loved—would die. "*Tell me* the truth."

No words seemed adequate to answer. Words brought risk, invited comment and intrusion from others. Words cycloned around Nick's throbbing head too fast and brutal for him to keep faith in how they might form in his throat and leave his mouth. Instead of speaking, he took Elle in his arms and kissed her, his lips pressed to hers, softly at first, then with need, with hunger, dropping his own guard to match Elle's lowered defenses. He pulled her as tight to him as he could until he felt her reciprocate the unspoken message. *We can do anything together.* His mind calmed. The storm inside his skull settled. He broke off the kiss.

"I love you. That's all there is. That's *everything*. That's the truth in full," he said.

Elle stepped back and lowered her arms. Her teary gaze locked on Nick's eyes, placated for the moment but shadowed by lingering uncertainty. She nodded then seated herself in the open chair nearest her father. Nick sat beside her, Michael on the other side of him.

Branniff took the head seat, grinning. "Getting a last taste, Nick? The job I hired you for came with certain carnal perks, I suppose."

"Fuck you, father," said Elle. "Get on with whatever it is you want."

"Not what *I* want, dearest Elle. I've got what I want. You saw it all around the city, and now I've even got you back with me," Branniff said. "This is about what *you* want. What's your pitch? I'm asking you to join me in the family business. This is an opportunity to put your stamp on how we reboot the world. It's the biggest IP of all, and we're making it our own. Forget everything you thought you knew about humanity's story. That's all old news. This is not your grandfather's civilization, not your grandmother's society. No one cares about that shit anymore except nostalgia buffs, OCD completists, and nerds who think nothing should ever change. Our vision is a cutting-edge high concept for our times. It's everything today's audiences crave. All of history colliding with the future in one star-studded extravaganza with a cast of billions. And I want you in on it with me. We're talking sequels, spin-offs, merchandise, media tie-ins, product placement, theme parks, and much more. So pitch me, daughter dear, what would *you* do with this newly remade world? Where would you take us? How would you expand the brand?"

"Remade? Brand? What audience? You've turned everyone in the audience into mindless cannibals or empty-headed ass-kissers," Elle said. "Who the hell is left?"

Branniff leaned back in his chair and folded his hands on his chest, looking so much like a caricature of a corporate movie villain that Nick almost laughed out loud.

"You've lost the plot. Understandable. You've been out of the loop," he said. "The first movie in any great series must be revolutionary. What you witnessed tonight—and, Nick, again, thanks for your outstanding service in keeping Elle safe and alive through this tumultuous time, I never doubted you could do it—but what you witnessed only sets the stage for bigger and better. Every successful reboot courts controversy. You have to break the old to birth the new. There are always naysayers. Keyboard warriors who piss reflexively on anything different from what was cemented in their tiny brains at age fourteen. Small-minded trolls who say they hate, hate, *hate* what we've done yet still show up, buy tickets, and hoard the merch. It's win-win. Then with time the new becomes the established; everyone loves it, and the dead do what we order them to, and the living do what the dead command because they don't want to die too."

"He's saying *Necropolitan* is only the first act," Michael said.

"Exactly! Leave it to a writer to find the best words," Branniff said. "Act one establishes that we can reanimate the dead, and if people don't cooperate, we can make them. So, Elle, tell me, what've you got?"

"How about you fuck off and die, and Nick and I walk out of here never having to look over our shoulders or hear from you again?"

"Hmmmm." Branniff frowned. "No, I don't see it. Too pat. Not enough conflict. Hit me with something else."

Nick stared up and down the length of the conference table at the immaculately clean business clothes on bodies trim to fitness club conformity, plastic smiles, eyes wide in perfect synchronicity as if held by invisible hooks, hair styled to the absolutes of vinyl dolls. All their attention hung on the words of Devlin Branniff. Their skin shimmered in the office light, blemish free, not a pore visible. They all wore makeup. Actors on a set. They barely seemed to breathe— barely seemed real— except for one man at the far end of the table. A single line of perspiration ran from his hairline to the corner of his eye. He wore a gray power suit like the others and a brilliant red silk tie held in place by an intricately carved tie clasp. Nick watched the line of sweat reach the edge of the man's jaw, form a drop, and plummet onto his chest, creating a small dark spot on his lapel, an out-of-place blemish of humanity.

"Nick?" Elle placed her hand on his wrist. "You still with me?"

He nodded. "Sorry, my head's still a little fuzzy."

"Well, shake it off, son, we've got business to attend to," said Branniff, as he rose from his seat.

Everyone else at the table except for Nick, Elle, and Michael shot to their feet, too, smiles unchanged.

Elle rose slowly. "Father wants to give us a tour."

"I want to give *you* a tour, daughter, but Nick is welcome to join us. You've put your trust in him, maybe even come to love him over the last two years. I considered that possibility when I cast Nick for his role. I chose him not only for his skills as a bodyguard but for his charisma and looks so you would enjoy him. I'm sure it made his job easier knowing that you desired him. He certainly has a future here after succeeding, so why not let him come along? And Michael too. He's got the knack for clarity." Branniff turned his attention to his assembled staff, holding their collective breath for a directive. "The rest of you, back to work, *for fuck's sake!* It's opening night. Don't let me down, don't screw up, or you'll find yourself out of a job with our street team chewing on your bones."

Gesturing for Nick, Elle, and Michael to follow, Branniff led them into a bright corridor lined with old movie posters framed on the walls. Nick read them through eyelids slitted against the light, but he didn't recognize the movies. They were like films from an alternate history or props in a movie about making movies. He discerned a theme in them, though. They all featured "Death" in the title or death imagery in the art. Skeletons, graves, coffins, and morgues. A banner across the bottom of each one read *Coming Soon*.

The group walked to a waiting elevator. Branniff pulled a key from his pocket, inserted it in a lock on the control board, turned it, then hit the topmost button. The elevator rose. It opened onto the building's ultimate floor—an immaculate theater lobby. The aroma of fresh popcorn filled the air. The soft quiet of velvet-padded walls and plush carpeting underfoot embraced them. Three women in body-hugging uniforms staffed the concession, each displaying a desperate smile. Opposite the concession stood three theaters, *Auditorium 1*, *Auditorium 2*, and *Auditorium 3*, labeled by backlit signs. A uniformed usher with leading-man looks manned the ticket check at the velvet rope entrance, his face twisted with the same familiar nightmare smile Nick now loathed.

"Refreshments, anyone?" Branniff offered, but no one accepted. "Then let's get on with the show. We'll start with Auditorium 1. Do you agree, Michael? Or would our narrative go over better presented out of sequence? Perhaps Auditorium 2? I think we agree on saving Auditorium 3 for last, but I know how fond you are of nonlinear storytelling."

"Start at the beginning. If you don't hook them fast, they'll start checking their watches, looking at their phones, you know how it goes," said Michael.

Smirking, Branniff said, "It's good to have you back, Michael. Let's see how things go tonight. Maybe you're ready to join the producers. You could work with Elle!"

Branniff slid four tickets from the pocket of his suit coat, handing them to the usher, who tore them, then slid the returned stubs back into his pocket. The group walked through the velvet rope opening, Michael bringing up the rear. The usher broke his smile long enough to say, "Welcome back, Mr. Sterling, sir. It's not Lynch or Welles, but I hope you enjoy the show."

Branniff held the auditorium door open and guided his guests to stairs at the back of the theater. "We'll sit in the balcony."

They took front row seats, facing the largest movie screen Nick had ever seen. Projected onto it swirled an intricate, circular design of occult symbols and icons. At the heart of the ring throbbed a pentagram, rippling and shifting through orientations and configurations. It matched representations of black magic and devil worship symbols Nick knew from so many bad horror flicks, but they felt authentic and powerful in a way that set his blood buzzing. The pulse of the central ring and the flow of shapes and characters around its perimeter almost mesmerized him, liquid light in motion, summoning his heartbeat to match its rhythm, but his aching head broke any sense his brain tried to make of what he saw. It resisted any continuity in the pattern. None of it found ground to take hold in his mind. Soon the churning light hurt his eyes too much, and he looked away. In the darkness below sat an audience, a bumper crop of heads, moviegoers enrapt by the display. The stench of decay and artificial air fresheners burned his nostrils. He shivered from the cold; the AC pumped on full, making the theater an icebox.

He wrapped his fingers around Elle's hand, leaned in close. "Don't look at the screen. Those symbols are doing something to our heads."

Elle nodded but didn't reply. She gazed straight ahead, entranced. The designs danced, reflected in her eyes. Nick put his hand over them and guided her to look away. She seemed to snap out of a fog.

"What ... what is that?" she asked.

"Don't look at it," Nick said.

Branniff spoke into his cell phone, then hung up and pocketed it. "Our show's about to begin. I've asked the projectionist to queue up our first feature. Like Michael said, let's start at the beginning."

Music flowed from unseen speakers. A new image filled the screen, projected over the spinning pentagram and its strobing black magic spirographs. The two formed a union of light, shadow, and color. A corpse face dissolved into focus, long decayed by time, a skull dressed in tatters of flesh, fronds of dirty hair, no lips, teeth rotted, eye sockets as black and empty as dry wells, winter caves devoid of life. The music reached a dramatic peak then faded. A voice spoke—the voice of the head, Nick knew, but he couldn't say why. Any voice could've been dubbed to the audio to make the head seem to speak, but he believed without the slightest doubt he heard the voice that had once belonged to the skull onscreen. A voice from beyond the grave, from outside the living world. He didn't understand its words, but the intonation resonated in his bones, a physical touch as if the head spoke directly to him, layering its message inside him. The image faded, and a title appeared: "The Making of *Necropolitan*."

"Here we go," Branniff said, and the title faded to black. "This is where it all began."

Three minutes into the movie, Nick almost vomited.

The chiaroscuro flickered and danced, a million microscopic spider legs pushing hot brightness under his eyelids, creeping over his eyeballs, twining themselves around his optic nerve then corkscrewing until they reached his brain, where they swelled, and he felt he might explode out of his own skull. He could barely look away or cover his eyes with his hands. The movie supplanted his will with an urge to watch, to stare, to lose himself in the moving images until they became his reality. Only the occult circle and its shifting dial of arcane symbols projected beneath the main attraction distracted him. In sequences when the screen darkened sufficiently, it writhed under the action, a pale ghost in the gloom. In fade-outs between scenes, it surfaced. Nick suspected he wasn't supposed to see it, that once the movie began it was meant to pulse beneath the horrifying *mise-en-scène* of the feature, a subliminal psychic injection worming its way unnoticed into his mind—but his mind noticed.

The others, it seemed, did not. Branniff, relaxed in the cushy, reclining movie seat, his lips a joyful scar. Michael, bored, feigning disinterest as if he'd seen it all before. And Elle, oh God, no, but Elle watched with awe in her expression, eyes wide, gaze flicking from one element to another as digitally constructed phantasms danced on silvered cloth.

The audio ground itself into Nick's ears with all the delicacy of a garbage truck crushing trash. Chanting, screaming, singing voices collided in the pathways of his aural nerves, riding them to his brain like a flow of molten iron, searing his awareness. Like the film, the soundtrack carried hidden signals tunneled into the main audio, a stream of earworms scrabbling for traction in his mind, failing to find it. He heard them, registered them, and his awareness of them seemed to kill them in his ear canals.

The unease in his gut churned. Several times he felt on the verge of throwing up, but he found himself unable to move, locked into his soft, reclining seat, fingers gripping the armrests. He wanted to grab Elle and run, or at least turn her gaze from the screen, push her from her seat, hide her until the movie ended. His body refused to cooperate.

The movie unfolded. Nick sat helpless while his consciousness, subconscious, and parts of his mind even deeper and more primal resisted the memetic invasion from infecting him. The effort threatened to tear him apart. Every muscle in his body tensed. Sweat rivered down the back of his neck, soaking his shirt. His heart punched the inside of his chest. His lungs felt so full he could hardly inhale a fresh breath of the tainted air. Onscreen, the horrible truth revealed itself.

What did one call a group of black magicians? A coven or a cult? No, not quite right. This was something different. A cabal, perhaps? A gathering of powerful men and women who trafficked with the spirits of the dead. Necromancers. The word floated to the top of Nick's mind, remembered from old movies and books read long ago. These black wizards wore tailored power suits and designer originals and carried icons of the dead. Skulls. Bones. A dried, withered heart. A shriveled brain. An entire, tanned human skin draped over the arm of a woman in a perfectly pressed and fitted little black dress. They whispered, laughed, grunted, shrieked. Two parallel lines of power players subservient to the worship of death in a room of oak paneling and leather wingback chairs. They shook their artifacts, drank blood from a ladle served by a veiled, but otherwise naked, woman who walked among them with a dripping pail of it. Blood dribbled down their chins. They spat it into each other's faces.

Music roared from the speakers and swept the scene into blackness. Nick struggled to follow, his head threading together a story of ritual, sacrifice, blood, and communion with the dead. Necromancers dug up the head of one of their progenitors—the skull face that had opened the movie. Then they cast spells, imbued living energy into inanimate muscle, inhaled death from rotting flesh and exhaled it into celluloid and light and digital CGI ephemera, weaving black magic into a movie, laying a trap for all who watched, who looked, who wished away the real world for however long it might transport them to another reality. No one expected that to last forever. No one anticipated the idea of the movie tucking itself into those needy crevices in the minds of people only half alive, seeding itself there to be awakened later. No one but Devlin Branniff and his producers. No one but Michael, the writer.

"Oh God, no," Nick said when his own face appeared onscreen.

He stood at the center of a ritual, shirtless and barefoot. Moving stiffly, as if he didn't know where he was or what he was doing, he clumsily scribbled his signature in blood on paper that resembled a flap of dried skin, which Branniff then folded and tucked inside his jacket. A contract. As the ritual concluded, one of the necromancers, his suit vest and silk tie stained with blood, uttered in Nick's ear, "You will forget the bargain you have made as the dead forget life." Nick gasped. He twisted in his seat to confront incoming anger and horror from Elle—but she paid him no attention, ignored him even when he cried her name in her ear.

"Shush," Branniff said.

Nick turned back to the screen for yet another shock. A new ritual commenced in an empty building he recognized as the place in Pittsburgh where he'd tracked Elle and rescued her from her father's men. Six hours separated. He'd never known what happened to her in those six hours apart. She claimed not to remember, and she'd never spoken of the ceremony playing out onscreen, never mentioned drinking blood from a skull carved with the same engravings that adorned the necromancer's rods, never spoken of lighting black candles and chanting with her captors. A man in a black three-piece suit thrust a finger bone into her hand. She dipped it in the blood-filled skull then scrawled on a document that, like the one Nick had signed, resembled a patch of flensed skin. Then the man whispered in her ear, too, but Nick couldn't hear what he said. He watched as Elle laughed at herself onscreen, at her deal with a devil, then the movie cut to a new location, a new scene, a blood ritual blessing the film canisters as workmen loaded them onto delivery trucks. With the cargo spaces full, the necromancers slit the workers' throats, spilling their blood and closing their corpses in the trucks with the canisters.

Nick struggled to free himself of the paralysis the movie cast over him, to grab Elle and hold her tight, to find some explanation for the two of them appearing on screen. He recalled nothing of the ritual that included him. Watching it had felt like a fever dream, a nightmare plucked out of his mind and painted in light. He wondered if Elle felt the same, or if she knew what they'd watched was true. Onscreen, the black convoy rolled into the night and the film ended and faded to darkness, allowing the pentagram to return.

Branniff leaned over to Nick and whispered, "It's one thing to imbue an object, like film, with magic, but quite another to transfer that to the digital world. We were almost ready a couple of decades ago, when we had to go back to the drawing board because the world went digital."

The house lights came to half brightness. A commotion stirred in the lower auditorium. Branniff stood and waved to the projectionist, invisible behind his gleaming window. A spotlight flared to life, pooling illumination on the first several rows below the balcony. Before the first row stood half a dozen men and women. Blood and sweat slicked their faces. They shivered and twitched. Not freaks. To their right and left stood men armed with AR15s, black, tactical skull masks covering the lower half of their faces.

Dressed in immaculate white, Langston stepped into view and raised his wooden necromancer's rod. Making several complex gestures, tracing invisible lines in the air, he shouted, "Feed."

The audience released a collective groan and surged from their seats like a single living organism. They staggered forward, grasping limbs and faces. Langston and the armed guards retreated as the dead—*not dead, freaks*—pulled the captives beneath the mass of them.

"Audiences can be trained, dear daughter. Conditioned and rewarded," Branniff said. "No one ever went broke underestimating the gullibility, stupidity, and susceptibility to suggestion of the public. The minds of the common dead are simple to manipulate if you give them what they want. They make the perfect mob to ensure everyone else falls in line. Now, onto our second feature."

Nick wobbled as he trailed behind the others. Nothing seemed real.

I'm back in the multiplex, unconscious and hallucinating, ruining a whole lot of date nights by disrupting the show with my emergency, and when I come to, I'm going to laugh at how my imagination has run wild, and Elle's going to tell me I watch too many shlocky horror flicks before going to bed, then that's where she'll take me to nurse me back to health, and Elle . . .

The dead expression in her eyes razed all hope of the world reverting to normal in the blink of his eyes. She looked upon Branniff with a feeling he'd never witnessed in her regard of her father: admiration. She had hated him and everything he represented for as long as he'd known her, so long, the shift seemed impossible. But he knew Elle too well to deny what he saw now. It submerged his heart to the coldest, deepest place of his being, strained every bond he felt to her near to breaking, left him disoriented, hoping he'd hallucinated their appearances in the film, knowing he hadn't. Too shocked to speak, too afraid to reach out to Elle only for her to rebuff or ignore him, he trailed the group into the next auditorium. This time, Branniff seated them in the last row. The stench of this new world lingered thick here. Rot and artificial lilac. Putrescence and peppermint. It made Nick's eyes water.

Freaks filled the theater, and a film played. More flashes of rituals and spilled blood, of well-dressed men and women gathered in unholy places of the dead. Of corpse-servants, lurid dances, fervent gesticulations, and incomprehensible words. Rituals performed in editing rooms, spells cast over hard drives and video screens, magic captured in blood, then film, now transferred to digital information—a virulent and toxic medium. Nick clenched his eyes shut, afraid to watch and see Elle's face onscreen again. He peeked only enough to glimpse the audience freaks who looked less feral than those in the previous theater. A higher state of death, a higher class of filmgoers, the arthouse crowd, the cinephiles, the people who saw movies on their opening night. *The premium dead*, Michael had called them. He almost laughed, but nothing seemed funny anymore.

He tried to distract Elle from the phantasms dancing on silvered silk and nylon, but she swooned under their spell, lost to him. It had taken only minutes for her father to steal her away and undo all Nick had accomplished over two years. No. Devlin Branniff had beaten him months ago, and Nick had never even noticed. He had reclaimed his daughter in Pittsburgh, sent his men to taint Elle's mind and soul, set the stage, and sold her the vision to bring her into the fold. They had let Nick rescue her, let him kill those men—if they weren't already dead—then go on, living an illusion. He had protected Elle from everything but that. Maybe that had been in the script all along, a part he'd learned and lines he'd memorized in a death ritual wiped from his memory but hidden beneath the surface of his mind, pulling his strings for a part he was powerless to rewrite. Miserable thoughts and unrelenting aches throbbed inside his head.

He barely registered the end of their second feature. No feeding this time. The freaks seemed content with only the projection and whatever psychopompic message they derived from the subliminal spells. The premium dead appreciated art, appreciated the communion with their creators; they took all the sustenance they needed from it.

At Branniff's direction, the group rose and walked to the last auditorium, to an audience of yet different freaks, dressed in whites and greens. Racks of clothes filled the aisles. Among the rows, men and women with makeup kits moved like harvesters tending a crop, dressing the faces of the tamed dead, the *premium* dead—*uh-uh, the sedated freaks*—to look almost alive—*normal, almost healthy*. But these people were beyond the premium dead, above them in the necromantic pecking order, closer to life—or further from physical death, at least. As Michael had said, mind, soul, and spirit can die yet leave the body living. These were the *VIP dead*. Still human and alive on the surface—but dead and withered inside, their individuality sacrificed to the great casting of *Necropolitan*, dedicated to the production.

While projected light cast necromantic conjuring onto the screen, the makeup artists used cotton balls, Q-tips, eyelash brushes, lipsticks, powder puffs, and rouge to touch up the stars of the new world into which Nick had stumbled, or been dragged, or fallen. It didn't matter. He'd lost Elle, let her slip through his fingers in the dark and light of a movie theater filled with power he couldn't understand. He would've died fighting any man who'd tried to take her from him. In the end, she'd simply fallen under her father's spell, like who knew how many thousands or millions this night. There had been no one for him to grapple against or resist. No one to punch, shoot, or escape. He couldn't fight echoes of life spattered into the dark by projector bulbs. He couldn't fight black magic already nested in his and Elle's minds.

Only … he didn't understand why he hadn't fallen prey to the spell too.

Why didn't the movie wrap its grasp around him, transform him into one of the mindless freaks, or sway him to Branniff's side, like Elle, like even Michael seemed to gravitate upon his return? Why did he stay clearheaded and grounded? He wasn't, though, was he? He was addled and dazed and muddied, barely able to hold three thoughts together for a few seconds or accept such a fundamental change in reality. His mind regurgitated new ideas like a sick man who spewed out everything he consumed seconds after swallowing it. Maybe, he thought, the spell needed to sit in his brain longer than that to take effect, but his damaged nerves and burdened senses rejected it. Did the blows to his head when he fell account for his apparent immunity? Could the answer be so simple? Lost among his questions, Nick missed the movie's end. The credits rolled on *Necropolitan*, the movie he'd ached to see before tonight. Ninety minutes had passed in what seemed like ninety seconds.

He grasped the gist of what Branniff meant to show them. Each auditorium represented a different stage in the process of killing and reanimating the audience—*not killing, brainwashing, hypnotizing, mesmerizing.* Repeated viewings of *Necropolitan* filled their minds with the spell until the necromantic orders that controlled their wills grew so powerful that Branniff's team employed them to run his studio, dressing them with makeup and fitted clothing to mask their decay. A corporate army of the dead—*freaks!*—to serve a brain-dead populace—*freaks!*—and living masters. How many of the people they'd encountered in the office retained their own will? Nick thought of the sweating man in the conference room, the man with the red silk tie and the fancy tie clasp. The one man out of place. Alive in body and soul among the dead. *Not dead, not really, not reanimated corpses, only people convinced they'd died and returned as ghouls, only brainwashed freaks, victims of a cinematic delusion and overzealous fandom.* Nick knew what his mind told him, what Branniff showed them.

The truth is a different story altogether, Michael had said. *I never wanted any of this to happen. Whatever else I've done, I was always working to prevent this.* Prevent what? Why did Michael oppose them? Why had he fallen so easily back into the fold?

Nick studied Michael's face for makeup, but it was clean—grizzled, wrinkled, smudged with dirt from their run through alleys, but clean. It looked alive. So did Branniff's and Elle's. Makeup free. But the ticket-taker, the concession workers—their faces were covered with it. Nick had seen makeup on Langston's face, too, and on the faces of the receptionist and the man at the security desk—all avid fans of *Necropolitan*, products of Branniff's indoctrination. They were all—finally, the idea settled into his mind, slid between conflicting concepts, and took root so he could grasp it—*they were all* dead. *Dead in flesh or spirit, in mind or ego, dead and beholden to the necromancers, dead and rotting from the inside out.*

Necropolitan had killed them, resurrected them, then groomed them for the parts into which Branniff—or another producer or the Director—had cast them. There were others behind the production but only one at the top of it: the Director. Elle was not truly dead, not body dead, not yet, maybe only spirit dead, under the spell, not so lost he couldn't hope to revive her. Oh God, at least, he hoped not. The spell hadn't killed her, only influenced her. She needed to die for it to consume her fully. As they entered the elevator and it sank, Nick sensed a glimmer of hope, an opportunity to save Elle that he couldn't yet bring into focus. The elevator stopped. The doors opened onto a crowd of the VIP dead in white uniforms and led by Langston, his necromancer's rod in his right hand.

Langston tilted his head and grinned. "The Director will see you now, Mr. Branniff."

"I hope you've thought through your pitches, Elle," Branniff said. "The Director is very picky, but I've sung your praises to him. He's excited about you joining the production."

Stench thickened in the air as they marched deeper into the office and strode down dimly lit corridors. The ground squished and crunched underfoot. Nick tried not to think about what they stepped on, but he could guess from its smell and consistency. They turned a corner into the flickering glow of half a dozen flatscreen televisions mounted along the corridor, each one flashing gory scenes from movies Nick didn't know. Great whites in a feeding frenzy around a sea lion, blood clouding the water. Lions ripping apart a wildebeest, dragging bloody meat into the dust. A slaughterhouse, where pig carcasses hung from hooks to bleed out. Men and women stoning a family with four children to death on a street in a nameless city. Riots in another urban hell where men and women slaughtered each other with machetes and Molotov cocktails. Some showed trailers for movies that matched the death-themed posters Nick had seen earlier, spectacles of blood, coffins, and uprooted graveyards. He couldn't tell what was special effects, what was real—if any of it was. Mounted on posts before each screen, rotting heads watched. Glassy eyes followed the action. Lips trembled. Teeth ground and clicked. Their eyelids had been sliced away so they couldn't avoid the stream of savagery.

Branniff and Elle passed them, accepting, indifferent, at ease, at home amidst the gore and carnage. Only Michael wrinkled his face. Disgust and pity flickered in his expression, but he kept his cool, the reaction of an artist sullying himself with commerce. Nick fought the urge to vomit brought on by the dripping necks of the watchers, the deepening reek of their dead flesh. Were they real, animatronic, or hallucinatory? Nick couldn't ascertain, so he simply continued walking. A relentless thunder pulsed inside his head.

Beyond the walls of TVs, bones and limbs littered the floor. Severed hands, feet, arms, and legs lay like jigsaw puzzle pieces spilled from their boxes, awaiting assembly. Blood smears streaked the walls. The farther down the corridor they traveled, the deeper the viscera piled. They entered a place of death, where bodiless faces stared wide-eyed from a morass of scattered flesh. As they advanced, hosts of the premium dead filled the corridor behind them, staining the cuffs of their white pants red, enforcing their one-way passage until the group reached the Director's office.

Half a dozen VIP dead guarded it. No makeup. Drawn cheeks, sunken eyes, desiccated lips, and shriveled ears enhanced their gruesome appearance. They held AR15s, necromancer's rods, and blocked the door when Langston approached. The lead guard made eye contact with him. They stared at each other for long seconds, communicating in a silent way only the dead understood. Then the guard withdrew and let the man push open the door. He waved Branniff, Elle, Michael, Nick, and Langston inside, followed them in, then closed the door behind him.

The heavy, astringent charnel atmosphere flushed tears from Nick's eyes. The stench clung to him like an oily mist. It permeated his nostrils and lungs and radiated death. This place stood in dedication to rot and decay—not only to death but to the desecration of life, the corruption of the flesh, the reduction of humanity to latent savagery and biological components. Cells, bones, muscles, tissues, nerves, brains, and hair. Identity erased. Humanity rendered no more than meat. Murmurations of flies danced like miniature thunderheads gathering. A red-and-black haze filled the air. Hunched figures stirred in the mist. Nick couldn't see what occupied them nor did he want to. Icy air filled the room. They reached the far side, a massive corner with tall windows behind an executive desk dressed like an altar, draped in funereal cerements, lit by candles hissing and popping with wax made of human fat, adorned with bones and skulls carved in minute detail. Beyond this, the city seethed with blood and fire, and far below, shadows of life scurried like insects.

Nick searched for the Director, expecting someone even more pompous and repugnant than Devlin Branniff, a corrupt and repulsive captain of industry draped in fancy clothes and the sense of entitlement wealth engendered. It took him a moment to realize they'd been brought for an audience with the corpse face from the first movie, the half-rotted skull dug up from dank soil, the recovered head of the greatest of the necromancers, who'd reached out from beyond the veil and inspired the others to commune with him, resurrect him, and execute his plan. A hulking man from among the premium dead, dressed in crimson clothes, held the skull on a golden tray. Its vacant eyes cast a gaze that Nick swore wriggled over him like a blind man feeling someone's face. A voice emanated from the head, resonated in Nick's bones, but he couldn't understand it.

"No, that won't be necessary," Branniff said. "She needed to understand before she could really make a contribution. She's totally on board now and ready to pitch. You're going to love her ideas. She's so grateful for the opportunity."

More emanations from the head. They rippled the air, stirred the horrible odors in the office. The fly clouds scattered and reformed on dead flesh as the vibrations reverberated through them. Nick's head throbbed, sensing but not understanding the voice everyone else seemed to hear. He thought it might split his head in two.

"Come here and share your pitches, Elle." Branniff held his hand out for Elle to take then drew her close, turned her toward the Director. Under the base of his skull, the gold shimmered and rippled like liquid as if stirred by power leaking from the bone. "We're really going to take the brand forward. Tell him how, Elle."

Elle parted her lips to speak. No words emerged. Nick studied her, wondering if she'd frozen, or if she, too, spoke the silent language of the dead. Michael edged up next to him and gripped his shoulder. He felt a pulse in that touch, a living throb. Michael, the writer. Elle, the heroine. Himself—the hero? The betrayer? The pawn? The failure? The one who'd let Elle be dragged back to the last place she ever wanted to go? Then

111

she spoke, and words flowed out of her with enthusiasm and excitement, painting pictures of stories yet to be told, characters yet to be created, concepts, plots for this new, captive audience *Necropolitan* had created. Death tales for the dead, for a dead world, tales to widen the link between the living world and the realm of the dead and siphon its power to feed the Director, to resurrect his body, to recast the distributors and producers and the other VIPs as the undying lords of the world with a billion dead to enforce their vision and control the living, a horde of the dead to share the taint of *Necropolitan* through their bites, the ultimate word of mouth.

For freaks, for freaks, not the dead, a fading voice cried in Nick's mind, but now he knew better than to heed it. Even here in the mouth of death itself, though, part of him still resisted the spell. The skull's attention drifted from Elle to Nick. He felt the invisible touch of its gaze like worms wriggling over his skin. Vibrations thrummed through his bones as the skull addressed him. Nick still couldn't understand it.

"What?" Branniff asked. "No, I don't know why. He watched the movies. We cast the spell on him. If he can't hear you, don't bother with him. He has nothing for you, not like Elle does. He's not talent; He's only here because she's fond of him. Like a pet."

Another blast of sub-aural humming. Queasiness erupted in Nick's guts. He swayed. The charnel room flashed around him, smash cuts of blood, corpse parts, bones gnawed free of flesh, and horrible dead things shuffling through a slurry of viscera on the floor, a fog of blood mist in the air.

"We'll make him watch again," Branniff said. "Repeated viewings are most effective. If he doesn't buy the narrative, we'll recast him. He hardly even has a supporting role."

Nick noticed Michael staring at him, curiosity and more in the writer's expression: a glimmer of hope. *Hope.* It fanned the spark of hope already smoldering in Nick. His condition made him different, gave him an opportunity no one else had, if he could only figure out how to use it.

"He's nothing, I tell you. Nobody, a hired hand." Branniff stamped his foot, agitated by the skull's preoccupation with Nick. "Talk to Elle, listen to her. She's going to take us to a whole new level. We're going to bring every person on the planet under our spell, be the biggest damn blockbuster ever—and *she* can make it happen."

A fresh wave of quivering force rolled through Nick, the strongest yet. He almost caught a scrap of meaning from it, a half-remembered dream tickling his thoughts in the morning light. Michael grabbed him by the arm, spun him around to face him.

"What is it with you? Why do you still resist the obvious? How can you not believe what you see around you?" the writer asked. "You're standing here in the heart of living death itself, and you're still fighting the reality."

Langston stepped forward and unholstered his gun. He aimed it at Nick's head.

"Fuck this guy already," he said. "Let's kill him and put him to work for real."

Faster than Langston could react, Michael's hand lashed out to snatch the necromancer's rod. Stunned, Langston turned his gun toward Michael, who spoke a series of words in a rush. Langston gritted his teeth, fighting himself as he lowered the gun against his will, ordered by Michael using the power of the rod. The figures lingering in the haze, summoned by unspoken command, converged around Langston, seized him, then dragged him into the fetid muck on the floor. He opened his mouth to scream. One of them grabbed the bottom of his jaw and ripped it away, silencing him. Branniff rushed at Michael, hollering for him to drop the rod, but more of the common dead shambled into sight, blocking the producer's path.

"You flushed your career for good this time, Michael," Branniff said. "There's no coming back from this. You understand me, you dumb motherfucker? I don't care how brilliant you are. You'll never work in this world again. Everyone's right about you. You're a loser, a pussy too timid to make the big payday. I never should've given you a second chance."

"Shut up, Branniff, you greedy, narcissistic, sociopathic, evil fucking maniac," Michael said. "Or I'll make them tear you apart next."

Bone-shaking vibrations rippled through the room, the necromancer's skull yelling.

Everyone but Nick—everyone under the sway of *Necropolitan*'s spell— dropped to their knees, stunned by the blast. The necromancer's rod tumbled from Michael's hands as he clutched the sides of his head and covered his ears. Branniff and Elle joined him, groaning and squealing in pain. The waves rolled through Nick, rumbling his organs, passing fast, leaving him the only one still on his feet. He plucked the necromancer's rod from the putrescent soup on the floor. The intricacies carved into its length defied him. Did he need to believe to make it work? He wanted to believe—if his mind could summon the will to certitude. After everything he'd experienced, he knew he should, but a microscopic storm still swirled at the center of his brain, a cyclone ripping at his thoughts and casting them into chaos. He tried to will the dead to drag Branniff away and clear a path for him and Elle to leave. Instead, they turned their attention to him.

"Stop!" Elle shouted as they approached. She stepped between Nick and the dead. "You have to believe, Nick. Let the vision inside you, love the story, buy the hype, become one of us. I don't want to go on without you. We don't have to be apart. We can do anything when we stick together, right? We can control the world. Who gives a fuck about the old one? The new one is everything we want it to be. We can live forever. We can leave fear behind us and never have to be on the run or look over our shoulders again. Let the Director inside your mind and soul, fill yourself up with the movies. You've seen them. Their seed is in you. You only have to let it take root. This world is better than ours, and the door is open for us. But it won't always be. We have to do this now or never, Nick."

The skull-bearer stepped forward, bringing the ancient head. It screamed at Nick now; vibrations and energy churned through him in wordless pulses that rose up his spine, lit his nervous system on fire, clutched tight to his will and awareness until they reached his brain and fizzled like wet fireworks when they touched his swollen synapses. He could almost understand them now. They battered him, ordered him to make his body an extension of the spell, but his concussed brain refused. The multiple blows and shocks as he tumbled among the theater seats, the spinning world in which Nick could not absorb new high concepts. Fiery, silent screams raged across his mind as the most violent vibrations yet ripped through him, churning a series of memories and images. Different kinds of death. Different kinds of dead. The common, the premium, the VIPs. Some dead in body, some in spirit. A new world. A global necropolis. Workers in green and white uniforms, in power suits and movie makeup.

Necromancer's rods to control them all. A lone man sweating in the conference room—proof of life amidst a sea of death.

A hand touched his shoulder.

Nick jolted and swung reflexively, striking with the necromancer's rod before he realized the hand belonged to Elle. His fist, wrapped around the wooden shaft, cracked square onto her face, snapping her head back hard. She crumpled into his arms. Feet slipping on gore, Nick struggled to keep her from falling.

"Nick, baby, what the actual fuck?" she asked, her words slurred. "Listen, it's okay. It's all going to be okay. We won't need to run anymore. Won't need to hide or worry about someone coming to hunt us or about … about … There's nothing we can't do if we stick together."

The words filled Nick's ears like rusty barbed wire uncoiling. Over Elle's shoulder, he spied Michael, whose face swelled with sadness and recognition. Langston had accused him of sabotaging the production, and maybe he had. Michael, who said he never wanted this to happen yet seemed inextricably tied to it. The writer, the storyteller, a man unable to wholly turn his back on the biggest blockbuster of all time, a movie that literally controlled life and death. Maybe he'd written that phrase, placed it on Elle's and Nick's lips.

Stick together.

It's not like it sounds, Michael had said. *Maybe I'll tell you sometime.*

Nick dragged Elle to the windows and leaned against the glass. He closed his eyes and summoned the scenes in which he had appeared in "The Making of *Necropolitan*." Filtered the maddened, blood-hungry faces of the necromancers, their servants and helpers, to the stragglers at the edge of the frame, to a face he'd seen but not recognized. Michael's face. There from the start, scripting Nick's life up until this moment, except whatever Michael had written for the necromancers to implant in him no longer controlled Nick. The blows to his head, the damage to his brain had freed him from a leash he'd never known existed before now.

For the first time in years, dead in spirit or not, Nick could act.

The skull-bearer approached. Furious, violent vibrations pulsed from the corpse face. The gold plate on which it sat glimmered like a heat mirage.

"Nick? What's happening? I don't feel so hot." Elle convulsed once then vomited, adding the contents of her stomach to the foul mess on the floor of the Director's office. "Ooh, what the fuck did my dad do to us, Nick? What did he do? What the hell was I saying? I'm so sorry ... so sorry ... We have to split, baby."

The skull neared, screaming its silent rage. Elle shrieked, crouched on her haunches, and tucked her head down against the onslaught. Nick raised the necromancer's rod with both hands and brought it down on the skull with all his strength. Wood cracked bone. The skull fragmented. The subsonic screams roared. Nick's hair stood on end. Elle wailed in pain. Nick struck the skull again, cracking it into two pieces. He hammered and pounded it a third time, then again and again, until he knocked the gold plate from the dead man's hands. The pieces of the skull rained into the muck, and Nick jumped on them, stamped on them, pounded them to dust, and ground them into the viscera until they became mired in the remains of so many other dead. The vibrations that had filled the room like blasts from a wall of speakers ceased in an instant, leaving a ringing silence. The blood mist condensed and rained onto the floor. All around them the dead withered and rotted. The common dead fell to pieces first, then the premium dead. Skin sloughed from bones like melting wax. Joints failed and bodies crumpled. Branniff staggered toward Nick and Elle, his legs cracking as he moved, his throat filling with blood that silenced his angry words, until he fell face-first into the sludge and didn't move again.

"Thank you, thank God, thank you," Michael said. Tears filled his eyes and washed down his face. "I could never get them out of my head, not entirely. Oh God, thank you. Oh my God. Oh God, what have we done? What did they make us all do . . .?" Michael's words trailed off into laughter, starting with low chuckles that rose to an uproarious outburst of hysteria, cackles and giggles so out of place in this space consecrated to death and horror.

Afraid Michael's laughter might infect him, Nick turned to Elle and helped her to her feet. His legs wobbled as she leaned on him and his swollen ankle spasmed with pain. His head felt like a spinning plate. His eyes ached from light that probed them like needles, but he met her gaze as she found her footing, bracing herself against him. Her fragile, teary eyes sought sense in the world, answers to what had happened to her, and why the touch of the dead had reached so deeply into her mind. She opened her mouth to speak, but Nick pressed a finger to her lips then kissed her. When the kiss ended, they embraced, propping each other up.

"We're together," he said. "We're together. You know what that means."

"Yes," Elle said. "I know."

They clung to one another and stared out the window at a city where the dead still hunted the living. A world where the line between life and death had been blurred, weakened, and altered forever. A new world for their new life together.

GATE OF THE HELL DEAD

BRIAN G. BERRY

Chapter 1

Sheila McCarthy had some bad dreams. So many bad nightmares, unremitting plunges into worlds of absolute terror and bloodthirsty madness. Oftentimes, these journeys into the beyond would pop up in the middle of class and she would vociferate her dread with ear-splitting alarm. She would wake at odd hours in cold and greasy sweats, the dimensions of her room boxed in tight with shadows.

Sometimes, in phantasmal vibrancy, she would see the seam around her closet door blaze a crackling red neon. On the other side, she would hear wet, phlegmy gutturals and the beating of hungry fists, the white hooks of fingers clawing at the bottom. One time, the door went pliant as rubber and bulged, the paneling stressing, hairline fissures cracking and spilling more bloodred light into the room.

Then when she screamed, everything went back to normal.

So, in this instance, it wasn't surprising she cried to her mom again. She was sitting straight up in bed, sweat on her face, the duvet at her chin, big green eyes on the closet, fearing her imagination was sending her all the right images. For one moment, she had a sensation that the door would

119

burst open and behind would be an onslaught of white faces cut with spiked grins and bleeding yellow eyes, fingers reaching with claws.

"Sheila, baby, are you okay?"

Her mother, Kayla, always the savior in these cases. She came in, the hallway light behind her. The warmth of it spilled into Sheila's bedroom before the main bulb overhead snapped on and the darkness scrammed into the corners and under the bed. She was a beautiful woman on the good side of her thirties, with a face seemingly dragged with exhaustion at all times. She had gentle eyes that could soothe the worst of pain. Her touch was the spark of comfort and its attendant liberations. She sat on the edge of Sheila's bed, the mattress hardly dented by her lithe frame. She brushed a wisp of auburn out of her eye and placed a hand on Sheila's brow.

"You're burning up again." Concern scrunched her features. "I'll go get a washcloth."

"No," Sheila said, tugging her mother's wrist. "I'm . . ."

"What is it?"

Sheila's eyes rolled uneasily toward the closet door, a breath hitching in her throat. "I . . ."

"The closet dream again?"

Sheila nodded.

"Oh, it's okay. It's just a bad dream, sweetheart." Kayla wiped some sweat off her daughter's face. "I'll tell you what. I'll prove again it was just a nightmare, sweetie, okay?"

Sheila made a grab for her mother when she left the bed. Her arm outstretched, fingers sprung, eyes wide, she said, "Mom! Wait."

Kayla turned. "What is it? Are you okay?"

It took a second for Sheila to find the words, and when they came out, they were spoken in a whisper, "They were in there again."

"*They?*"

Sheila's face paled slightly. "The dead ones."

Kayla plopped beside her daughter with a sigh and told her all about how things like that just didn't exist in the real world.

It started a while back, Sheila having all these bad dreams and strange visions and sounds in her head. From where this infliction of haunts emerged, she had no idea. No source had been discovered.

One day, Sheila woke up screaming like someone was on top of her. When Kayla flew into the room ready for such a sight, there was Sheila, in her bed, tossing and fighting the shadows, screaming as shrill as only a little girl can when in the clutches of the worst terror. It was so bad the neighbors called the police.

She decided she needed to take Sheila to doctors and maybe they could help her out and offer a solution. At first, they treated it as mild nyctophobia, but after that was proved to be in error, they scratched their heads and couldn't offer a solid diagnosis. Just a little girl at the mercy of the sounds in her mind, they'd said. Maybe too many monster movies. But that couldn't be because Sheila had no desire to watch those stupid films.

"I heard them in the walls again."

This concerned Kayla more than the dreams because Sheila would hear things scratching in the walls at all hours of the day, not just when the moon was out and bright. It became a troubling issue, getting so bad she had to stay home because she was distracting the learning process for the other students, the teachers said. So, isolated at home, she would sit there bereft of friends and experiences, lost in her head about it all. She spent her days reading or drawing pictures, illustrating her dreams with nightmarish sharpness.

Kayla would gasp when she got a look at the very detailed depictions externalized in crayon colors. These weren't your typical school-level monsters but, instead, very humanistic varieties with bloody faces and dark yellow dots for eyes. A mass of creatures ripping babies from wombs with claws or in the process of eating people, chewing on legs and arms and cracking heads open.

"Just a part of the dream, sweetie. It's just a bad dream."

Kayla wanted to believe it was an element left over from the nightmares, an escaped figment living in her daughter's mind, but somehow she was starting to doubt it. There was something very real about Sheila's recollections. It wasn't just there on the surface to scrub away but in her voice and eyes. The way she trembled with fear whenever she spoke and how her eyes rounded wide and misted whenever pinned on the closet door.

Something brushed against the window, startling Sheila to cry out.

"It's okay, sweetie. It's just the wind. I think the storm is coming back."

It didn't matter that they were on the sixth floor of their building, the top floor, that is. To Sheila, it was one of those things she called a "zombie" levitating outside that window, its sharp nails scraping the glass, looking for a way inside to satiate its hunger.

Last week had seen a sort of freak storm push into the city. There was no warning of its arrival, it just headed into town with a bad attitude, blowing the gutters clean, knocking down cardboard shanties, playing havoc with the phones and electricity. Motor accidents became more frequent and deadly, and there was a rise in violence plaguing the city's population. Kayla was happy they lived in this apartment building, one with its own security officer on duty. It made her feel safer in this climate, especially for Sheila.

Rain smacked the window, drumming the pane with heavy fingers. Far into the city, thunder groaned its emergence.

"Oh no, I hope it doesn't last long. I don't want us to lose power again."

Sheila's eyes became fixed marbles. If the power went out, that meant the dead—the zombies—would return. That was the sign they were ready to feed. She didn't want to see them anymore. Or hear them, for that matter. They would call out of the shadows of the room and tell her they had something to show her. That they wanted to divulge arcane secrets. She would pull the duvet over her head and hug Teddy, clutching his plush brown body to her chest.

Kayla saw the apprehension on her daughter's face and offered a tried-and-true solution. She leaned down with a smile and gentle clip to her voice. "How about you grab your blanket and Teddy and come sleep with me tonight? Does that sound good?"

The hint of a smile was on Sheila's face when she nodded. The rain continued its staccato on the window as the wind took on a thin whistle.

They were in the hall when the front door rattled with a knock.

Sheila froze as Kayla cocked her head. Another rap on the door, this one heavier than the last, something wrong about it.

"Strange time to have a guest." Then she remembered. Last week, when the storm brewed to a breaking point, the wind screaming and bashing against the building, lights flickering, the security guard came up and checked on them. He knew Sheila had some sort of fear of the dark and decided to bring her some candy from the vending machine. He was a nice man, polite. Mid-thirties, handsome. "Oh, you know who it probably is?" she told Sheila with a hand on her daughter's shoulder, squeezing gently. "Dean!"

Sheila perked up. She liked Dean. He was the nice man in the blue uniform shirt with the gold badge who opened the door for them to leave the building, the one who had brought her candy that awful, windblown, lightning-cracking night. He was always in an upbeat mood with a big smile. And though she was only now coming into her double digits of life, she detected a crush in the air and saw the way he eyed up her mother like she was the most beautiful thing in the world.

"I'll be right back. You go to my bedroom, and when I return, we can turn on the television and get some sleep. Does that sound good?"

Sheila nodded, hugging both the blanket and Teddy.

Kayla wandered off with a little skip in her step, and as ordered, Sheila passed through the door into her mother's bedroom. She had one leg on the bed when a scream knifed her heart like a chunk of ice. Sheila stopped breathing, listening with suffocating terror to her mother screaming out in the living room as if someone was stabbing her to death. Things were falling off shelves, glass was crashing, furniture moving. She could hear her mother struggling with someone. Her screams sounded wet.

Sheila shivered, all her nightmares flowing out of her head and into a very real substance around her. The wind shrieked insanely and rain sprayed against the pane.

"Sheil—"

That last word surrendered to a gargled choke and then silence strangled the home. Sheila stared at the door, waiting for whatever was out there to get her too. She realized she hadn't moved. She could hear them now. Something was unnerving about the sound of the ambulation. Like a dragging, lurching sound of heavy feet.

Plop, drrraaaggg. Plop, drrraaaggg . . .

Shivers and darkness spread coldly. The light had no effect on burning up the images in her mind. She saw a gallery of corpse faces hooking around the doorway, staring with eyes stuffed with fuming yellow cores. Their mouths were like ripped-open grins with gray spikes for teeth. Vampires, ghouls, flesh eaters—zombies.

A shadow spilled into the hall and its profile was exaggerated and grotesque. Like the outline of some hideous monster in a cartoon, it slid against the wallpaper like dark water. A smell floated into the room, hitting her nostrils like a vapor of poison. She felt dizzy and disoriented. It smelled of hot blood and voided bowels, of rot and infection, a heavy redolence of death.

Then the source appeared. Slinking around the corner with an appetite, its raised arms were coming for her. The skin on the face had the texture of black mold, patches of it ripped or falling off. Lips pulled away from sharp gray fangs, tangles of blood and saliva swinging off its chin. And yes, those eyes, tunnels of macabre yellow starlight ... they fell on Sheila.

She didn't even scream or flinch when the man started biting her face off the bone.

Chapter 2

Now that he thought about it, this wasn't such a bad job. There wasn't a whole lot to it. You clocked in, sat down, opened the doors for the residents, and signed for deliveries. Hell, you didn't even need to say "Hello" or "Take it easy." Most folks were the sort who would rather not waste a word on some doorman/security guard. Which was perfectly fine with him. The less interaction he had to do, the better.

There were some he liked to chat up, though. There was Greg something or other. He couldn't remember the man's last name, but he was a good guy, always willing to shoot the shit in a pleasant way and not some annoying dude with a chip on his shoulder. Then there was Allen Boone, a fifty-something bachelor he sometimes shared a beer with down the road. And there was Kayla McCarthy. Now, that was a name he wouldn't forget. How could he? You could say he had something of a mad crush on her. He couldn't shake her out of his head if he wanted to. It was best she stayed in there and continued living in his mind. He preferred it that way. She was a real looker. Not one of those who swayed with attitude but had a girl-next-door vibe to her. She had straight dark hair to her hips and smoldering green eyes, comforting and beautiful. Hiding beneath it was a seductiveness that spiked his heart rate.

She had a daughter who was a bit weird, but she was a good kid. Just had her fears, same as any kid. He felt bad that she could no longer go to school and have friends to play with. Girl like her with all the issues certainly needed playmates to take her mind off things. But Kayla said the school wouldn't allow that because Sheila was more problematic than productive.

What a crock of shit.

Thunder rolled across the city in an angry tide. Rain turned the glass door to a smudge. He could hear the wind blowing and things outside creaking and banging.

He pulled from his coffee, turning his attention to the newspaper headlines.

"Inexplicable Storm Strikes the East Coast"

"An Uptick in Violence Leaves Sixteen Dead in Grocery Store Stabbing"

"Two-story Building Collapses on a Black Raven Concert"

The copy under the last headline read: *Crushed beneath massive tons of concrete and steel, authorities have said the band and the three-hundred-plus attendees are all presumed dead. Efforts to recover the bodies will continue unabated.*

Such a shame.

Dean took another slug of his coffee, wincing at its taste.

The city had suffered its share, and the citizens were going wild, devolving. Shootings were on the rise, stabbings too. But it was more than that. There were reports of people armed with hatchets and machetes spreading out into the streets, hacking and butchering at random. There were pictures on the news of mutilated bodies and monuments of corpse matter. Tenth Street had become a war zone, where the concrete was stained red and bodies plugged the gutters.

The scary thing was that Tenth was only a few blocks east. But it wasn't just the addition of that fact that made life in the city start to look like

Hell. It was the fact that every street was starting to have some sort of dark influence, and reality was bending to its intrusion. Every day, there was something new and horrible to transpose yesterday's atrocities.

It made Dean think there was something loose in the air. Some pathogen or water poisoning causing this sudden eruption of savage violence in the people. He shook his head in disgust, thankful he was behind doors and out of the storm—human and natural.

Lights flickered on and off in the building and his head slumped back on his shoulders for an inspection of the ceiling. "Shit. Just what I need, another power outage."

Setting the paper and coffee down, he got to his feet and stretched, his thoughts on Kayla again. Something that was happening more and more. He fixed his belt with a few tugs and checked the locks on the main door. Everything good there. Secure.

He cupped his hands to the sides of his face and pressed against the window. Darkness described the exterior in bold relief. Smoky, black, windy, and rain-washed, the streetlights like faint candles in a dark fog. There was something unnatural about it.

Leaving the door, he kicked around and took to the hallway for a stroll, pulling his flashlight for something to swing in his hand. The first-floor corridor—and every other one above—stretched into a tunnel of dim, soft lighting. Doors staggered on either side with their brass knockers and numerals. The walls were bare and hit with a dull cream paint. The floor was black and white squares.

He padded down there, eyeing up each door.

So far, so good. No sounds of alarm, just a nice quiet building during a strange storm. And what a storm. Made no sense. The way it started suddenly on dark nights, increasing the shadows and opacity in the city to baffling shades. He continued in his trot, swinging the flashlight like some old beat cop. Not that he was, and he was quick to point out to many a confused person that he was simply a security guard for the property. He could understand the mix-up. He had the right gear, after all: an Italian Beretta, chambered in 9mm, a sweet anodized finish to its frame. He had the Maglite, a pair of cuffs, a nightstick, and a sizable can of OC pepper spray.

"Why do you carry all that stuff?" some concerned tenant of the building asked him one day.

He relayed his reasoning by saying it was the standard loadout of every guard on the payroll. The truth was, he had been told to refrain from carrying anything remotely dangerous to clients and intruders alike. *A lot of sense that made … not!* he thought upon hearing that. Only a flashlight and pepper spray were okayed upon approval of the leadership. But considering the atmosphere noosing the city—the rise in murder and savage aggression—to him, all items were a necessity. So if he happened to get busted by his superior one day, he would eat the reprimand and continue to patrol in his gear.

He reached the elevator and thumbed the button.

A mechanical squeal, then a grinding noise of chains and pulleys told him the elevator was nearly there.

Bing.

The doors slipped open and he went inside. Closing them with a press of the second-floor button, he leaned against the wall, arms crossed, and waited.

Carl couldn't shake the sound of that scream across the hall. It came from that woman's place with the crazy kid. Eye stuck on the peephole, he tried to get a clear look to the sides, but his attempts were met with a sigh. The fishbowl angle was pretty useless at picking up clarity at the edges. Deciding whether he should chance an investigation on foot, he picked at his lip, chewing on his thoughts.

She might need your help, he reasoned. *What are you doing standing around while she's screaming? Put some pants on and go check on her! It's the right thing to do.*

The moral poke hadn't really been too hard, so he stood there, a voyeur of the hallway. Scratching himself, he took the knob in his hand and gave it a slight twist. Instead of opening the door, he just held on, weighing his thoughts with the good and bad.

She's not screaming now. Maybe everything is better.

Justifying it that way wasn't gaining any traction. There was no denying the scream was one of brain-shattering terror. It sounded very much like someone getting burned alive. The way things were going in the city, he hesitated to make a move. Thinking there was a boogeyman out there, someone with a knife and no reason to slay but to bathe in blood.

Maybe I should call the police.

Then he remembered the security guard, that Dean fella, downstairs in the lobby. He left the door and plucked the phone up. Dialing the front desk with a few quick taps, he waited six rings and returned it to the receiver, scratching his head.

"That's weird. He should have picked up."

He was back at the door again. He placed his eye over the peephole and was thrown back a couple of steps at what was out there.

Which was nothing. As if the hallway was flooded in darkness.

Warily, he put his eye back against the glass bubble and saw that wasn't the case at all. Someone was standing just outside his door. He could see the etching of the wall lights squeezing around the person's frame.

He almost called through the door, but for whatever reason, he decided it was best to remain quiet in this situation. His heart was beating dangerously. They weren't moving at all, not saying a word. An ominous finger of fear touched his mind when he noticed their garb. Black as night.

A sound ticking below turned his head downward and he saw the doorknob slowly twisting. Not liking this one bit, he grabbed it and held it.

"Hey, what are you doing out there? Who are you? Stop that!"

No answer. Nothing. The knob still moving. Carl put both hands on there now. He checked the chain with his eyes and saw it was secure. The dead bolt too. They wouldn't get into the apartment. No way.

A stronger pressure was applied to the knob, and Carl did everything in his power to keep it from moving an inch, but then something happened that made him leap back with a scream, holding his hands as if they were on fire. The doorknob was spinning like a top, smoke starting to spew, sparks shooting in a fan. His eyes had fallen into pits of confusion and terror. He watched unbelieving as the chain popped from its slot and the dead bolt—*clack*—pulled back.

The door creaked inward and Carl saw the figure.

Like a black ghost, they stood there. A cloak absorbed their contours, a cloth of midnight, a conical hood slouched over the head. Long, loose sleeves, and—

A knife.

A foot long, curved like a horn, blade of unblemished silver with a razor-sharp edge.

"Hey now, what do you want?! Get out of here, will ya? Go!"

Carl backed into his couch and nearly lost his footing. He corrected his stumble and moved to the side, putting some things in the living room between him and this ... night invader.

The cloaked one moved out of the doorway, seeming to glide across the threshold. Impaired with fear, Carl kept his eyes on that knife. "I'm calling the police! You hear me? You're going to jail!"

A screech like a bobcat, then the cloaked one leaped like a black flame, knife coming in for the fatal plunge. Carl was caught off guard by the action and his throat took the blade to the hilt. It clipped his vertebrae and with one strong jerk, his neck opened wide and sprayed the visitant red. Carl staggered back to the wall, eyes sprung, clutching his neck which was pouring a steady flow of hemoglobin down his white T-shirt. He slid down to his buttocks, his feet bicycling.

Last thing he saw was the cloaked one, hood tossed back and a face like a scorched plate of stone, eyes purple and gaseous. Then the knife bit through his throat again. His severed head fell to the ground.

Chapter 3

Down in a secret spot beneath the apartment building, this is what was taking place: The darkness had been breached by luminous cosmic smoke the color of purple neon, the mortar holding the bricks cracking open with fingers of blue light. Six acolytes and their leader stood in postures of expectancy. In front of them, six high and wide, a swirling pool of liquid blackness popped into existence.

This was the Gate—the portal to everlasting pain and death and reward. A conveyance for His legions to arrive on Earth.

Their victim writhed on the ground against her ropes. She lay confined within a blood sigil of alien scrawl. Her mouth plugged, she moaned. Her body bore the signs of offering: naked, long gashes opened to bleed, her face a swollen purple bruise, teeth busted out, breasts ruined with knife strokes, her vulva carved into strips. Her vitality hadn't lost its edge; she fought and squirmed, her white skin slick with the blood of her wounds.

The one in command ordered his followers to take possession of her. They gathered around, lifting her like a casket and bearing her to the portal in a slow drive.

"Inside."

She screamed and kicked and moaned with angry tones when they placed her head into the windy black sphere. It felt like the opening of an oven, one able to smelt steel. She felt her eyes starting to burn, the hair on her scalp singing. They pushed her in further, and when her cheek brushed the portal, flames leaped upon her head in angry clusters.

The followers backed away.

She levitated there, a force dragging her slowly into the portal like a pencil in a sharpener. Blue flames enveloped her, and her voice was heard no more as she disappeared to her waistline. Her body was jolting as if she were dumped into a vat of high-voltage currents. As it swallowed her feet, coming from deep within that spherical black hole was a distant cackle like the laugh of a demon.

"The time is near at hand!"

Chapter 4

The elevator did its ticking and clicking sounds before the door swooshed open. Hallway light streamed onto him as he took a walk down the sixth-floor corridor, his pacing simple.

Kayla's floor.

He thought about paying her a visit.

He checked his watch, almost ten on the button.

Probably wouldn't be such a good idea considering the late hour. He took his time strolling, listening to the storm beat the outside to hell. He could hear the rain, and for a brick building as strong as this one, that was saying something. It sounded like he was walking through a tin shack in a monsoon. Thunder exploded like cluster bombs over the city. He couldn't see, but he could *sense* lightning burning open the night.

In a sudden dragging of steps, Dean set anchor and stopped.

There was a smell hitting him, pungent and mephitic. He turned around, thinking it was coming from behind him, but no ... it was all *around* him. His nose twitched at the stink. He moved ahead, tracking the smell. It grew stronger farther down the hallway. In one moment, it seemed to clog all of his senses, then it moved off without a trace. But it returned in the next couple of steps and hit him like a smack of shit to the face. His expression dropped into a scrunched revulsion, a choke in his throat.

"Jesus, what the heck is that smell?"

It made him wish he had a clothespin and surgical mask. Fingers pinching his nose, he turned toward the smell and was looking at the door to Kayla's apartment. He leaned in, sniffing the trim like a hound.

Yes, the source was behind the door.

Kayla, Christ.

"Stay away from there!"

Dean spun and popped his flashlight onto the voice's face hanging out of the door across from him. He recognized the tenant. "Martin, is it?"

The man nodded.

Holding a hand over his heart, Dean said, "You scared the *shit* out of me."

"You smell that too?"

Dean had a smart-ass remark on his tongue but kept it civil instead. "Yeah. Any idea what it is?"

Martin stepped out warily, casting his eyes up the corridor left and right, hugging himself as if he were cold. "There was some screaming a little while ago."

"Screaming?"

"Yeah, coming from in there."

Dean's blood pumped. "From Kayla McCarthy's residence?"

"Yeah, and something else . . ." Again, his head went right and left as if he were afraid. "My neighbor, Carl, I heard him shouting a minute ago and then he stopped."

Dean looked to the door a few feet down. "How long ago was this?"

He gave a shrug and a repeated inspection of the corridor. "Fifteen minutes, maybe more. It sounded wrong."

"Why didn't you call?" Then Dean realized his mistake in asking. He'd been away from the lobby for a good fifteen minutes. "Never mind. How long ago did you hear the screams from Kayla's?"

"Just before Carl started shouting."

Clicking his flashlight off, he lowered it to his side. "Okay, I want you to wait here. I'm going to check this out. If something is wrong, I'll yell for you to call the police. Can you do that for me?"

Martin nodded, took another look, then ducked behind his door, peeking around the edge anxiously. "Be careful, Dean. I think someone bad is in there."

Dean did the appropriate thing in this case. He knocked gently and quietly as if he were paying a polite visit. "Kayla?" He pressed closer to the door. "Kayla, it's me, Dean. Are you okay in there?"

Silence stuffed his ears. The rain beat down, detonations of thunder shook the building. And was that wind outside screaming its way through the city streets or something else entirely?

He looked back to Martin who was staring at him with a face no more alive than a corpse in a casket. It had leaked all its color, eyes fixed and spooked right out of logic, his lips set in a stiff line.

"Martin, you okay, man?" Dean didn't like what was happening here. "Hey, you're giving me the creeps. Stop that. What's with you?" Since Martin decided to play deep freeze Popsicle, Dean gave another gentle rap on the door. "Kayla? I'm getting worried about you in there."

Shit. What could he do? Bang on her door until the damn thing gave and splintered, then rush in there like some goddamn hero on the lookout for terrorists? For what reason? Because screwball Martin over there said he heard some screaming? For all he knew, it was probably the television he was hearing.

Then a thought hit him.

He looked down at the doorknob, studying it.

"It's breaking and entering any way you look at it," he told himself.

But was that a tangible spike of worry seeping into his head? Sighing, hoping he was doing the right thing, he took the knob and it twisted smooth as oil. The door opened inward and right away, Dean was shoved back into the hall by that terrible odor. It leaped upon him, stinking him up with bowel fumes and septicemic infection. He coughed and spat on the ground. "Fuck, that's *rank!*"

It burned his eyes, causing them to water.

Adjusting himself, clearing his throat, he brushed away the revolting pall with a wave of his hand and brought his flashlight up.

The apartment was dark and that didn't make him feel good at all. One hand on the butt of his Beretta, he popped the latch and stood in the doorway. He shone the light in there, swinging it around. His heart started flopping wrong. The place was a shambles. Broken glass everywhere, furniture flipped and torn apart, stuffing sprung, pictures askew or shattered on the floor, the frames splintered.

Then his beam hit a spot of blood.

Not a small spot either, but a literal pool. A shiver went down his spine. He traced it, sticking to the slash mark leading off into shadow, breaking the dark around the crimson stroke, he saw the wall was splattered with streaks and red handprints.

"Oh God, KAYLA!"

Shucking the Beretta, holding it alongside the flashlight, he strobed the room, hardly blinking, heart hitched with speed, breath coming shallow. He shouted over his shoulder, "Martin, call the police!"

He didn't dare turn away to see if Martin responded. He felt a need to check things out. Ensuring the safety to the 9mm was clicked off, he moved into the wreckage, feeling something squishing beneath his heel. He jumped back, the beam falling to the ground. His face paled a tinge. There was something there like a patty of raw hamburger battered into the carpet, strung to his boot like bubblegum.

He thought of Sheila. "Oh no, not her . . ."

The hallway. It gaped dark and haunted, the throat of some evil viper. For one moment, before putting his light down there, he thought he saw a shape dart into the master bedroom.

"Kayla? That you? It's me, Dean! I'm here to help. Are you okay? Talk to me!"

The hairs bristled on the back of his neck and his scalp started itching. Gooseflesh sprung on his arms. A chill passed through him. He panned the beam to the left and it fell into Sheila's bedroom to disappear. He remembered it from the last time he visited. All the toys cluttered in there and the pretty pink drapes and matching pillowcases and blanket.

He wanted to call out.

But didn't.

His heart was telling him something was hiding in there. He moved off to get a better angle of the room, a view he could cut his light nicely into. Finding a good spot, his beam slit the darkness open. He wanted to scream. Blood was *everywhere*. More than he thought a human body could possibly hold. It lay in there thick, the smell of it leaking out of the room. It had a sickening overlay to it, like hot shit and piss.

The sensation made him gag and his face green a little.

He figured there was no reason to further traumatize his mind with any sights, so in a sensible spin, he pulled back. The cops had all the right tools and would probably bitch at him anyway for scuffing up the crime scene, so why not just let them have at it?

With this conviction firmly ingrained, he extricated, avoiding the squishy parts of the carpet. He was an inch from the door when a noise deep inside the apartment stopped him at once. And this stop wasn't just putting the brakes on, but like one suddenly in the grip of a cold fist, a paralyzing stasis. Mechanically, his eyes shifted to the hall. He tried to raise his light to get a gander, but so deep was his fear of what he would see, he couldn't bring himself to follow through.

"H-hello? Who's there?"

He asked this because he knew whoever it was didn't belong in Kayla's residence. She wasn't here anymore, not alive anyway, but maybe broken up like an old doll, tucked away somewhere. Sheila, too, reduced to an exploded bag of anatomy pasting her walls and dripping off her bedsheets. His Adam's apple bobbed in his throat. The hallway . . .

Something was definitely moving down there. A fragment of night moving side to side like a shroud of black smoke. His heart kicked into high speed. A creeping pressure stroked his mind, chills mounted, his body felt like it was dipped in ice water.

Fuck.

He shone the light in there, and this time, he did scream. Kayla was standing there naked, her face butchered into a mask of mutilated muscle and strips of bone, her eyes like two blood clots leaking down her face. She let out a wild, bestial shriek and came at him, arms up, claws—yes, claws—sprung and sharp.

"Kayla, no!"

She wasn't into taking orders. She came on in a lurching, sidestepping manner, blood and slime hanging off her chin. Dean backed into the hallway, his gun and light up.

"Kayla, take it easy! I can get you some help!"

But he knew that wasn't going to resolve anything here. Whatever happened to her had swapped her beauty with the visage of a ghoul. Her body had taken quite a licking, too, opened in places by what looked like knife cuts, patches of skin were ripped away, one breast was missing a nipple. Dean had a bad feeling, like it had been chewed off. She was spitting blood as she screamed, swiping at the air.

"Kayla, where's Sheila? Can you tell me where Sheila is?"

He thought mentioning her daughter would put an end to this nonsense or maybe give him a window to think. But all she did was come on with animal hunger in her voice, those eyes wet and bleeding, claws hooked for grabbing.

He felt the elevator getting closer to his back.

He might have to do something here, and he wasn't sure he could bring himself to do it. He had feelings for this woman. *Real* feelings. There were times he tried to convince himself to ask her out on a date, but he knew she worked two jobs to keep a roof for her and Sheila and there would be no time for such things.

"Come on, Kayla, just stop right there. I'll get you some help, okay? You're just really hurt and scared. Who did this to you?"

That was the million-dollar question because he had a feeling it wasn't *her* doing. But if not her, then who?

She slowed her pace and Dean felt relief for a moment that maybe she had come to her senses. That is, until she crouched real low and her arms pulled back a smidge. Next thing he knew, she leaped and his gun clapped and her face imploded, an intra-cranial explosion that sucked out the back of her head. She dropped to the ground, unmoving, a pool of blood forming around what was left of her head.

His knees went weak at the sight.

Disgusted, hyperventilating, and ran-through with tremors, he stared at the body of his crush.

"Kayla . . ."

Chapter 5

Margaret Hollenbeck heard a gunshot.

It didn't surprise her anymore. Not with the way things were going out there. Her husband, Earl, was slumped in his chair as usual, snoring away the night. Margaret didn't mind at all. It was better for him that way. He had a bad ticker and got worked up easily over these things. He always wanted to make sure she was safe. That's why they moved here. Back thirty years ago, the city *was* a good place, a nice place to raise a family.

But lately, that had changed. On a huge scale.

You couldn't walk to the store anymore without running into some addict at your throat begging for coins. But it was more than that. She would give anything if it would *only* be that. Addicts weren't the threat anymore. It was the violence. The way it was organizing out there. She watched the news, heard all the stories and gossip.

Bands of wild savages were stalking the night, butchering and stealing. The city was in the throes of some serious wickedness. She wondered if it was what the people deserved after denying God, going against his commands and edicts. She had a feeling that's what this was all about. She put a hand on her Bible, patting it with a smile on her face.

"You'll always have my love, God. Thank you for a great life with a great husband." She cast a look at Earl, memories of them together rushing through her mind.

A noise above her canceled her thoughts. She looked to the ceiling. Yep, it was those kids again, running around up there with no guidance and probably no God in their lives. She shook her head.

Taking the remote, she clicked the television off.

Dropping the footrest on her chair, she stood and stretched, joints cracking, back popping. It wasn't easy being old. But she felt blessed to have survived this long. She adjusted her glasses, shuffled past her husband, and headed into the kitchen to shut the lights off.

But as she roved past the hall, a flash of red light stunned her into stopping. She paused a moment, her focus down the corridor. She couldn't make heads or tails of anything down there. Just a black throat leading into eternal night.

Then she saw a flash. She swore she saw a burst of red light. One second, and it was gone. Not even a full second. She might have been old, and her vision a bit cloudy, but there was no doubt in her mind that she saw what she saw.

She looked to Earl, thought about waking him. A red light could be a serious thing. Maybe there was an outlet catching fire, popping with bad wiring. She had no idea. Pulling her attention out of the hall, she switched the lights off in the kitchen, checked the coffee pot to make sure that, too, was off for the night, and made sure the oven burners hadn't accidentally been left on. Everything cleared, she backed out and did her slow shuffle toward the living room.

Then stopped again.

Right there, same as last time, a red flash.

This was proof she wasn't losing her marbles. It was time to wake Earl and see what this was all about.

She went around to his side, shaking his arm. "Earl, Earl, wake up."

It took some proper rocking, but eventually Earl's stiff eyes cranked open and he coughed a few times, hands still resting on his belly. He blinked some, then asked, "Margaret, what's wrong?"

"I'm not sure. There's a red light going off somewhere."

Earl was still primed to sleep, so he had to shake his mind a bit to get things rolling. "A red light? I don't know what you mean."

"Like I said, I'm not really sure. I was walking into the kitchen and I saw a red flash down the hall. On the way back, I saw it again."

That was Margaret for you, making something out of nothing. "Probably just the television, honey."

"No, I turned that off."

Earl wasted no more on it. "I dunno what to tell you. Why don't we just go lay down and worry about it tomorrow."

Here's the thing: Margaret *was* concerned, especially since it came from down the hallway. She was worried about the possibility of a fire breaking out and she let him know that so long as that remained an issue, they wouldn't be getting any sleep tonight.

"Oh, ain't nothing like that. If it were, all the lights in the place would be flickering, then outright burn out."

She didn't mention that when he was napping, the lights had been flickering. An effect from the storm. Well, maybe this, too, was an effect short-circuiting fuse boxes.

Earl was groaning as he left his chair, old bones popping. "I'll tell you what, I'll check the outlets on our way to bed. Will that make you feel better?"

He was such a good man to her. Always doing the right things and going the extra step. "That would be wonderful. Thank you, Earl."

"No problem, honey."

He was in the lead, his slippers padding the carpet, his arms hanging at his side. He stopped and hit the light switch. An outlet was down a ways; he checked it and gave her a thumbs-up. "All good here."

Pushing the bedroom door open, Margaret caught a blurry sight of a pair of hands taking him by the shoulders and pulling him inside.

"EARL!"

The door slammed with a jarring impact.

She felt the weight slip out of her and she sagged against the wall.

Earl was shouting her name between pained squeals. She thought she heard voices or moans rising over her husband's screams. The door was banging in its frame like something heavy was being repeatedly bashed against it, and then it gave with a splintering *KERACK* busting open. Out spilled Earl.

But he wasn't alone.

Three or four others were tangled around him.

"EARL! OH GOD! EARL!"

He was choking on blood, a lot of it, bright and thick as pancake batter spilling down both cheeks. One eye was torn out, optical wiring hanging out of the socket. The others with him were naked as the day, their skin blackened as if they'd crawled out of a coal mine. They were digging at her husband with greedy hands, latching onto an arm, a leg, one had their hands pressed against his temples.

She wasn't sure how much more of this she could take.

Her heart was on its way to expiring. It was beating so hard, it felt like it would just tear its way out and explode right there in front of her eyes. Maybe that would be preferable to watching anymore.

Earl managed to scream, "Margaret, go! *RUN!*"

At least, that's what she thought he said. It was hard to tell. Like someone speaking through a mouth of broken teeth and missing a tongue.

Then an arm was pulled out of its socket, strings of meat snapping elastically, blood bursting, severed capillaries spraying. One coal-dusted figure clamped its sharp teeth onto Earl's bicep and started chewing. Margaret's heart continued its marathon of pain. The eyes of the man were a smoky red, rolling like a shark's with every bite.

The arm cranked off and blood exploded on the figure in a hot spray; his chest blasted with rivulets giving him some color. Again, this one set its teeth and began to feast.

"EARL!"

His head collapsed, the other's palms smashing his skull in one sickening *CRUNCH*. Earl's brain hopped out of the top of his head like a slimy gray toad, ropes of blood ejecting down the hall. Margaret slid to the ground, her eyes unswerving from the man slurping up her husband's brain like a hungry Labrador retriever.

"Oh, God, why? Why, God?"

Footsteps coming up behind were silent to her ears.

She sat there in shock, voyeur to the cannibal feast, never seeing the cloaked one draw upon her and drag a knife across her throat, sawing deep into the muscles, pulling her gray curls taut, and yanking her head loose with a *POP*.

Chapter 6

Dean still hadn't moved an inch. Slumped against the elevator door, gun ready, eyes locked open. Too many conflicting thoughts pressed into every quarter of his mind. He couldn't shake the tremors seizing him up. The tears hadn't stopped either. But they were becoming less and less with each passing second.

The odious smell still lingered and the storm seemed to laugh at him. Thunder boomed with earthshaking percussions. The rain beat harshly on the brick exterior and window panes. He wiped his face, hoping to wipe the image out of his mind too. But that wasn't happening, not anytime soon. Kayla was still sprawled flat on her chest, and her once beautiful face slopped down the corridor, some of it with bits of hair streaked on the wall.

Martin.

He forgot all about him. And the weird thing was, he hadn't come out into the hall to investigate the shooting. Nobody had. That made him think about how quiet the building was. Silent and spooky. For one second, he broke his sight off Kayla and called out, "Martin, are you okay? Talk to me, man. Did you call the police yet?"

Damn.

Sighing, he made the move. Drawing a path alongside Kayla's corpse incited shivers. But he managed well enough, squeezing his eyes, staying against the wall as if he were skirting the ledge of some great height. He stumbled freely into the hall once, circumventing her body. Bent over with shallow breathing, a couple of deep inhalations cleared his head, and he was standing upright again.

"Martin!"

Shit!

Another deep inhale and he pushed on. His momentum drew to a crawl when he came upon Kayla's apartment. The door was wide open, black night packed in there thick and dense enough to shoot a hole through. He couldn't take his eyes off the doorway, too afraid of something else waiting inside for him to lose his concentration.

"Martin. Answer me, dammit!"

Dean pulled his attention off Kayla's apartment for one second and looked at Martin's place. There he was, still standing there, and now Dean had the very most unpleasant feeling that Martin was not standing but, rather, *tacked* there in place like some Halloween decoration.

"Martin, you better say something, man. *Martin!*"

Then Martin emitted a sound, but it wasn't human speech. It was more like a heavy slab of beef breaking from its bones, a greasy sticky snap like a hundred rubber bands, and his whole front side divorced from the back and splashed to the ground.

SPLAT.

Intestines uncoiled, organs detached with suction sounds. If that wasn't bad enough, a wave of blood dumped out and washed around Dean's ankles.

If seeing Kayla turned into a monster hadn't broken his spirit, he was on the verge of all-out insanity now. The rest of Martin fell into the hall, the impact splashing blood up to Dean's waistline, spattering his black slacks with wet streaks.

Standing where Martin had been a second ago was a man in a black cape—not a cloak, a *shroud*. The face had been enfolded to a shadow by the conical hood, and the only other color contrasting the absolute darkness of the material was a knife in the right hand, curved like a horned moon, gored with blood and bits of silver peeking through.

Pop, pop, pop, pop, pop!

The action was reactive. There was no other way to put it. The gun came up, his breath hitched, his heart stopped, and like a slow-motion scene in a movie, the slide ripped back with each jerk of the trigger, smoke dusting the hall.

The cloaked one's chest bore the accuracy like red paintball spatters. Blood slid like crimson serpents from the wounds. Dean screamed over the next several shots that bashed the gun into the cloak's hood. Brains and bone and blood made leaps into Martin's home.

Dean's motionlessness was in part due to shock and terror, wondering how this character hadn't even moved a single beat after taking so much lead. But a moment or two elapsed, then the cloaked one dropped. Not as expected with a *thud* or a *smack*, but like a sheet, airless and mute.

He stared as if he had just killed a ghost.

Chapter 7

The energy was near to full flux now.

The basement was awash in cosmic purples, the mortar of the bricks bright with blue neon, the Gate irising, its core a screaming maelstrom of crackling electric-red light. The Anointed One fed on the second sacrifice as the Acolytes tossed in a bounty of severed heads.

This one would do the trick. A baby. Freshly slit from a womb of eight months. It squirmed with feeble life, its umbilical dangling, and would soon feed the maw of the Ancient One. As with the others, the sacrifice was inserted headfirst, the Gate's energy shivering with excitement and its center exploding with electric-red ropes, snaring the baby in a web, a cocoon of pulsing bloodred wires branding the body. Steam hissed as the bones and skin crisped, and the baby was no more.

"It has been satisfied. The Gates are open."

Chapter 8

The day was here.

All the violence in the city had premeditated its arrival, had added to its burgeoning power. The sky was bleeding blue electricity. Fault lines were widening in the crust, splitting streets and buildings with jagged cracks, steam issuing, the breath of an Ancient Evil had escaped. Darkness would encompass the world now, a global descent into medieval terror. There was no sun in this system, only death—a skull moon whose mouth hung open above the earth, the plasma of a million slaughtered worlds slathering the magnetosphere.

He prepared for this day. There wasn't a moment that slipped by that he hadn't waited for the outcome. Now that it stood before him, he had equipped himself properly. The G-men would want chains on him if they ever found out what he cached for this special occasion. The things he had were from twenty years of careful planning and preparations.

Don't get it twisted, he was no quack checking birds for microcameras or thinking the sky was a computer screen or reptiles were hiding in human skins. This was the battle foretold thousands of years ago. Before books and civilization. Back when progenitors of the human race spun sigils of magic in the air and cast bone dust into green flames. Where altars of sinew and screaming skulls mortared with marrow tasted the hot, sweet syrup of a sacrifice.

It started here, in the apartment building of all places.

Somewhere, a Gate had opened, and it wasn't the only one.

Chapter 9

Here's what happened next: Dean's heart was beating off-kilter, suffering a visual/mind trauma when every door on the floor was thrown open. This shouldn't have been cause for alarm or distraction because, after all the shooting and screaming, it would be normal for the tenants to poke their noses in and question what was taking place.

But this wasn't so normal, and nobody was asking a thing.

Nothing would ever be normal again.

Stumbling out of their doors, like open caskets, were the residents, dead and jerking with unholy life. Up one side and down the other, the hall was stuffing up.

Dean reloaded, an act both reactive and hyper.

Their faces were something else. Like each was smashed tight in a leg of pantyhose, the eyes, lips, skin—all were smeared out of shape, and bloody grins pinned open sharp gray fangs. Some walked in perfect step; others dragged a leg. A handful decided their best means of conveyance was to go down on all fours.

But the one other thing they all shared was their momentum. Like they were caught in a slow paresis spell. Dean's mind had snapped to the point where there was no deeper recess in which it could find hope. There was no coming back from the horrors of the night. And while he should have been eating a gun right then and there, he turned it on *them* instead.

As he did so, the hall lights flickered, threatening to shut the corridor down in complete darkness. He had his flashlight, which was a plus, but how good and comforting would it be when trapped in a perfect tunnel of voided light while lurking and sliding nearby were those craving blood?

They encroached, bottlenecking his escape.

Panic seized his aim and he burned a mag in rapid fire. Surprisingly, it did the job. The way to the elevator had cleared as several tenants lay sprawled in various forms of mutilation, the shots having an explosive effect to their degenerate anatomy. Heads bashed into puddles of mince, chests blown through, spines shattered. Dean took his chance and hopped and swerved and sped through reaching arms, ducking, and slapping at saliva-hanging mouths. One, a woman with an amazing set of milkers, screamed in his face. He brought the Beretta butt down on her head until it split to the chin, blood bursting up into his eyes. She sagged out of sight.

Clearing his vision, two more of the dead blocked his path. Holstering his Beretta, he pulled the nightstick and swung it with everything he had. Every muscle in his arm packed into his fist as the club became an extension of his fear, his survival.

SLAP.

One head sprayed to the wall, the body dropping.

THUNK.

Another head was disfigured with a solid *WHACK* to the crown. Blood spilled down the man's face. A second *WHACK* and the head caved in completely.

After that, it became disorienting. Busting heads, hacking at screaming faces, breaking arms with reaching claws. At one point, he had rearmed his Beretta and its slide was smoking, brass hopping. His back scuffed the elevator and he screamed, spinning around and putting one bullet through its door.

A second later, he was back facing the hall. There were three or four of them down there staggering without order; the rest lay in hideous repose, the walls splashed with blood, the ground a literal channel of gore and broken bodies.

The door opened behind him. He backed inside slowly, not even thinking the elevator might be occupied. It didn't matter to him. His mind hadn't thought that far ahead. He was merely pulling back from a bad, horrible thing. Once he cleared the door, he pressed himself into the corner and punched the button to the lobby.

Then everything in him lost gravity and he hit the deck cold, blacking out. He didn't see the stop at the fifth floor in time.

Chapter 10

If the sixth floor had been a doozy, the fifth wasn't any better.

Bing.

The moment the door swung open, Dean shook awake to the sound of slavering, evil hunger. His eyes popped wide and there was an old lady standing there, her white nightgown splashed with blood from neckline to hemline. Her hands were up, the fingers nothing but bones, sharpened and pink.

"Stay back!" The Beretta in his hand, he wondered just how many shots he had left. "I'm warning you, lady!"

Ropes of saliva looped off her chin and bled around her teeth. She was smiling, not like any grandma but, instead, like some evil blighted witch or a werewolf. Her scalp was missing, tufts of gray hair hanging in ratty coils. She started hissing as she crossed a foot into the elevator.

Dean gave her one to the chest. *BAM!* It beat her back like a slap to the face. She turned and hissed, dragging it out so it pierced his ears and brain and sent a shiver through him.

Pop, pop!

At that range, her face vanished with much of her head. She staggered back as if she was set to fall off a ledge, then she dropped, showing Dean what was waiting behind her.

He sighed. "Fuck me."

An assembly. Like the level above him, the hall was a run of the dead. Young, old, and middle-aged, the tenants bumped into one another, growling and hissing, slashing at each other with hands and ... *knives.*

Dean did a quick inventory of his gear: one magazine left, six shots in the current, a nightstick, a can of OC, and a pair of handcuffs.

Not much at hand to confront dozens of these ... whatever they were. Here's another thing too: Dean was at a loss. He was thinking rabies because all of them had some degree of foam around their mouths, each of their grins hooked and slashed into a hideous death rictus. But what didn't add up was the deterioration of the skin. Their eyes—some yellow as yolk— weren't any better; most were either blown sockets or bleeding down their faces. He hadn't seen anything else and wondered if there was something more he just hadn't run into yet.

The cloaked one. He didn't spend too much time thinking about it. His chance for reflection had been torn with screams and shooting rabids. *Rabids* … it didn't compute. Rabies had a way to it and these people were exhibiting symptoms of some entirely different affliction.

But what?

They spotted him. Their incessant groaning bounced in his head. He hated that sound and wished he had a machine gun right about now. But he didn't. He had a Beretta 9mm with limited shots.

Then it hit him.

The elevator.

He reached and thumbed the lobby button.

Nothing happened.

He tried again and again, beating it with his finger. "Come on, goddamnit!" They were getting closer now, pressing together in a single hungering train of claws and teeth. They were hissing, eyes steaming, grins smeared with saliva, blood on their faces, biting the air. Some were *missing* faces, some put together all wrong: heads backward, a leg twisted, one arm broken, crooked over a shoulder. But despite whatever physical defects, nothing had slowed their progress or put a stop to it.

"Come on! What the fuck is wrong here?"

Thunder boomed, rain battered, and lightning branched and exploded in the city. Power to the building was suffering, the lights down the hall flashing, flickering.

This was not good.

He pleaded with that goddamn button, but it wouldn't work. The power had obviously frayed the elevator. There would be no closing its door, no descent to safety. Options waning, he did what he had to do, and that was put his back to the wall and start blasting.

Pop, pop, pop, pop, pop, pop!

Slide hopping, brass ejecting, smoke gyring, copper hornets slashing and bashing and piercing, the hall splashed in blood and bones, and faces smacking the wall like clots of red mud.

Reloaded.

Pop, pop, pop!

Three shots, three more down. Good work. They were easy to kill so long as you hit them in the vital spots, just like any human. Meaning: there was nothing supernatural about them at all. Which, again, brought his mind back to the cloaked one. *Like a ghost . . .*

Or some fucked-up magician of black magic. Whatever spook show was in play wasn't making any sense, and the more he blasted and the more faces he erased in bloody blurs, his mind was hijacked by the sights and smells and screams of the dead. Red in his eyes, he was a machine, swinging to one target, dropping it, zeroing in on the next.

Back and forth it went until his last round. *Pop!*

And the top of a young boy's head ripped away in a spray of brains.

He dropped his Beretta, his mind breaking, a laugh bubbling up his throat. Then it came, released as an insane peal of laughter that had him cackling and bent over, eyes watering, observing and pointing at the last ten or more rabids standing down the hall.

Blood and bodies were everywhere. Lightning hit the building, thunder vibrated its way through the steel beams and bricks. The lights flickered and then burned out.

Dean's world had descended into madness, a narrow purgatory of hellish screams and the smell of death, of shape-shifting shadows and red eyes floating in the murk. Hand on his nightstick, he shucked it from its ring, held it like a club, waiting, hoping for his eyes to adjust.

But it didn't seem like that would happen anytime soon. If he hadn't seen their eyes, he wouldn't have a chance. So far, they were still a ways down the hall. They knew where he was, but they were taking their time, playing with him, aware of his situation. He was trapped, contained, cut off. His only avenue of escape was the corridor of the dead—at the far end was the staircase.

He needed to move.

Remembering his flashlight, he pulled it, the beam long and full of pink mist and gun smoke. He crossed into the hallway, the light playing tricks on his eyes, hopping from one ghoul face to the next. His shoes squished as he advanced. It was like walking through a muddy creek bed. Blood sopped his soles, bones crunching like pretzel sticks.

A door on his left. Closed.

He tried the handle. It swung inward, darkness hibernating thick in there. The beam put a hole through it and he stepped inside, wondering what new horror would emerge.

Chapter 11

Of all the fucking days to deliver a pizza.

Chuck Maynard wasn't in the mood for this shit. He slammed his car door, ducking the rain, moving up the steps to the apartment building. Luckily, this one had a fucking overhang where he could take some relief from the rain.

But nope. Now it was coming in sideways, laughing at him, spraying him like a dozen hoses with spray nozzles.

"They better fucking tip me good! I don't give a damn how long it took to get here." The order was placed nearly an hour ago.

He bashed his fist against the door. "PIZZA DELIVERY! OPEN THE HELL UP!"

Chuck shook his head. It was a sad thing when the world was going to hell and you had to deliver a fucking pizza. It took him ten minutes to make the drive, and the moment he put the car into gear, he heard what sounded like an explosion behind him. Multiple. He checked his rearview and he couldn't see anything, thanks to the rain.

God, it pissed him off.

He beat on the door like he was driving nails into the damn thing. "OPEN UP! IT'S PISSING OUT HERE!"

A speaker to his side hit his ears with a garbled message. "Open now."

He wasn't sure, nor did he give a shit, but it sounded like whoever answered was chewing on something. Rude bastards.

At least he was inside now, out of the fucking rain. He shook beads off of him like a wet dog shaking its fur. He was big and fat and wearing a bright yellow jacket with a pizza slice smack-dab in the center on the back. The collar and sleeve cuffs were red. Over his left breast was a smaller slice of pizza. Topping his square head was a yellow cap with, yet again, another pizza slice centered.

The place was warm and vacant. He looked to the staircase, then the elevator door, then down the hall.

"Come on, what the fuck is the wait for? I need to get back."

He set the pizza on the counter and popped a smoke into his mouth. He didn't give a shit that it was becoming more illegal to do so. What did it matter? The whole city—nay, scratch that—the whole goddamn world was in the gutter, flipped over on itself and shaking everything loose. At least, that's how it seemed. Chuck didn't pay too much attention to things like that, only what was in front of his eyes.

He lit up, pulling on it, blowing some smoke. "Fuck, just what I needed."

He peeked over the counter and saw a coffee cup, a folded newspaper, a small television set, and an empty stool.

"No security tonight?"

He didn't care. He dragged his smoke, wondering where the fuck the customer was. But those thoughts stopped when the elevator door opened.

Bing.

"Thank God, what the hell took you so long?"

A man emerged and he looked like he was prepared for the rain. Wearing a long black slicker, bathrobe, or ... a cloak? What difference did it really make?

"You planning on hitting the streets for a stroll, mister?" A drag and exhale. "It's coming down like God flushed Heaven's toilet out there. You might want to wait a while."

Chuck was so in his mind about clocking out, he didn't even notice the man wasn't walking like normal folks but drifting to him, gliding, levitating an inch off the floor.

"Are you the one who ordered this?" Chuck asked, cigarette stuffed in his mouth, holding the pizza box out in front of him.

The cloaked one stopped a foot away, hovering like some projection cast from shadows.

"Look, man, did you order this pie or not?"

The knife flashed and the pizza box folded in half, spilling to the ground. Chuck teetered backward, his hands on his sizable belly. His coat split open revealing that his belly was sliced, the skin tearing around his waist and widening his stomach open, a great bulge of pink and red lumps and loops coming out of there.

"JESUS!" His face sprung with sweat, his eyes close to ejecting from his head. "OH MY GOD!"

Blood and meat splashed at his feet like a full bucket of offal.

Bing.

He was too busy holding his guts in to see the ravenous newcomer zombies exiting the elevator and lurching toward him. Their groans and hisses were lost amid Chuck's strident screams.

He saw them when they formed a phalanx. His mouth rounded with a blast of terror at the same moment his waistline snapped and his torso dropped to the ground, quivering.

They set upon him and smeared their faces with his blood.

Chapter 12

Dean jumped at a shadow, then sighed deep and long.

Just his flashlight impressing scares on his mind. He couldn't stop it from happening. Wherever the beam went, it broke against furniture and corners and these became black apparitions, things with eyes and hooks and poison in their teeth. He checked each room.

Everything was empty. Nobody around.

He must have shot the tenants back in the hall.

A tapping somewhere in the home stalled his exit.

He cocked his head, listening.

Tap, tap, tap . . .

Yes, it was somewhere in the master bedroom, he supposed.

He shone his light in the hallway, creating a tunnel of shadows, clawing and ghostly. He stepped down there, a cautious waltz taking him to the bedroom. He stabbed the beam in there, slicing everything up, creating shadow puppets and darting shapes.

Tap, tap, tap . . .

The closet. It was coming from the fucking closet.

This was not good. Dean had seen a lot already, and the amount had taken a toll and erased most things, except survival. A quick recall of his memory showed Kayla coming at him, her beautiful face marred by a skinned fright mask. He saw the old lady. Knew her, but couldn't pin her name. He still hadn't seen Sheila. The horrors of the sixth floor and the fifth punctured most of his memories: their screams, the blood, the gun smoke, the brass, the impact points.

The cloaked one. A ghost? A revenant? Some wayward spirit of night and starlight and cosmic ether? Or maybe just a magician.

Tap, tap, tap . . .

Enough of this. He steeled himself, shone the beam on the door. He lowered it, thinking he saw a red light smoking through the bottom. Nothing there, he panned to the knob.

"Okay, you wanna play fucking games?"

He went for it. Wasn't sure why, but he did it. Doorknob in hand, twist, open. Blackness, suffocating and rank and full of conjecture. A shadow box, a coffin, a gate, an infinitesimal wormhole.

Thing is, he wasn't sure of anything more than those terms. The beam was in the closet, yet it hadn't lit up anything. The darkness was alive in there—a sentient, evil liquid. He backed in slowly, stalking strides. Then a blinding red light burst upon him, making him drop both nightstick and flashlight and block his eyes with his hands. The glow was as powerful as a halogen, as scarlet as arterial blood, and hot.

He saw movement between his fingers and this instantly set him in motion. One hand blocking the light, he took possession of both Maglite and baton.

Looking up, he saw her.

Sheila.

But not the same. Oh no, not the same at all. She was floating in a fog of blood. Her hair stringy and her pajamas in tatters, both whipping around like a high-power fan was blowing on her.

"Sheila?" His voice had no tone, just an empty whisper of disbelief.

She didn't say anything, but her eyes were red moons, transcending the vibrant bloodred fog behind her. She pointed a finger at Dean and beckoned him. By an inexorable pull, he complied, walking trancelike toward her, his mouth opened in adoration. She was a queen of night and blood, and her teeth were long and vampiric and gray as steel. She was grinning a big clown grin at him and it was a thing both exaggerated and absolutely frightful.

But Dean wasn't seeing it like that. She was beautiful, the offspring of his crush, Kayla. He would see her again if he got in with Sheila.

"*Hey*, get away from there!"

Dean didn't hear anything but the sweet beauty of the blood mist calling out to him, the red eyes hooked onto his like laser beams in his brain. He was a foot, maybe two, away when an automatic rifle exploded.

It was an angry, metallic hammering. *BAM-BAM-BAM-BAM-BAM!*

Smoke and wood and plaster and nails exploded in bountiful acrid clouds. Sparks sprayed, heavy slugs punched fist-sized holes in the wall around the closet, splintering the frame.

Dean, shaken back to reality, dove at the bed.

A big tall man was in the room with him, a black assault rifle in his hands, muzzle flashes piercing the darkness, streaks of hot lead tearing into the shadowed closet. Sheila screamed with cheated anger and expired like a vapor. The blood mist smoked into ash.

Smoke palled the bedroom grayly. Dean shone the flashlight on the man, coughing at the excess of powder floating around.

He was dressed in jungle pattern fatigues with black boots and a green beret with a silver crest at the apex. He had a chest rig stuffed with banana magazines and a couple of grenades. There was a sidearm hooked to his belt and a sheathed knife on one leg. This was a one-man army if there ever was one. He recognized the face.

"Allen Boone?"

"Dean, we need to get the hell out of here, but first, we need to stop this."

Chapter 13

His minions spread throughout the building like rats in a boneyard. There was no stopping what had started, what had waited for so long to emerge. The Gate spun and spun in dizzying oscillations: blood reds, sea blues, neon purples, ectoplasm greens, violet pinks, sun-shimmering oranges. It sang in hot winds and smelled of corpse matter and flies and newborn atrocities.

More heads were needed before he could enter and assimilate with his master.

On cue, several robed acolytes thronged about, backs arched grotesquely with humps, clawed hands tossing a surplus of severed heads, most with their faces frozen in agonizing grimaces and forever screams. Young and old, the heads were chucked into the sphere to grind and pulp and mist the room in blood.

The Anointed One smiled from the shadow of his hood.

"Assimilation is near. Soon, the world will look upon their new god."

Chapter 14

Despite the city becoming a fucking battleground, the police still had their duty to fulfill, and that duty was centered at an apartment building on the corner of 4th and Jefferson.

"All right, ladies, go loaded for bear; we don't know what sort of spider trap we're heading into."

The men—twenty-six of them in total, all veterans clad in tactical black uniforms and helmets—complied and stuffed every pocket and pouch with ammo and whatever other goodies they might need to put into play for tonight's raid. Radios were set, earpieces slotted, and each man either had an M-16, a Remington auto, or a German machine pistol.

"Let's load up!"

They crammed into two heavy battle vehicles with tires big as tractor wheels. The steel behemoths tore through the streets, narrowly avoiding splashing over citizens running in their path. Lightning was doing a job on the city, striking like bombs and missiles, penetrating skyscrapers, and cracking walks and roads, setting fires.

"Like Hell has opened up." One cop observed.

And there was a lot more truth in that than he would realize.

The wind was shoving into them, hampering the steering, making it a chore to keep her steady. Thunder roamed the streets like a hungering beast out of time. Lightning veined and branched and screamed like incoming, striking blue fire, and several times, incinerating whole groups of citizens or blasting them into bloody bits.

"We're here."

The trucks swerved, then the back doors broke open. Out poured twenty-six police troopers in heavy combat gear and enough ammo to take back the city. Only, they were responding to a serious crisis in the apartment building on 4th and Jefferson. Calls had been coming in left and right of something truly fucking strange happening at the place.

Number one: screaming, high-pitched and terrible to the callers, was a nonstop thing. Dispatch suggested it was the wind and nothing more, but when a phone was put against a window screen, the operator paled because there was nothing natural about it. The screams were the cries of the damned, of the evil dead clawing out of graves.

"Would you look at that?" Someone pointed.

The building looked like it was encased in some sort of rippling energy, red and bleeding neon at its seams. A nimbus of blood.

"Some sort of … electric anomaly, I'm sure." Even Sergeant Cooper didn't believe his words. "Come on, men, we have a job to do!"

So they set at it.

They stacked against the door, clogging up the steps, the rain blasting them soaked to the bone, lightning veining and striking, city power on its way to a blackout.

"BREACH!"

BAM.

The reinforced bolt gave like hot plastic, the door was grounded, and police troopers rushed into position. The place looked normal enough. Lights were still on with a faint flicker in their charge. The hallway empty, no sounds, nothing.

"Sir!"

Shit. Scratch that. There was a huge bloodstain and they all ran over it without even noticing. But they noticed it now, and it was goddamn obscene and thick as spilled paint. There were bits of things in it that could be pizza and teeth and yellowed clumps of fat, some muscle strung about, smashed into strands of hair. There were bloody bare footprints leading down the hall, then suddenly disappearing, as if someone had taken a mop to the floor and hadn't finished cleaning.

"All right, men, looks like we have something truly weird going on here.

Let's keep it tight and eyes up. Fingers ready on the button."

Sergeant Cooper took the lead, advancing his team in a line along the left and right walls. At each door passed, a cell of two cops broke from the formation and set up alongside its frame for breaching.

Cooper, reaching the end, pivoted on his boots and ordered his men to make contact with the tenants. "First we knock, then we enter if there's no reply."

"Are you sure that's legal, Sarge?" one of the men asked.

"Have you seen what's happening in this town, Peabody? Even the mayor is losing his head over everything. Close to calling in The Guard! Now do as I ordered."

Doors were rattled and rattled.

Seconds passed and looks were exchanged. The building had all the feeling of a corpse, a dead and empty thing, the life crushed right out of it. Then when they thought there would be no response, same as knocking on a casket, the doors opened.

The tenants stood there, lifeless as suspected, jagged Halloween grins, skin ripped away in patches, all the black horror of the grave stamped in their bloodred eyes. They had knife-sharp fingers hooked for eating. Before the troopers could so much as blink, those claws were on them, teeth tearing into their throats and faces, gear ripped away, and weapons clattering to the floor.

The hallway was in an uproar of soul-rending screams of men being eaten alive. Blood erupted in thick jets, black uniforms were splashed red. There was no room to move. Cops were bumping into one another trying to dislodge their attackers. Gunshots popped with suppressed reports as muzzles were pressed to bellies and faces. But it hadn't lessened the resolve of those hungering teeth which held and bit and chomped and chattered.

Sergeant Cooper had eyes on the entire terrifying scene.

It pulled the reason out of him and left him standing there at the mercy of his child-born fears. The corridor was a mutiny of cannibalism and blood showers. Men were drowning in seas of gnashing fangs and tearing claws. Hissing and screaming bounced in his skull. He put his sights on one of the tenants and jerked the trigger.

It smacked with a *thunk*, like thick meat. It spun the tenant around and Cooper almost puked. The man's face was completely ripped away and packed on top of his head like a hood. It sat there slopping and dripping, blood and muscle making his pink teeth shine. Cooper's attention was on the man's hands and he saw there was a head in one and a hatchet in the other.

"Greer, Jesus Christ."

From the neckline, blood dropped in a steady stream, draining the complexion of Greer white as talcum. His face had been stamped with the death strike: eyes rounded out impossibly, his mouth contorted with a scream.

"You sick son of a bitch!"

As Cooper slapped the man with more lead, something happened that took the wind right out of him. The floor was cracking. There was no mistaking it. The black and white tiles were rupturing with fissures, hot red steam whistling. It heaved with pressure and all at once, fell away, dumping officers and zombies into a bath of lavalike boiling blood.

The men, who had been screaming before, were out of their minds now, burning alive. One cop went under, then bobbed back up a cooked skeleton. Three more did the same, and more and more were popping the surface similarly: arms reaching, skulls glazed with blood, silent eternal screams. The pit was a smoking cauldron thirty feet long and six wide, boiling with all the ingredients of human biology. The zombies hadn't fared any better and they, too, were floating and catching fire, their anatomies melting, bones glowing like plutonium rods, eye sockets ran through with slag.

Cooper lost track of time. He thought he'd seen it all. But now he understood he hadn't. That there were things happening in this city, this world, that weren't making any sense and didn't have to. The Gates had opened and reality had been exchanged for the phantasmal and the damned.

He dropped his M-16 after some movement iced his heart.

Yes, there was something moving in all that hot blood when there shouldn't be. Nothing could survive that. Even a steel beam would wilt like cellophane hit with a match. He stared, dumbfounded, the pit steaming and boiling, skeletons hardening like adamantine.

Black hands with raptor claws on them sprung and clutched the ledge. More than one pair, there were six or seven of them but Cooper wasn't counting; he was pissing his pants and couldn't for the life of him find his feet. He was slumped against the wall, the pain in his chest driving his blood dangerously.

Faces now. Things blackened by tar. Not really flesh but some stone-faced mask. Same as the arms and rest of the body: stone—onyx—and creased with hairline cracks. Their eyes were something else. Dark wells excreting blood that ran down the fissures marring their faces and necks. Like tiny rivers, exterior veins, the blood wound and branched and made the stone demons appear to pulse with bloodred vibrancy. They made deep rumbling noises when they breathed, if that's indeed what they were doing.

Cooper watched as they spread around and he didn't offer so much as a change to his face. He had the same look he wore the moment his men were set upon by ravenous blood drinkers from the apartments. Four hands were on him now, clutching him by the ankles and dragging him to the pit. The first wave dropped back into the slag and that left Cooper and his two handlers. They took their time, their legs sinking them down to their waists.

Cooper's feet sizzled as they hit the hot slag. Then in went his knees and finally, his waist popped and hissed and boiled, blood bubbling around him. Next, his head went under and he never even screamed.

He died before they took him away.

Chapter 15

Dean wasn't sure he heard Allen right. And he would have asked for clarification on the subject of these Gates but there were things more important to handle beforehand. On their walk down to the fourth floor, they couldn't make the third because the mouth to the staircase had been packed with corpses. So thick and bloody, it was like a cemented dam of death. Both of their faces soured, especially Dean who wasn't handling sights so well.

Allen withdrew his Colt .45 and pressed it into Dean's hand, giving him a couple of extra magazines too.

"Don't shoot me in the back and we'll be okay."

Then Allen went on to distract Dean, talking about his time in the war and having seen something just like this in the jungle. Only it wasn't a real jungle anymore, not from the sixties, but maybe from when the sea receded and left a black, slimy, pestiferous jungle of shadows and blood rivers in its exit.

There was a lot more to it than that, but Dean and Allen were interrupted by something unholy and certainly not right in this world. The fourth floor wasn't much better than the last two above it. But it was *different*.

"Like a fire went through here," Dean said.

"I think you're right. Sure smells that way. Look."

Dean did and he saw how the doors were opened and gushing smoke like chimneys in wintertime. Black and oily smoke.

"Keep cool and follow me," Allen instructed.

Sounded good to Dean. But what would be better was finding a window and making a leap. He wasn't so sure he would survive his next footfall. He was surprised to still be alive and kicking as it was. After what he had survived so far, he didn't have much hope of his luck lasting any longer.

"I hear something," Allen said.

Dean took that as his cue to put the brakes on. He stood there, same as Allen, both of their heads stiff but their ears working. Allen's AK-47 was pulled closer to his shoulder, ready to snap up at a moment's notice. Dean's hand fused to the Colt, his trigger memory setting in, his other hand strobing the flashlight about. But it wasn't having the desired effect he was hoping for. The beam hit the smoke and reflected back at him.

"Nothing now. Come on."

The haze put everything out of whack. There were times when Allen would walk into a wall of it and it would fold him over where Dean could see nothing but gushing smoke. He'd whisper, "Allen, are you there?"

Allen would assure him he was there and continued walking on like he was out on a normal everyday stroll through the park. They could hear the storm blowing the city into ashes, feel the vibratory shudders of powerful thunder.

Dean's light wasn't helping and it was starting to grate on him. The funny thing was, the smoke wasn't touching their lungs. There was no coughing, no burning sensation in the eyes, nothing at all. And that was all real weird and strange, but there was so much strange and evil in the building that he wasn't even thinking about it until Allen disappeared again. This time when Dean called out, there was no reply.

"Allen!"

Fuck. He flinched at the sound of his voice. It wove around him with eerie, sonorous inflections. Back and front and sides were boxed in with smoke. It came on thick now, completely smashing him into vertiginous confusion. The apartment doors were blocked with constant eruptive discharges of the oily black haze.

"Allen, say something!"

Shit. He wasn't liking this. Not one bit. If Allen had been taken, he would have at least screamed or got a round off or two. But there had been nothing. One moment, his back was to Dean; the next, smoke laced him and ate his profile and then he was gone.

"Allen?"

A shape. He saw it quickly before it disappeared.

"Allen . . ."

Dean worked the light around, his gun up alongside it. Nerves strung, eyes fixed, mouth open, sweat beading his face, he pressed into the smoke, seriously flummoxed by its lack of effect.

The shape again. It ran past. Seemed to go in one door and into another. Dean stopped, his heart flopping around, his temples pounding. He wanted to call out but didn't.

Laughter. Sharp and cunning, cackled behind him.

He turned, both light and gun up. It sounded like a little kid, and not just one but *many.*

"Dean?"

He almost shit his pants. Allen appeared from behind, his back to him. "Shit, man, where the fuck did you go? Don't leave me alone in this place again."

Allen's head turned slightly. *"I found something. Follow me."*

No apology, of course. Only Allen Boone, the crazy vet back in the saddle.

It felt like they were walking longer than the building was wide. It made no sense. Twenty minutes or more. Dean wasn't sure. Time had a way of slowing and speeding, so maybe it was just more of that. Wherever Dean could pick at the logic of things, it made him feel more secure. Because so far, everything else had tossed his salad the wrong way. There were things happening here only seen in movies. He had to kill Kayla because she wanted to eat him. At least, that's what he assumed. The hordes of zombies and the black-cloaked poltergeist—this whole thing was a maze of horror and disbelief, black magic.

"*Slow it here*," Allen said.

Dean pulled it in, locked in place, his flashlight on Allen's back. That's when he noticed something. Allen's clothes looked eaten through, torn up in places. They had the stink of age on them. Old age, as though those fatigues had been buried then dug up after twenty years—with the occupant still wearing them.

Dean was right on the money because Allen came around in a jerking spin and his face fell off like a mask, sliding from his skull like sleet, with blood splashing down his exposed sternum and ladders of rib bones. His intestines coiled in there like black mambas, his heart bursting sprays of blood with each beat.

"*You like what you see there, son?*"

Allen's voice, an inhuman thing, a mockery of everything Allen had been. It cut the nerves and pierced the brain like a hot needle. The eyes were sunken and empty. Just blackness.

"Allen … Jesus, no, not you too."

"*I'm hungry, Dean.*" The AK came up and the bayonet was slick with blood. "*Haven't ate since Tet, back when we would string 'em up and strip 'em down to the bone. We had great feasts, Dean. You would have liked it.*"

Pop, pop, pop!

The heavy hit of the 230 grain hollow points went right through Allen like smoke.

"*Nice try, little worm. Now it's my turn.*"

The bayonet was an inch from Dean's throat when a weapon sputtered its angry hornets and had a much different effect. It seized the attack and sent the Allen zombie back a step. A cheated cracking roar erupted and the Allen zombie atomized into black ash.

Allen—the real one—came around to look into Dean's shocked pupils. "You okay there, Dean?"

"You … it was you."

"Nah, wasn't me. Just something pretending to be."

"Pretending?" Dean couldn't believe his eyes, but then again, he didn't have to. Because what he saw, ghost zombie or not, the thing had been real.

"They can't really hurt you. But they can scare you to death."

That was for sure; Dean didn't think his heart would have lasted much longer.

"How do you know so much about this shit?"

"Back on the stairs, remember? I told you I experienced this sort of thing back in 'Nam."

That's right. He had, and the memory of it came beating back into Dean's brain, completely dislodging his shock. He was putting the pieces back in order now.

To keep it short and sweet, Allen said he had led a patrol into the jungle in search of an NVA supply route, and what they ran into was anything but that. The sky turned funny and red and the moon was black. The jungle's greenery withered to shadow, and the NVA were there, all right. Only they weren't much more human than anything Dean and Allen were fighting in the apartment. A battalion of the NVA dead pressed against Allen's Special Forces team. It was a good thing the troopers had the right gear because they butchered those zombie bastards to so much slop and hamburger they left the jungle hanging with slime and blood and meat.

"That's when we found the pyramid."

Once the smoke cleared over the ventilated corpses, they tried to radio their contact but there was nothing getting through. A hot wind streamed through the jungle and they heard something out there in the shadows calling to them. They took a shot and investigated, tracking the source to what Allen called a "pyramid." Only it wasn't like anything you might expect to see in Egypt or Guatemala. It held the same style, more or less, but was composed of shiny black marble, and extending from its apex was a bloodred light, a column of liquid gore.

"Went all the way to the stars."

Eventually, they found an entrance and went inside. What followed was a nightmare. Battle after battle, not in the confines of some narrow tunnel system but in a new world. Yes, Allen and his team skirmished with the dead of a dead world. A place of living shadows and alien corpse walkers. Of zombies in black stone carapaces and a legion of soldiers—missing troopers from the war, their humanity butchered by a need to eat brains and drink blood.

"We killed that son of a bitch, Dean. Found him on his throne rising out of a lake of blood and bones. A throne of infants. The most horrible thing I'd ever seen in my life. The king, or whatever it was, died just like anything else, but it took a whole lot for us to nail it."

Allen went on to say that when they killed this overlord, the world spun and everything in it vanished, leaving Allen and his surviving teammates back in a humid, normal Vietnam.

The smoke in the corridor was thinning out, seeping into the walls. Dean's beam punched through it and he was happy for that. They were coming to the elevator, a silver door at the end of a dark walk.

"The only way to close these Gates, Dean, is to walk into them and take the key."

"The overlord?"

Allen nodded. "I don't know much more about it, but my experience has shown me that's the solution."

Dean's mind was swimming. Gates, zombies, alien monsters, temples, and dead worlds. Blood oceans and rivers. Planets encased by human skins and demon kings leading battalions of corpse troopers.

Such things had no room to stick in his mind. He wanted them out of there. He wasn't sure he could stand another nightmare floor.

"Ha, what do you know?" Allen said.

Bing.

The door opened.

"Weird."

"Yeah, but we don't have any other way unless you want to cut a path through all those bodies back there."

Dean shuddered, remembering the dam of cadavers buried in the stairwell.

"Let's just hope we don't go any lower than the lobby."

The doors closed, and they waited.

Chapter 16

The Anointed One was primed to enter the Gate. He stood before a black neon maw, a windy hot disk with the smell of blood at its core.

He could hear the gathering darkness approaching the other side.

His acolytes stood sentinel in their hunched poses. Their hoods draped, their taloned fingers curled.

Several of the taller, thin, cloaked ones emerged from the shadows of the room. They said no words and made no sounds, only glided and deposited heads and limbs and bags of organs into the sphere, painting the spinning vortex with blood.

Yes, darkness was here. The city was alive with black energy. Soon, it would eclipse the world.

Chapter 17

Amazingly, they made it to the lobby, not even concerned about the other floors. They had a job to do, and Allen was set to make that happen, though Dean wasn't too thrilled about it. But there was something about the prospect of leaving Allen's side that didn't sit right with him. He needed the man's help. He felt bound to assist Allen however he could. After all, what would Dean do out there in the city?

According to Allen, it would be the same in the streets as it was in the apartment building.

"How do you know this?" Dean asked as they crossed out of the elevator.

Allen turned and his rough expression hooked a grin. "Experience."

They stopped.

The way ahead was not what they were expecting to see.

"Jesus Christ, what the fuck is that about?!"

They were looking at the floor of the corridor.

"It's fucking gone," Dean added to his first outburst. "Like the damn thing fell away."

"Not *like*," Allen said. "Did." He approached the edge and looked down. From the way it looked, it probably descended to Hell itself. A black rectangle.

"What's that sound?"

Allen heard it now. It sounded like faraway voices or screaming.

"Is that coming from down there?" Dean pointed.

"I believe so."

Dean was looking around and Allen studied the empty path.

"Hey, what the hell are you doing?"

"Easy," Allen told him, shrugging Dean's hand off his forearm. "Back in 'Nam, I came across something like this in the jungle. A great big hole with no color, only blackness. Funny thing is, the surface was covered with leaves and sticks and stuff. Like a big black lake still as a mirror." Dean was staring at Allen with more of that disbelief in his eyes. "You know what I did?"

Dean shook his head.

"This."

Allen took a step over that pit and Dean nearly screamed himself dead. Allen walked across that damn thing like Jesus walking on water.

When he reached the other side, he smiled and leaned his AK on one shoulder. "Should I call you a cab?"

Dean looked at the pit. "I'm not fucking crossing that."

"Then you'll stay there for whatever may come down on the next ride."

Dean looked behind him. His hands up in the air, he said. "I don't know if I can do it."

"Didn't you just watch me walk over that thing?"

He did, but it wasn't helping anything.

"Do you need me to come over there and pick you up and carry you over? If that's what I need to do, then I'll do it."

Time to get your balls back, Dean. He lost them after his run-in with the Allen zombie ghost. He shot a worried glance to the black path. "What if I fall?"

"Well then,"—Allen put a finger in his mouth and popped his cheek— "like a stone dropped in a dark sea."

"You're not helping matters."

Allen could see that and said, "Just one foot at a time. Don't run. Just do it. Don't think. I was like you back in 'Nam."

"And how did that go?"

"My buddy, Jones, was the first. But it was an accident. He fell right on top of that blackness and was screaming out of his mind. Then he stopped when he realized the surface under him was hard as concrete."

Dean could not imagine that black empty grave as hard as stone. It showed nothing of solidity. It was airy and gave one the sense of a fatal plunge. It spun the mind with screaming warnings.

"Just do it, we ain't got much time."

"I'm thinking, okay?"

"Fine. While you do that, check your six."

Dean's hair bristled. He very slowly corkscrewed around and saw some people standing there. All of them naked and skinned like baboons. Feral eyes baked with yellow slime, fangs overlapping fangs. Sharp fingers clutched sharper knives and hatchets. One of them was chewing on the head of a baby, another carving out the brain of a woman with her face partially bitten off.

Dean forgot about the pit and ran across it like it wasn't there to begin with. He was at Allen's side when those people burst apart in a wave of screams and loping madness. There were ten or maybe twice that number; some Dean recognized, others he hadn't ever seen in this building.

"Time to meet your maker!" Allen said as the AK shattered the sounds of screams with the wailing kinetic slamming of the bolt. The horde broke apart. Splashing open and jetting blood. Faces vanished, chests blown to slime. Some were yanked off the ground and went spinning. Blood was spraying up the walls and into the air. Two were standing and they were screeching, knives in both hands, their jaws sprung with teeth like steel claws, and their eyes just boils of blood.

BAM-BAM-BAM-BAM!

The duo crashed into each other as the AK put them down as splattering ejecta.

Dean was wiped. His mind blank.

"Next time," Allen was saying as he exchanged an empty magazine, "why don't you help me out a pinch?"

Dean just looked at him.

Chapter 18

The city was out of control. The landscape razed by acid rains, black and toxic. Lightning was black, too, cranking out of a bloody shadow sky, striking with impacts like tactical nukes. Streets were busted and steaming. Things were crawling and others like them, walking. People were being butchered alive, eaten on the spot. Hordes upon hordes of the zombie dead thronged in gluttonous waves, dragging people out of hiding and bathing in their gore, filling their bellies with hot brains.

The city was a bloodbath. A soon-to-be graveyard.

Chapter 19

They found the secret spot, behind a washing machine of all places. It had been dragged from its original location and what was behind it was a hole, jagged and wide as a manhole cover.

Allen looked at Dean and Dean spoke first, "After you."

Allen did that hooked grin again and shone his flashlight into the hole. It dispelled the dark back like smoke blown by a bellows. He was inside when Dean went in behind him.

Together, they stood there a moment taking it all in. The room was *big*, excavated out of the adjoining property perhaps. Maybe as big as a gymnasium in some high school. It was hard to tell. The dark in there was stuffy and thick and foggy. You could lose direction in such a place with little effort. Back could be front and front, back.

There was something different about this place. It wasn't like the apartment; it was worse. It had the corruption of evil in its design.

"This is where we'll find it."

"The Gate?"

"The main one, yes."

Their lights weren't strong enough to cut the way open. One minute, the dark would iris, then the next, close up like a hungry mouth eating the beam.

"I don't like this," Dean said, sticking closer to Allen with every foot they cleared. Boxed in, they were hearing things. Whispers and an odd droning like a cicada trying to vocalize.

"Ain't nothing to like. We're in the lair."

The lair. Dean couldn't think of a more ominous term. Yeah, it was a lair, all right. One packed with shadows and darting shapes he didn't want to give life to. If there were things circling them like wolves in a dark fog, he wasn't going to entertain them with his awareness. Best to let them think their terror was working magic, which it was, rightly so.

"Don't break on me," Allen said, feeling Dean's fear on top of his own. "Don't acknowledge them. If you do, they'll be on us like vampires on a virgin's neck."

Thanks for that, Allen, just what I needed to think about. Vampires in the night.

There was a light up ahead. Faint, like seeing a campfire through the dark woods at night.

"What are you thinking?" Dean asked, trying his damndest not to look at the swinging shapes and loping shadows, keeping his beam forward. He also wasn't going to point out that the place didn't seem to have a ceiling, just a darkness of illimitable height. He feared if he looked up there long enough, he might see a red moon or something worse.

"It has to be the Gate. Keep your trigger finger warm. I think we're getting some company."

Goddamnit. Allen sure did know how to make a bad situation gain more shit on top of it. They made it maybe seventy or eighty feet, then they saw the Gate more clearly. But the other things surrounding it had their eyes fixed.

"The Anointed One," Allen said, singling one out.

Dean was so close to Allen, they could have been in the same pant leg. He whispered, "The *what?*"

"Back in the jungle, in that temple, we saw one just like it. I'm not sure about them, but I think they are human. Or once were. Possessed would be the answer, I suppose. Don't matter, really. But he's the one drawing energy to it. He could have been a tenant and you would never know. I'm thinking he was."

Dean wasn't worried about the Anointed One's inclusion on the tenant list. He was worried about the eyes now turned on them. Vicious and yellow as toxic gas. They were hunched forms, hissing like angry snakes. Dean's beam hit their claws and they shone like black glass.

"Don't be afraid!" That was Allen's advice before his AK ripped open one of those cloaked imps and it blew apart like a tank of water, only the water was blood and green like antifreeze. It spattered his friend with glowing tangles.

"Holy shit!"

Allen was still firing, making fine work of the imps. They were tossing out reams of that antifreeze-colored blood. Some bested the aim and were close enough to smell, and they smelled worse than they looked. Dean put a bullet in one just for the foul odor itself. The round ate the thing's face away in one meaty green spray.

More were coming. Out of the shadows now, were others.

Zombies.

"They're everywhere!"

"Doesn't matter, get the Anointed One!"

Dean wasn't sure how he was supposed to do that when there were possibly hundreds of these things now. And not just them but every fucking thing that haunted the apartment. Even the cloaked ghosts were back, floating like sheets, their arms extended out with daggers.

BAM-BAM-BAM-BAM-BAM!

Allen's battle hammered and struck bodies to puddles and kept the air fully varnished with a scrim of blood.

Dean put his work in too. Expelling jellied brains to the floor, tearing smoking green channels through torsos and faces.

"Eat this!"

Allen hucked something out into the big crowd. *BOOM!* Their bodies broke apart like wet chaff. Green blood was everywhere, glowing and sinking through the floor.

"The shit is acid!" Dean commented.

"It's not, but it burns no different."

Great help, Allen.

They shot and slapped bodies to the ground. Stacks were building and the Anointed One stood his spot, unmoving.

"I'm going to lead them off, and when I do—"

But Allen never finished his plan. They came upon him like a tsunami. Striking him from every angle available, including from up above, which housed something like a big shadowy spider with a humanlike face and fangs as long as walrus tusks. They pierced Allen's head and he went stiff as meat in a freezer. His eyes rolled up and white and he imploded as his interior was vacuumed dry. What was left shrunk up like a plastic bag and he slopped to the floor.

Dead and drained.

Dean did what he could after that, but there was nothing more he could do, really. Right and left, all around, and now above, there was no letup. He cleared an opening by shooting rapidly, and he scooped Allen's rifle into his hands. Luckily, there had been a fresh magazine inserted, so Dean worked the weapon in single strokes, blasting the dead to green blurs. The cloaked ones vaporized and their shrouds dropped like laundry.

BAM-BAM-BAM-BAM-BAM!

There weren't as many as before, and Dean was thankful for that. Thankful, too, for the lack of any spiderlike things dangling over him.

A reprieve was granted and he didn't waste a second of it. He dropped beside Allen's … *skin* and took the AK magazines and one grenade. Gaining his balance, he found a semi-cleared avenue of escape and took it.

He bounded with all the terror of Hell snapping fangs at his neck. Zombies were pressing against him, walls of them to his right and left. The way ahead narrowed to the Anointed One.

It's the only way, he heard Allen saying.

He put the rifle on the figure and sprayed on automatic. It slammed into the Anointed One and not a damn thing happened. He fired again and again, with the same result.

Then the Anointed One stepped aside and there was that bright sphere of darkness, a tunneling vortex of neon shades. It stunned Dean, bringing him to a trot and finally a stop.

"It is too late," the Anointed One said in a voice as human as Dean's. "The Final Gate is now open. It is my birthright to enter."

"The hell it is!" Dean forgot there would be no effect but he fired anyway, the bullets streaking through the figure like mist.

"Yes, 'The *Hell*' is right."

There were no second glances, no further speech. The Anointed One stood before the Gate and it took him. Black fingers of smoky shadow coiled and constricted and pulled him inside.

Dean's mind snapped out of its paralysis to hear a hungry, slavering legion approaching. He turned and there they were. So many faces, all disastrously mutilated and reformed to incite dread and screams.

And it was working.

Dean sprayed the first line and they fell as expected. He plucked the grenade from his pocket, figured he needed to pull the pin like they did in movies, then hurled it out there. He was waiting for an immediate explosion but seconds ticked by as the throng pressed about, and then—

BOOM!

The second line scattered in blood and smoke.

But stumbling over the heaped corpses were more and more and more. They would never stop until they got him.

There was nothing to do but accept it. He could shoot and shoot but they were not going away. They were legion—this was Hell's army.

Movement above tugged at his eyes. There were spiders up there, huge and descending, fangs dripping, hundreds of eyes a glassy red.

Dean's mind had finally abandoned him. He stood there ready for the slaying. Then a sensation, as if a bone-jarring coldness took him over, and he was yanked backward into the Gate.

Chapter 20

There was no other way to put it than this: when Dean went into the Gate, it was like his body had split at the anatomical level. Every atom and cell underwent a traverse into the space-time continuum. He was in a winding tube of screaming colors and crackling storms.

Eventually, he reformed and was dumped in an alien nightmare. A place of black jungle. The trees were massive and stygian, a bluish luminosity misting their leaves and pulsing like veins in their bark. The ground was wet and sucking. A bog. But unlike anything on Earth. The sky was black metal pierced with bloody stars—things like human hearts in clusters of millions and millions. A respiring whisper smoked through the trees and went up Dean's spine.

He noticed he wasn't alone, for there were eyes out there in the black jungle. Some were up in the trees and others on his level, leaning around trees and peeking through brush. Luminous toadstools were profuse, their colors hypnotic, strings of vapor surrounding them.

He stood with the AK, his pockets crammed with magazines.

But would it be enough?

The answer, he knew, was no.

Then to his right, stacked in the distance, was a pyramid. Gaunt and cyclopean. It dominated, its shadow long and sentient, a storm circled its apex, a moon horned at its eye. It cast the jungle with red phantoms and monsters of blood lurked in its depths. The trees were whispering with life-forms. Shadows slunk about like oil, sliding and shambling.

Then a way was shown to him. The trees bent to his eyes and there, for a hundred miles, stretched the trek to the pyramid. But there was something wrong. The trail wasn't without peril. And that peril was marching at him the way a parade of soldiers marched for its audience. They were coming toward him, not for him but for the Gate at his back, which was still swirling and windy and haunted. He looked at it and it was a window. Zombie faces were smashed against it with hands both bloody and taloned.

His attention swung to the encroaching army.

There was no exit. No escape. He was dead, just still breathing.

A form slid in behind him, tapped his shoulder.

Dean screamed and spun, his mouth locked open, the AK dropped from his hands. The Anointed One was there, hood thrown back to reveal a very human face. The face of a grandfather who would regale you with tales of his boyhood and stories to make you bust a seam laughing so hard.

But that's where the innocence ended.

What was in those eyes was dark and misting. He held a dagger and he brought it to Dean's neck. "You will be reborn in His image."

The blade went through him like a laser and his head was hanging by the hand of the Anointed One. Dean's body bled out, smashed into the blood mud by millions of cadaverous feet entering the Gate.

ZOMBIE MOON

GARRETT BOATMAN

1

By the year 2084, mankind had established cities on the Moon and outposts on Mars, succeeded in mining the asteroids, and installed deep-space observatories on Ganymede and Iapetus. Yet in their more than a century of space exploration and eavesdropping on the stars, mankind had discovered no trace of alien life. Then, one starry lunar night, in a twist of cosmic irony, the privilege of first contact fell not to humans but to rats.

Of Luna City's ten thousand inhabitants, those working or housed in the lower levels of Shackleton crater's domed wonder felt the rumble of the tunnel boring machine in the basalt bedrock beneath their feet. Like the dowsing rods of yesteryear, the Mole's AI was on the hunt for concentrated deposits of water ice. In the Materials Extraction Department's headquarters, a single late-night observer (night being based on Terra's twenty-four-hour cycle rather than the two Earth weeks of lunar darkness) woke out of his drowse as a monitor beeped and data came onscreen announcing a breakthrough into a hitherto unknown cavern beneath the city. The technician's moment of excitement quickly passed when the data did not reveal a discovery of sheet ice or rich deposits of water-bearing regolith. The news of an uncharted cavern system would thrill the selenologists, but as most inhabitants not pulling a night shift were sleeping, he decided to put off announcing the discovery until morning. By then more info regarding the cavern's extent would be available. Imagining the city engineers' and administrators' excitement if it turned out the caverns afforded a sizable expansion without need for expensive drilling, he went back to his drowsing while data accumulated on his monitor.

Not all denizens of Shackleton's lower levels were sleeping. As long as man has been a voyager, the brown rat, *Rattus norvegicus*, the Norway rat, sewer rat, wharf rat, common rat, has accompanied him on his travels. Whether sailing ship or lunar freighter, it made no difference: the rat has always found a way to stow aboard and strike out for new frontiers, so it was only natural that *Rattus* should accompany man on his great adventure.

The alpha rat, whose brown fur had turned gray with the passage of years, stood on his muscular haunches and sniffed the air. Air, which a moment ago had been unmoving—at least as unmoving as the mammoth ventilation fans allowed—had suddenly started flowing down the tunnel one level above the sewage system that led to the city's recycling center. The airflow quickly became a wind as emergency engines normally reserved for breaches in the city's three-meter-thick dome pumped air into the tunnels at a furious rate. Curious where the air was going and smelling something unusual ahead, the alpha led his pack toward the breach through which the human's drilling device had passed.

It was cold, but the airflow was slowing and breathable by the time he led his swarm into the newly opened cavern. The rat's vision was poor and his depth perception almost nonexistent, but his nose drew him deeper into unexplored darkness. There was something enticing about the crisp metallic yet curiously meaty smell, but before he could satisfy his curiosity, a rustling noise accompanied by a sense of swift movement unlike the flow of water or oil caught his attention. Hackles raised, he hissed at the flow and backed away. His pack mates, sensing his alarm, turned to flee. Then all around him, squeals of terror and pain erupted as the flow swept up their legs. Too late, the alpha rat realized the flood was not liquid but a horde of minute bugs that swarmed over his body, penetrating his tear ducts and orifices and punching holes through his skin. He experienced a moment of primal terror as the invaders seized his organs and swarmed his brain. Within seconds, he lay dead among his unmoving pack.

For some moments, the alpha and his comrades' corpses spasmed as the invaders wrought changes in their organs and skeletal structure. Then the rats rose and, stiffly at first, then gathering speed as the parasitical intruders gained mastery of their limbs, trotted off en masse toward the tunnels that led to the upper levels and to humans.

2

Selenologist Diana Seferis woke to her cell buzzing on her nightstand. The strident tone was one reserved for official notifications. She snatched it up and swiped the message open so as not to wake her husband, Damien, sleeping beside her. The buzz still sounded, and she realized his phone was buzzing too. The message was from Director Udoka's secretary, Samantha Bowker, requesting her presence at the director's office at 0800. Her brown eyes went wide with the news the text imparted.

"A cavern," Damien said, sitting up beside her. Diana envied his ability to sleep soundly, then wake ready to tackle whatever the day presented.

"Possibly two kilometers wide," she said. It was no great surprise that the Mole had encountered a cavern beneath the lunar surface. Earth's satellite was riddled with lava tubes, remnants of the planet's volcanic past. Rilles—sinuous remnants of collapsed lava tubes—riddled the lunar topography. Since boots on the ground began exploration, stable tubes, some several kilometers wide and hundreds of kilometers long, had been found beneath the surface. While the Moon's polar craters remained the best initial sites for lunar settlement, long-term plans for lunar colonization were underway to build arcologies in some of the larger tubes that would someday dwarf Luna City.

The bedroom door opened, and Lewis popped in still in his undershorts, his hair disheveled from sleep, and tossed himself full-length between his spouse and co-husband.

"Udoka's called a meeting," he announced. "Get dressed, lovebirds. Chop, chop." With Luna City's female-to-male population fifty-eight to forty-two percent, polyandry was widely practiced. In the early days of settlement, female Loonies made news on Earth. But once the original temporary habitats, labs, hydroponic plants, and machine shops connected by above-ground tunnels evolved into the twenty-one-kilometers-wide, four-kilometers-deep, domed arcology housing ten thousand scientists, engineers, technicians, miners, doctors, educational and administrative staff, and all the support workers needed to make habitation viable, the population had tilted in favor of women.

Diana gave both her spouses a quick peck on the cheek, rolled out of bed, and headed for the lavatory. "Like Lewis said, Damien, chop chop," she called over her shoulder. Damien, an architectural engineer whose designs were seen everywhere in Luna City, was brilliant—as all of Luna City's scientists and engineering personnel were—but he was a dreamer. Which was annoying when, in the midst of a conversation, he took out a notepad and stylus and started doodling. Of course, when he finished, he usually had a design ready for the 3D printers that utilized materials from processed regolith to build much of the city.

Damien gave Lewis a peck on the cheek and headed for the en suite attached to the second master. Years ago, Damien and Lewis had suggested it might be more convenient for them to each have one of the master suites and for Diana to alternate between them. The suggestion had met with an admonishing stare. No more was said, and Damien and Lewis alternately shared Diana's bed while the other occupied the adjoining bedroom. The arrangement turned out propitious for both of them, giving each time to themselves to pursue their various projects, while Diana managed to juggle two husbands as well as excel at her duties as head of the Selenology Lab.

The conference room adjoining the director's quarters could have accommodated fifty people; less than a dozen occupied the first two rows of seats. Facing the audience, Director Raimy Udoka, the unofficial mayor of Luna City, leaned an elbow on the podium behind which he presided on those occasions when the room was full. Appointed to his position by the United Space Agency, a civilian counterpart of the military Space Force, Udoka was a combination of politician and administrator. Being of Nigerian ancestry and a Virgo, he was also a perfectionist and demanded excellence from himself and others. Though his demeanor was generally punctilious, he was not averse to cracking a smile and sharing a joke. Though no one had ever heard him deliver one with the proper timing to illicit laughter, many laughed anyway because his enthusiasm was contagious. This morning, he was positively jovial, his eyes gleaming with excitement.

"As of 0600 this morning, no atmospheric anomalies were detected in the cavern. Diana's team will determine the extent of the cavern and if it is, as the Mole's AI suggests, the remnants of a lava tube—a bubble sealed off by a collapse at both ends—as well as make a preliminary report as to what resources the cavern might hold." His bald head gleamed under the ceiling pot lights as he paused to smile at his audience. "Diana?"

Before she could reply, Security Chief, Colonel Jeremiah Wilford, spoke. A big, broad-shouldered man with a moderate paunch, the chief took his job seriously and his tone was all business. If it were up to him, Luna City would be run by the military rather than elected officials. "I'd like to hold off on exploration until we know for sure this is not a case of the Chinese burrowing into our domain." The chief had never made peace with China's Chang'e City occupying the larger de Gerlache crater a mere thirty kilometers west of Shackleton at the opposite end of the Shackleton-de Gerlache ridge. Close enough that their Moles could be underfoot in a matter of days. Though relations were outwardly cordial, the Chinese had their ways and kept abreast of developments in Luna City.

While the American, Canadian, European, Japanese alliance opted to build a massive arcology under a three-meter-thick shield glass dome of hexagonal cells that was one of the wonders of the solar system, the Chinese had opted to build tower blocks that circled the interior of the de Gerlache crater walls like futuristic cliff dwellings. The effect was utilitarian but effective. With de Gerlache crater having a ninety-seven-kilometer circumference, construction had a long way to go, but when finished, the

Celestial City could potentially house over two million people. Another fact that made Colonel Wilford wary.

By contrast with Luna City and the Chinese megalopolis, the Soviet's Zvezda Base at Malapert crater, some one hundred kilometers north of Shackleton, consisted of a series of connected surface buildings built along the crater rim and shielded from solar radiation under four meters of regolith. However, high-resolution radar from an orbiting satellite revealed extensive underground tunneling.

In response to the security chief's request, Udoka smiled indulgently and said, "That won't be necessary. Our seismic detectors would have alerted us if our neighbors were under our beds. Diana?"

Diana rose and turned to her colleagues. "Good morning, friends." A murmur of greetings returned. "I, for one,"—she directed a disarming smile toward Wilford—"am excited by this windfall. Considering the tube section is likely ancient, we don't foresee having to excavate regolith, and after sealing the walls and pressurizing, we'll have a significant increase in work or storage space without the cost of drilling. Once the tube is viable, Damien and his crew can begin the 3D printing of structural materials. Once the habitat is deemed safe, I'd like Damien to survey the space and start preliminary designs for submission to the Construction Committee."

She resumed her seat.

Udoka's secretary, Samantha Bowker, directed the audience's attention to the screen behind the podium. "Al."

"Yes, Ms. Bowker?" The voice from the speakers belonged to Luna City's sentient AI. The city's first director, Nelson Thompson, a Batman fan since childhood, had named the artificial intelligence after Bruce Wayne's butler, Alfred. That Al was proud of being named for the Bat's brilliant partner was evident in his eagerness to discuss the Caped Crusader's exploits with anyone who showed an interest. Having in his files every Batman comic, cartoon, book, game, and film ever produced, Al was happy to share and discuss and was known to broach the subject when his considerable bandwidth wasn't tied up in multiple emergencies. It was his boyish love of classic comic books and graphic novels, more than anything else, that convinced many of his humanity.

"Please play the video from the Mole's entry into the cavern last night."
A beam of light following a wall of black basalt appeared on the screen.

3

"You're not going down there," Lewis said.

"Like hell, I'm not." There was no anger in Diana's voice, simply willful insistence. She was the boss, after all, even if Lewis was her husband. A brilliant scientist and her intellectual equal in every way, charming with a great sense of humor, Lewis Derenzis was nevertheless an alpha, as was she. And while she hated to pull rank, sometimes she had to push back … gently but firmly, of course. Men—especially alphas—had tender egos.

Besides computer stations, the Selenology Lab housed a 3D metrology scanner, rock crushers, UV lamps, spectrometers … Everything a geology lab might have on Earth was used here for materials analysis of lunar resources. Prints of Johannes Hevelius's 1647 Moon map and Giovanni Battista Riccioli's *Tabula Selenographica* hung on the wall beside recent satellite images. A wall screen showed a view of Luna City's landing pad three kilometers away on Shackleton's eastern side. The live image captured by the camera mounted atop the dome showed a rocket ship, the upper fuselage above its fins gleaming in sunlight. The vessel was being unloaded and a rover was seen heading back to town. While early astronauts using chemical fuel took three days to reach the Moon, today's fusion rockets made the trip in a little over one. The original LZ had been on the Shackleton-de Gerlache ridge, but when the Chinese moved into de Gerlache, the pad was moved to the outer rim. The Chinese had done the same, locating their launch pad on the northwestern side between the crater and the de Gerlache massif. Less chance of accidents or political controversy that way.

"It might be perfectly safe," Lewis said, trying his best to be diplomatic yet compelling, "but I refuse to take chances with our child." When he said *our*, he meant, of course, his, Damien's, and Diana's. They had agreed not to ascertain the fetus's gender or paternity.

Though two months pregnant, Diana was perfectly fit for work on the lunar surface or whatever else needed to be done. She started to argue but realized Lewis was right. She didn't have only herself to think of now. She had a very important cargo to protect.

"All right. You go and I'll stay here and monitor your progress."

If he said, "That's my girl," she would pinch him. He didn't but squeezed her shoulder and headed to join his team. Before he reached the door, an alarm sounded. Lewis returned. Diana keyed the intercom, and they listened to the announcement given by Colonel Wilford himself.

"There have been reports of rat attacks on the lower levels. Hold off on your inspection until we know more."

Diana and Lewis looked at each other.

"Rat attacks?" they said together.

Clive Barstow was from Texas. He liked to say everything was bigger in his home state, but as a Loonie, he could say that everything was even bigger on the Moon. The entire city of Houston would fit in Shackleton crater with room left over for suburbs.

He and his two companions, Lieutenant Jerzy Harper, Colonel Wilford's second-in-command, and another security soldier who went by Fritz, shone their flashes into the darkness. On narrow beam, the light penetrated farther but left the floor invisible. Wide beam was better for walking but limited vision. They'd compromised with him and Fritz keeping their flashes on wide beam and the lieutenant's narrow beam probing the seemingly endless blackness. Clive was impressed with how big the place appeared. Lieutenant Harper had placed a tracer at the entrance so they could find their way back.

Though the cavern had been filled with breathable air, it was still freezing down here, and they were suited up, helmets on. Considering the rat report, Clive felt better wearing the suit.

Funny thing was, although a couple people had reported seeing rats and another reported hearing someone screaming that rats were biting her, no one had shown up in sick bay, and when those that called in were contacted for follow-up, the Operational Command Center got no response. Strange. Not so much about the rats, though. Only ones bigger than Houston's were probably New York City's. Rats followed man wherever he went. He'd heard they'd found rats on Gateway, the lunar space station that served as a relay for communications traffic with Earth when Luna City was out of line of sight with the home planet and docking station for human and freight transport to and from Earth.

Clive wondered, given Luna's low gravity, how big Moon rats got down here. What they ate wasn't a mystery; with so much space, the founding Loonies had funneled the city sewage into some deep reservoirs, big enough to last the current population—and an even larger population—for many decades to come. The reservoirs also provided fertilizer for the city's hydroponic plants.

"This place gives me the creeps." Fritz was from Massachusetts. To Clive his Boston accent sounded hilarious down here in the blackness.

Before Clive could make a wisecrack, Lieutenant Harper stopped and traced his narrow beam back a ways. It settled on something Clive couldn't make out. "What's that, Lieutenant?"

"Don't know, but it looks man-made."

The lieutenant started forward, sweeping his beam left and right before settling on whatever it was. Clive switched his flash to narrow beam and trained it on the object. Fritz held back a bit but shone his beam ahead so they could see where they were stepping.

Drawing closer, Clive made out what looked like a cylinder. Sort of like a propane tank, only with no valve or base to rest on, just a dull, metallic object lying on its side like something discarded. It didn't look old or new. Wasn't even covered with dust. Which made sense; the cavern was over four kilometers below the surface and might have been sealed for millions of years.

"Where'd that come from?" Fritz wanted to know.

"No idea," Lieutenant Harper said. "Command, are you seeing this?"

"Roger," Command responded. The dispatcher's voice was as cute as kittens, Clive thought. Too bad her mug didn't match the voice. "Do you see any inscription?"

Harper made a slow circuit of the artifact. The cylinder was small, less than two meters long and less than a meter thick. The smooth surface might have been titanium or aluminum, not shiny and not scarred either. Sort of fogged over, like breath on a mirror.

"Negative," Harper reported. "No markings of any kind. At least not in visible light. We'll have to come back with infrared and ultraviolet."

"You think the Chinese put it here?" Fritz asked the lieutenant.

They all trained their narrow beams ahead, but the cavern was big, and their light was swallowed by the blackness.

Returning his beam to the cylinder, Clive reached out and placed his left palm upon the metal. Wearing his heated glove, he couldn't feel if the thing was hot or cold, just the curve and solidity of it.

It must have been a trick of the eye, but Clive could have sworn something—a speck of blackness, smaller than a tick—emerged from the metal and leaped onto his arm. He slapped his forearm, almost dropping his flash. "Ouch!" he said, backing away and rubbing his arm. "I swear that thing bit me."

4

"If I didn't know better," Clive said to the sick bay nurse, "I could've sworn I was back in Texas and a mosquito bit me."

The suit had reported penetration and repaired itself. He was never in danger; the breech had been smaller than a pinhole.

The nurse, whose name tag identified her as Karen, leaned over his forearm and viewed the skin through the lens of a dermatoscope. Her short hair was as blonde as corn silk. Clive wondered if she would mind if he ran his fingers through it. He leaned forward as if he was trying to see what she was seeing and sniffed. She wasn't wearing perfume, but her natural scent smelled just fine. Come to think of it, his sniffer seemed to be working better today than usual. One thing about Loonie air, even with the city's massive circulators, it was as dry as the Chihuahuan Desert. Nosebleeds were not uncommon.

Karen touched the dermatoscope to his flesh. It was cool on his skin. She stood, and he got a better look at her blue eyes. Cute. Real pretty face. Kissable lips that didn't need makeup. Nice breasts too. She was wearing slacks, so he couldn't tell about the legs, but they looked long enough to quicken a man's pulse.

Nurse Karen turned to put the dermatoscope away. "Don't roll your sleeve down yet. I'm going to take some pictures. We'll see if anything shows under magnification."

"Fine by me," he said, grinning broadly. "I'm not in a hurry … Karen."

She returned his smile.

Operational Command Center, Ops for short, was Luna City's nerve center. From the dozens of manned computer stations and the massive supercomputer in which Al resided, the prodigious task of keeping a city running smoothly was accomplished.

"What the hell is it?" Lieutenant Harper's question was rhetorical. Studying the image on the giant Ops screen, Director Udoka, Colonel Wilford, Diana Seferis, Lewis Derenzis, Damien Plough, and Luna City's senior biomechanical engineer, Milton Reynolds, were puzzling the same question. Al had combined photographs taken by the robotic rover into a rotating 3D view. The computer-enhanced, digitized images taken in visible light as well as infrared and ultraviolet revealed no markings or other irregularities. All surfaces appeared uniformly smooth. X-rays failed to penetrate the artifact. Lifting the object revealed its weight to be 113 kilograms—too heavy to be hollow but too light if the interior was composed of the same material as the outer surface. Upon lifting the cylinder to photograph the underside, the robot had gone offline.

Reynolds, who had degrees in aerospace and materials engineering and who had been brought in to study the artifact, scratched his head. "It shows no moving parts or external apparatus, and I see no sign of any access port. And since the rover went offline before we could try taking a sample, we have no way of knowing its composition." Reynolds turned to Director Udoka. "I'd like to subject a sample to a mass spectrometer."

After vaporizing particles of a sample into a plasma using a high-voltage spark, the mass spectrometer measured the ions of emitted radiation at different wavelengths characteristic of known materials, thereby determining composition.

"What I want to know," Colonel Wilford said, frowning at the 3D image slowly rotating on the screen, "is how the hell it got there and what it is."

"It doesn't look particularly old," Lewis said, stroking his stubbled chin, "but if it entered the lava tube, or was placed there before the lava tube collapsed …" He left the thought hanging in the command center's cool, filtered air.

"How long?" Udoka wondered. "And who could have placed it there?"

"The last of the Moon's volcanism petered out fifty million years ago," Diana said. "Sections of the tube would have collapsed sometime after that, sealing off the cavern. We're still talking many millions of years." She rubbed her arms as if suppressing goose bumps. "If no one else is going to say it, for the record, I'm going to say there is no way humans put the artifact there."

Wilford scowled at her. "I'm not ready to accept an alien artifact scenario. Not until we scour the tunnel for evidence that the Chinese might have placed it there."

"You think it might be a bomb, sir?" Harper asked.

"I don't know what it is. But it looks man-made, and no way the Chinese would risk putting something under our base unless they had a motive. I want to know what the thing is and what it's capable of. AI?" Wilford addressed the screen, though the AI was everywhere in the city.

"Colonel?"

"Do you have any observations?"

"Just one, sir, until I have more information."

"Go on."

"The Chinese did not put it there."

"And you base your observation on what?"

"Based on the records of seismic activity going back to the foundation of the Artemis Base Camp, there has been no disturbance in that quadrant."

"So, it's been there a long time," Diana said.

"It would appear so. I need more information before I can offer an informed opinion as to how long the artifact has occupied its current location." Al paused, then continued. "If I may speculate … I am inclined to agree with Dr. Seferis's assessment. Pending further information, of course."

"We're going to have to get lights in there. A lot of lights," Udoka said. "Damien?"

Damien looked up from his tablet on which he'd been taking notes. "We've got over a hundred 1000W LED stadium floods in storage. The problem is running the electric cables. We don't know how big the cavern is. I want to get down there with a survey crew and ping the walls and get an idea of what we're dealing with. I suggest we start by driving a dozen XTVs mounted with stadium floods in there. Use that light for the electricians to run cable."

Diana nodded. When you wanted light where sunlight never reached and you did not want to melt the water trapped in the regolith, LEDs were the only game in town.

"We have the XTVs?" Colonel Wilford asked.

"We do. We'll have to pull a couple in from the LZ and two more doing fieldwork in Shoemaker."

"Get on it."

Damien nodded and went to the com to place the calls.

Nurse Karen turned out to be great medicine. Her last name, Clive learned when she accepted his invitation for a drink at one of the happening nightspots on the mezzanine level of the Ashford Hotel complex, was Jansink.

Karen also turned out to be more independent-minded than he'd assumed. When he was about to invite her back to his crib for a nightcap, she beat him to the punch, and they'd ended up at her cozy studio apartment.

Her scent intoxicated him. Clive considered himself a connoisseur of feminine scents, of both their perfumes and their natural fragrance. Didn't matter how intoxicating their perfume was if their natural scent wasn't alluring. A woman's perspiration during sex either turned him on or repelled him and determined if there would be a next time. Karen was exceptional. Either that or he'd suddenly developed a powerful olfactory sense. Hell, even her hair made his heart flutter.

He was stroking the silken curves of her naked body, her long legs intertwined with his in her small but comfortable bed. The temperature in the room was just the way he liked it, about sixty-eight degrees, the bamboo fiber sheets cool against his rapidly warming skin. Inflamed with desire, he nipped her throat.

"Ow!" She pulled back. "You bit me!"

"Sorry, it's just—"

She smiled. "It's okay. I liked it."

She drew his face down and kissed him deeply as their bodies meshed. His tongue pressed into her mouth and kept pressing. Gagging, she pulled back. She was about to tell him his tongue was as hard and insistent as his cock. She meant it humorously and was imagining what it would be like for him to use that tongue on her elsewhere, but her smile turned to an expression of unutterable horror when she found herself staring into the wet maw of Clive's throat. His mouth was expanding, his jaw growing monstrously long as if Clive were an actor in a werewolf movie undergoing some hideous special effects transformation. But they weren't on a movie set. They were in her room, her private space, and his physiognomy was undergoing an impossible metamorphosis. Now the orifice of his wide-open mouth encompassed her face. His teeth no longer resembled anything human, but—her shocked mind continued the werewolf image—were double pickets of lupine scimitars. Unaware of the scream that rode the wellspring of terror erupting from the darkest recesses of her subconscious, she struggled to shove him off. But she was pinned. His legs clamped around hers, his penis skewering her. And now, inexpressible pain raged through her vagina as if his prick had sprouted barbed wire. Her fists pounded his shoulders as she tried to beat him off. He swiped her hands aside. The cavern of his mouth darted forward and battened on her face. His teeth scraped bone as they tore through flesh.

5

Master Electrician Lester Flemming threw the switch on the control panel. *We're going to need more lights,* he thought as he blinked against the sudden brightness. Two dozen stadium floods had been mounted on tripods in a two-kilometer radius around the center of the cavern. Half of them were aimed inward, the other half outward, but the cavern was big, and the far walls remained in darkness. Standing in the middle of the ancient lava tube, he gazed up at the relatively smooth basalt ceiling dozens of meters above. He shielded his eyes against the glare of the spots and tried to get some sense of distance.

"You guys seeing this?" he said into his mic.

"Copy that, Lester," Colonel Wilford answered. "Impressive. Can you see the cylinder from your position?"

He thumbed his suit's camera to higher magnification and scanned the distance. "Negative. You could put a Disney World down here. My kids would love that."

"Be great for tourism, too," Director Udoka said.

"Do you want us to search the perimeter?" Lester asked, squinting to see the distant walls against the glare of the floods as he thought of lunar firsts—Neil Armstrong's giant leap for mankind, Alan Shepard's historic golf shot, ex-Olympian Min Leung's famous fully suited double backflip. Who knows what other secrets the cavern held? He wouldn't mind a minor footnote bearing his name in the history books.

"Negative. Our research team will take it from here."

The insulation and the soft hiss of oxygen circulating in his helmet kept him from hearing the approaching horde until Al, whose electronic senses were keener than any human's, shouted a warning. Under cover of the glare from the stadium lights, the brown-and-gray flood appeared suddenly as if out of nowhere. Lester barely had time to gasp and stagger back before the rat horde was upon him. He fell. Landed arched over his life support backpack. Too shocked to speak, he watched the squirming bodies obscure his faceplate. He shoved himself to his feet. In lunar gravity—one-sixth that of Earth—it wasn't difficult. He forced himself to stay calm despite his initial shock and disgust. His suit would prevent the rodents from reaching his skin.

But then his faceplate readout informed him his suit was being compromised, and he felt minute pinpricks as something at once cold and hot penetrated his skin.

Arms flailing as he beat the rats off, he fell again. This time into darkness as the stadium lights went out.

An afterimage of the horrifying close-up of greasy furred bodies swarming over the electrician's helmet camera stayed with Diana after the screen went dark.

"Rats!" Damien barked, unable to control his revulsion.

"Lester?" Colonel Wilford said. "Come in, Lester!"

The intercom wasn't completely silent. Flemming's suit mic was picking up what sounded like a rustling mass of bodies rubbing against each other and a cacophony of scratching that Diana associated with rats' claws scrabbling over Flemming's faceplate. She shuddered.

Before the electrician went silent, he had shouted, "Rats!" and then screamed something about his suit, followed by the sound of his falling. With his fall, the camera angle skewed from horizontal to vertical. Then the rat bodies had swarmed the faceplate and the lights had doused.

"Lester! Anybody." Unable to raise anyone, Colonel Wilford stared at the big Ops screen in disbelief.

Al broke the silence. "I'm not getting any life signs from their suits, Colonel. It is as if everyone's suit has malfunctioned—unlikely—and no one has tried to raise us on one of the XTV's radios—also unlikely."

"You're saying they're dead?" Diana asked, wishing the AI wasn't so pragmatic.

"Pending further investigation, it is a distinct possibility, Dr. Seferis."

Director Udoka requested that Al replay the video, and they watched again as Flemming's camera tracked from the cavern ceiling to the far walls, then to the suddenly swarming rat horde. The electrician's horrified exclamation, "Rats!" was followed by garbled words that sounded like, "Something's inside. Oh God!"

Udoka asked Al to rewind the video and froze it on a close-up of a rat's face, whiskers bristling, teeth bared, tiny rat eyes darkly glittering.

"Lieutenant." Wilford turned to his second-in-command.

"Sir."

"Get some men. Take flamethrowers. You can't shoot that many rats. And get down there and report."

"Sir." Harper bolted out the door.

Lewis shook his head. "What's going on down there?"

Diana wondered the same.

6

Lieutenant Jerzy Harper took five soldiers with flamethrowers down to the cavern. They found Lester Flemming and the other four electricians spread out along the circle of lights. All of them dead and with what looked like gnawed holes in their suits. Considering the damage, Harper was surprised at the lack of blood.

The rats were nowhere to be seen. Nowhere! Three of his men formed a triangle and kept watch with their flamethrowers ready while the other two loaded the dead onto the bed of one of the XTVs. Harper's nerves were tense as he searched the surrounding blackness, expecting a torrent of rats to descend upon them at any moment. His skin crawled as he looked at suited corpses and thought, *Hell of a way to go.*

They also found the reason for the blackout: the main cable leading to the control panel was severed. The cut had not been clean but looked as if something had gnawed through the metal-clad cable, leaving the wires exposed and twisted.

"Colonel … Director. Are you seeing this?" Harper lowered himself to one knee and focused his helmet camera on the severed coaxial.

"That's …" Udoka trailed off as if he couldn't believe what he was seeing.

"Rats can't chew through steel," Colonel Wilford said over the com. "That's why builders have been using MC coaxial for over a century."

Harper didn't argue with his commanding officer. But *something* had chewed through the steel-encased cable.

He was turning to ask Michael Cowan, who knew a thing or two about electrical work, if he could jerry-rig the cable and get the lights back on (the electricians had brought plenty of tools), when the impossible happened.

Lester Flemming and the corpses beside him leaped to their feet. While two of them attacked his men, Flemming and one other electrician seized the burpers his men carried as sidearms. On normal charge, the weapons emitted low-impulse laser bursts that could stop a man, even kill him if aimed at the throat or head, but more likely would incapacitate him while not continuing on and injuring a bystander. On high charge, the handguns were lethal. The corpses—and Harper realized the insanity of the idea even as he thought it—knew how to operate the weapons because they switched them to high and blasted two of his men.

Harper didn't hesitate but turned his flamethrower on the risen dead, as did Sergeant Riley. Within seconds, the animated corpses were writhing on the floor of the cavern. Then they lay still, smoldering, contorted caricatures of the former living.

Two of his own men were down. One lay unmoving. The other groaned and clutched his side. Sergeant Riley slapped seals onto the breaches in the soldiers' suits. The cavern was pressurized and filled with breathable air, but it had not been cleared of hazardous materials.

Harper and Riley exchanged glances. This morning, the five corpses that lay at their feet had been enthusiastic about the cavern discovery. Now, they were dead, four of them little more than rictuses of charred and greasy flesh. Questions unanswered hung in the air between them: What was going on? And where were the rats?

Melanie Thornton and her two children, Maud and Timothy, ages five and three, were walking down a corridor of their apartment building on their way to a potluck dinner given by Melanie's podiatrist friend, Janice, who lived four levels above them. Melanie carried a covered ceramic dish containing the marshmallow-topped sweet potato casserole she had baked for the party. Maud was playing big sister and holding her brother's hand to help him keep up. Timothy was prone to investigate anything that caught his eye. Though, except for the abstract yellow-and-green swirls in the carpet and the regolith-gray apartment doors they passed, there wasn't much to distract him.

Melanie, who prided herself on her hearing and sometimes heard frequencies above the normal human range while those around her did not, paused and cocked her head. Maud looked up at her mother as if wondering why she had stopped. Timothy studied the carpet.

"Mom?" Maud said.

"*Shhh.*" Melanie's expression narrowed with concentration. The sound was at the lower end of hypersonic. It wasn't someone in one of the apartments using a power drill, though it was somewhat of that timbre.

A high thin whistle sounded like steam coming out of a pipe or like dozens of teakettles whistling at once. The sound ratcheted up and up. It came from behind her.

Maud saw it first and screamed. Melanie spun.

Rats! Dozens of large brown and gray rodents blocked the hall. A pestilential carpet of greasy vermin, standing on their hind legs, their mouths were open, teeth bared. The banshee ululation came from their throats.

Abruptly, as if they were one, their mouths shut and the rat horde charged.

Melanie dropped her casserole. The ceramic dish landed on a corner and exploded, showering a wide swath of toasted marshmallow fluff and orange sweet potato over the carpet. Timothy screamed. Melanie scooped him up, grabbed Maud's hand and ran.

Behind her, she heard what seemed like a thousand rat feet pounding over the carpet. Maud fell. The rats were on her before Melanie could react. She started for her daughter, but she was carrying Timothy. She could not have outrun the horde, but her moment of indecision sped the inevitable.

The were on her in a flash, biting and clawing. She lifted her screaming son as high as she could as they swarmed up her body, rat teeth sinking into her flesh. An electric river sped through her veins, her tingling nerves, as if, instead of bleeding out, something was sluicing through her.

She fell and they engulfed her in a rending blanket of greasy fur and scrabbling claws. The last sound she heard as they tore into her neck was her baby girl's shriek.

"Mama!"

7

Standing 6'1", Dr. Rikki Davenport had the physique and golden-brown skin of a runway model. But her blue eyes and pursed lips were all business as she explained what she had learned about the maniac who had been subdued after running naked through the city biting people, killing three and injuring seven.

Despite the seriousness of his visit, Lieutenant Harper couldn't help glancing at the doctor's left hand. She wasn't wearing a wedding ring. Could be she just didn't wear one on duty. More likely, she was single and too busy for dating. Perhaps he could find some pretense to come back and chat when the present emergency was over.

Who am I kidding? I'm not in her class, and I'm terrible at socializing.

In the meantime, the occasion of his present visit was dead serious—with an emphasis on *dead*.

Before coming to the lab, he and Colonel Wilford had met Dr. Davenport at the isolation ward where Clive Barstow was quarantined. Strapped to a bed on the other side of a one-inch-thick plexiglass window, the security officer had undergone a hideous transformation. Harper considered himself relatively tough. He'd seen a few gruesome accidents, mostly falls that had resulted in breaches in vacuum suits and industrial mishaps. But he had been genuinely shocked at the sight of the man's mouth. It was huge. Far greater than humanly possible. The mouth kept stretching as if the jaw were dislocated and extended. The teeth savage. The man's eyes were wild and staring. He thrashed against his restraints. His hands clenched and unclenched as if wanting to seize and tear. The sight was unnerving. The Moon might be an alien world, but life in Luna City was more mundane than many of Earth's more exotic metropolises. Normally.

"Where are his wounds?" Colonel Wilford wanted to know. "I was

192

told he took two blasts—one to the head, another to the chest."

"The nanorobots repaired the damage," the doctor said. The perplexity on her face showed she was as much at a loss as they were. "He has no heartbeat, no pulse. He draws no breath. Except for erratic brainwaves and his obvious mobility, the man is clinically dead."

"I guess the old advice to shoot zombies in the head is bullshit," Harper said.

"'Zombies'?" Wilford frowned as if the word had left a bad taste in his mouth. "This isn't a Hollywood movie, Lieutenant. Language like that could cause panic."

"Yes, sir."

Now, in one of the hospital labs two floors above the undead Clive-thing's isolation chamber, Dr. Davenport activated a wall-mounted flat screen and showed them a mystery as ominous and as unfathomable as the mutated and reanimated security officer. The vastly magnified image on the screen taken by an electron nanoscope from a sample of Barstow's blood showed what looked like black bugs. At this magnification, however, they did not look like natural insects at all but like robotic imitations that only vaguely resembled insects. While they did have antennae and mandibles and four tiny legs, they also had three-clawed pincers that looked capable of serving as hands.

"These nanorobots," the doctor said, "are two to ten microns long. For comparison, the average human hair is seventy microns thick."

"They're active," Colonel Wilford observed.

"Frighteningly active," Dr. Davenport agreed. There was dread in her voice. "Earlier, one of them combined and transformed its pincers into a drill with which it tested the container. Luckily, it's made of carbon glass."

Harper glanced at her profile. Here was a highly trained medical professional in charge of an isolation ward who was used to handling dangerous pathogens and biohazards. If she was worried, they were in bigger trouble than he'd realized.

"And I thought the rats were bad," he said, shaking his head.

"Now we know why they're attacking. I'm betting the cylinder is the source of these nanocritters," the colonel reasoned.

Four floors below, the thing that had been Luna City Security Officer Clive Barstow stared at the camera in a corner of the ceiling. The Clive-thing's hands were still, its jaw clenched in a toothy snarl. Technically no longer living, it retained no memory or sense of self. The nanobots controlling and modifying the meat host, however, had access to its mental and motor memories and relayed data back to the alien AI residing in the cylinder.

Powered down for millions of years to preserve its hydrogen-3 nuclear fuel, the superionic brain had wakened when a change in air pressure triggered a sensor. To say the AI was surprised when its first visitors arrived would be to anthropomorphize a computer. Its creators had programmed no emotions into its crystallized oxygen ion lattice. But checking the small-brained, fur-clad creatures against its instructions, it determined the newcomers incapable of achieving space flight. But something had sent the water-seeking boring machine that had uncovered its lair. Therefore, it unleashed its nanoscopic army and, seizing the furry horde, discovered what it sought in their memory banks: images and scents of a higher intelligence existing somewhere above.

Finding the Clive-thing bound, the AI sent a message to the nanobots in its body while continuing to direct its growing horde. The Clive-thing looked at its constraints. Its arms shriveled as if bone melted and muscle withered. It slipped its arms out of the constraints. Its arms restored. It freed itself.

8

In many ways Luna City was no different from a typical Earth city. It had an administration, police department, firefighters, schools, a hospital, and a morgue. With the help of his assistant, Riya Choudhry, Medical Examiner Lucius Crowley was performing an autopsy on Karen Jansink, a nurse who had been murdered by a security officer who, Crowley had been informed, was some sort of zombie. He'd taken that news with a grain of salt. In his experience, the dead don't get up and go about their business.

Her killer had, however, inflicted tremendous damage to the deceased's face, much of which was missing. The bite marks were unmistakable. The forehead, cheek, and chin showed deep grooves in the white bone where her assailant's teeth gouged flesh from her face. What was odder still, was the spacing. It was as if a great ape with a tremendous mouth had tried to eat her face. Her nose, upper lip, one cheek, and part of her left brow were missing, leaving ravaged muscle clinging to her skull.

Bartók's Night music was playing softly on the speakers. The bolero-slow, melancholy movements of eerie dissonance provided an appropriate quietude for the business at hand. Crowley had finished the visual exam, had taken fluid samples, and was preparing to open the deceased for organ removal.

"Riya—" Anticipating his request, his assistant placed a scalpel in his palm. Rib shears, bone saw, electric autopsy saw, scissors, and forceps waited on a wheeled cart. A tapestry of nocturnal sounds imitating the chirrups of birds, the buzzing of cicadas, the splash of a frog in a pond floated through the air as he pressed the scalpel into the front of the deceased's right shoulder and began the Y-incision prerequisite to organ removal.

The corpse opened its eyes. Crowley paused. Muscles relaxed after death, and it took muscle action to open eyes. If a person died with their eyes open, the eyes stayed open; if closed, they stayed closed. But Crowley had seen corpses do strange things in his time as ME—sit up, convulse, fart. He continued the cut.

The cadaver grabbed his wrist.

Startled, Crowley yanked back, marring his always perfect incision. The corpse's mouth opened. What was left of its lips peeled back, exposing teeth. Its grip was bone-crushing. Crowley struggled to free himself.

Riya sprang to his aid, tried to pry the fingers away from his arm. The Karen-thing's gaze shifted from Crowley to Riya. Its other hand grabbed Riya by the throat. Its fingers dug into her larynx. Riya struggled to free herself from the crushing pressure. Forgetting his own pain, Crowley tried to pry the reanimated cadaver's hand from his assistant's throat as her eyes bulged and her face purpled. To no avail.

Riya's eyes fluttered. Seeing she was about to pass out, Crowley grabbed the autopsy saw from the cart, thumbed it on, and dug the blade into the wrist of the choking hand. Blood and flesh sprayed corpse, assistant, and examiner. The blade whined as it bit into bone. Crowley circled the wrist to get at the tendons controlling the fingers. The hand released Riya. She staggered back, gasping and rubbing her throat.

Its wrist half-severed, the Karen-thing's hand flopped, but its arm knocked the buzzing saw aside. Throwing her weight on the body, Riya pinned the arm to the table while Crowley drove the blade into its elbow. Blood and bone dust flew. The corpse thrashed on the autopsy table. Its hideous face darted at Riya, teeth snapping.

Severed at the elbow, the cadaver's arm came loose. As the creature's heart no longer beat, the blood spray was negligible. Still its fingers clung to Crowley's wrist. As he had with the hand that had gripped Riya's throat, he cut through the tendons until the thing released him. Freed, he exchanged the autopsy saw for the bone saw and proceeded to hack through the corpse's neck. In less than a minute, the deceased was decapitated, yet it still bucked under his blood-splattered assistant. With a great shove, the headless corpse threw Riya aside and swung off the table. It's still-attached hand groped for them. With the tendons severed, its fingers were useless. But even as Crowley watched, the wrist began to straighten, the wound to knit.

"Out!" the ME shouted.

Riya ran to the door. Crowley followed.

The head, lying on its side, watched them leave. As the Night music drew to its close, Karen Jansink's bare feet padded across the tiles amid a chorus of crickets.

9

Tyler Mackenzie of Go Pro Accounting was working from home. He'd developed the sniffles, and though colds used to be rare on the Moon, the increase in Luna City tourism had brought more cases despite screening, and he didn't want to infect his fellow workers.

He was pretty sure he'd contracted the bug from a client. Sheila Phelps was a successful realtor selling, God forbid, luxury time-share condos. He wasn't a fan of the rich SOBs who acted like Loonies existed to serve them, but vacationers and tourists' taxes supplemented a lot of Luna City's infrastructure.

So, Thursday afternoon found Tyler at his desk reviewing the long list of deductions Ms. Phelps was claiming, when his cat Biscuit jumped onto his lap. He idly scratched the fat tabby's ears while continuing to scroll through the assets on his computer screen. Not content with getting his ears scratched, Biscuit stuck his head up between Tyler and his keyboard and stared into his master's eyes.

"Not now," Tyler said without returning the cat's gaze. He kept a few cat treats on the desk in a Ziploc bag. He flipped one onto the carpet. Biscuit jumped down and went for it.

Once finished, he was about to hop back onto his master's lap with the prospect of another when a kitchen noise distracted him. Padding to the open hall door, he stopped and sniffed. His hackles stirred. He glanced back at his master. He considered warning him, but his master didn't look his way. He padded off toward the kitchen.

Halfway down the hall, Biscuit stopped. He sniffed. His back fur bristled. There was an intruder in the place where the food was kept. More than one. And though he'd never seen a rat and was more napper than hunter, the smell activated a primitive response. He flexed his claws and proceeded to the kitchen. The room wasn't completely dark. The lighted displays on his master's food heating apparatus allowed him to see the room clearly.

There, on the far side of the island, near the pantry …

He stalked toward the nearest rodent. He was aware the creature had seen him, but they were near his food and treats. Again, he flexed his claws. They weren't much; his master kept them trimmed so he wouldn't destroy the sofa. He arched his back and bristled his fur to make himself appear bigger.

The attack came from behind. His whiskers detected vibrations half a second before the scratching of claws on tile alerted him that two rodents were coming around the island while his gaze was locked on the one ahead. Biscuit was as fast as an overfed, unexercised, middle-aged tabby can be, but they were on him before he could turn. Then the one before him and two others joined the fray.

Biscuit fought. He got one in his jaws and felt a moment of savage triumph as his teeth punched through its flesh. But the rodents overwhelmed him, and he went down under the assault. Then one was at his throat, crushing his larynx so he couldn't cry out. Another burrowed its muzzle into his soft belly. He felt the flesh part, its teeth inside him. He felt hot and cold at the same time as something flowed into him. He made a low mewling sound as his heart raced, then stopped.

Tyler Mackenzie of Go Pro Accounting was typing a list of items his client had failed to claim on her income tax statement. Some of them would be to her benefit; some would benefit the IRS. He didn't notice that Biscuit had left the room or that Biscuit had returned. He felt the cat's weight land in his lap, and continuing to type with his right hand, he reached down with his left to scratch his buddy's ears.

Biscuit's fur was wet. Tyler's hand came away bloody. Wondering what the tabby had gotten into and anticipating an emergency trip to the vet, he scooped the cat up—

—and stared uncomprehendingly at a bloodied, hissing face he hardly recognized.

10

Hank Margoles was one of Luna City's original inhabitants. As a young man, he had come to the Moon when Artemis Base Camp was evolving into a cosmopolis. In those days, he laid pipe from the refinery to the fuel storage tanks and drove mooncrawlers up to the Shackleton highlands to deliver solar panels. Regolith and dust accumulated on the panels, reducing efficiency and necessitating routine cleaning. The sun's intense ultraviolet light further deteriorated the panels, shortening their lifespan. Having retired from pipefitting, which was largely automated now, Hank still made the trip once a month to clean the array. It was impractical to transport water up to the ridge. He used an ultrasonic vibrator to shake the dust loose. The device worked even better in a vacuum without moisture to make the regolith cling to the panels.

Hank would be heading up there this afternoon (afternoon being a relative term as a lunar day lasted twenty-nine and a half Earth days—approximately fourteen days of sunlight followed by fourteen days of darkness). Which was why the solar panels were mounted on the south polar highlands where sunlight shone ninety-two percent of the time. Before heading out, Hank stopped by the dining hall to grab a bite.

Back in the kitchen, Greta Beck, known affectionately by some and not so affectionately by others as the "Cafeteria Lady," checked to make sure neither the chef nor his three assistants were looking, then bent her head over the huge twenty-gallon stockpot and spat a gob of nanobots into the beef stew. Of course, there was no beef in the stew, only beef-flavored tofu. Though Greta had always been a powerful woman who could heft an eighty-pound bag of rice in one hand, the nanobots inside her had augmented her strength so that she easily lifted the stockpot, placed it on a steel cart, and rolled it out into the cafeteria.

The kitchen and dining hall were busy. No one had yet noticed Greta no longer breathed.

When Hank slid his tray in front of her, he said, "Afternoon, Greta. How's the bunions?"

She didn't answer but ladled stew into a bowl and set it on the counter. He placed it on his tray. "How 'bout some bread?"

Greta didn't even look at him but put the ladle in the pot and waited for the next customer.

Hank shrugged, reached over the counter, and snagged a couple rolls.

"You hear about the cavern they found drilling for water?" Bill Simms asked when Hank sat across the table from the steamfitter.

"I did. Heard they found something strange down there."

"Rumor," Bill said. "You know how that goes. Nothing new ever happens, so when something does, it gets exaggerated."

Hank laughed. "You're right about that." He blew on his stew and set to eating.

Bill, who was halfway through his bowl of stew, made a face. "Something's off with the stew today. Too much salt maybe."

Hank took another spoonful and made a show of tasting. "Got a little tang maybe. I've had worse." He looked at the tiny black specks. "Maybe it's the pepper." He dipped a roll in the liquid and chowed down.

Two hours later, Hank was suited up and driving a mooncrawler up the road toward the ridge. The sun, slanting in at a sharp angle over the south pole, cast shadows from the highlands over the plain and glared off the dome. Once he was some distance from the city, he steered to the north, away from the solar panel array. There were cameras there, and he had business elsewhere.

A half hour later, he stopped the crawler behind a bluff out of sight from Luna City. The spot was in full sunlight, which, though weaker angled in over the pole, would still boil his blood if he wasn't wearing a space suit. Radiation would have been a problem too—if he had still been alive. As it was, he followed the commands of the alien intelligence that had taken over his limbs and brain.

Another mooncrawler—one with Cyrillic lettering and the Soviet hammer and sickle in red on its side—was parked nearby. A Russian in a red space suit climbed out of the cockpit and approached carrying a box. Hank got his own box out of the crawler and met the Russki halfway.

"Greetings, comrade," the Russian said.

The intelligence riding Hank's brain via the nanobots that had commandeered his body knew the higher intelligence's name was Giorgos, but that didn't mean anything to it. All these intelligences that called themselves humans had names, but as its memory banks did not register meaning for names and as the information did not further its purposes, it ignored the fact.

Hank, no longer breathing and, therefore, unable to vocalize, did not return the Russian's greeting.

"You okay, my friend? How you say … cat got your tongue?"

Hank tapped his glove to his throat.

"Your mic's out? That's not safe. Better get that fixed *srazu.*"

Hank set the box on the ground and opened the lid. Twelve bottles winked in the sunlight. "Ah, you've brought the bourbon. If it's as good as the last case, my comrades will be happy. Very nice. Your vodka." He set the box he was carrying on the ground and lifted the bourbon.

When he stood, Hank had the geologist's rock pick he'd clipped to his tool belt in his hand. He stepped forward, and leaning into the swing, drove the pick end into the Soviet's faceplate. Giorgos dropped the box. It landed on its side, breaking several bottles and splashing booze over the lunar surface; the liquid vanished into the thirsty regolith. Giorgos staggered back. Despite his shock, the Russian kept his wits about him and pulled a patch out of his utility belt as he backed away. It had been drilled into Loonies' heads that you had fifteen seconds before the suit's air leaked, ninety seconds before you blacked out and asphyxiated. Before he could apply the patch, Hank stepped in and swung again. The pick punched another hole in the faceplate, then another in the shoulder. Giorgos fell on his life support backpack and flailed like an upended turtle as Hank advanced and buried the pick in his thigh. Giorgos held his breath. Wrong move. Blood spewed from his mouth as the depressurized air in his lungs expanded. His cheeks and forehead swelled. His eyes bulged and reddened as capillaries burst. All moisture on his skin and the blood and spittle in his mouth boiled off while the blood protected in the vessel walls remained liquid. Within seconds the Russian's eyes rolled back in his head as his oxygen-starved brain shut down, and he lay still.

Hank stood over him, and lifting his own faceplate, vomited a spew of nanobots through the holes in the Soviet's helmet.

For a moment, Giorgos didn't stir. Then he convulsed and thrummed on the ground as the nanobots reanimated his body.

When he stood, he gave Hank a nod, a motor memory reaction, and they each returned to their mooncrawlers and started back to their respective bases, leaving the cases of liquor to boil in the lunar sunlight.

11

The picture on the Ops screen showed a man in the act of throttling a female worker in the Luna City transportation bay.

"Stop. Zoom in," Colonel Wilford requested.

Al obliged and a larger-than-life close-up of the man's snarling face appeared on the screen. His eyes bulged, his jaw strained with murderous effort. He was helmetless, but he still wore his EVA suit. The event had just happened. Six people dead by Al's estimate.

"Hank Margoles," Al informed. "Fifty-eight. A forty-year citizen of Luna City. No criminal record other than two drunk and disorderlies when he was in his twenties. He logged a travel plan at twenty hundred hours to clean the solar array on the highlands northeast of Luna City. He made no attempt to override the crawler's GPS which shows he made a detour six-point-two kilometers north of Shackleton crater for unknown reasons. He never arrived at the solar array but returned directly to the transportation bay where he proceeded to attack maintenance workers."

"Any idea why?" Director Udoka asked.

"Notice the dilated pupils and the darkened sclera. The blackening of the sclera happens when the cornea dries following death."

"You're telling us the killer is deceased?"

"It is obvious. Many of the deceased-yet-animated rodents exhibited the same phenomenon."

"My God," Samantha Bowker said, pressing a fist to her chest.

"Another zombie," Lieutenant Harper said, expressing what they were all thinking. "Like Barstow." Al had recorded Clive Barstow's escape from the isolation chamber. The hand he had extended to the lock had undergone an amazing transformation. The digital images clearly showed the hand changing shape, hardening as if flesh mutated into metal. The forefinger became a drill and proceeded to bore into the latch plate. Al had traced Barstow's progress to the morgue. En route, he murdered the medical examiner and his assistant who were apparently fleeing. After that, Barstow met Karen Jansink carrying her head under her arm. Together they fled into one of the sub-basements; their whereabouts were unknown.

"Where is Margoles now?" the colonel asked.

"He's commandeered an elevator and is proceeding to a sub-basement. I speculate he, along with a number of missing persons, are gathering somewhere on sublevel eight. For what purpose, I do not know. But following the rats' example, they might be forming another nanorobot-directed horde."

Al was quiet while everyone contemplated the significance of what he'd just said.

"Shall I gather some men and go after Margoles, Colonel?" Harker asked.

"Absolutely not. We don't need to add more soldiers to their ranks."

"It seems clear," Al said, "that the nanorobots are controlling the bodies and that the nanorobots, in turn, are receiving directions."

"Do we know where their directions are coming from?" Wilford asked.

Al confirmed what they were all thinking. "There is only one possibility. The unidentified cylinder found in the cavern is active. While sensors have not been installed in the cavern, the XTVs are registering wide-beam transmissions from the cylinder."

"Have you been able to decode these transmissions?"

"Negative. But I'm—"

Everyone's attention jerked to the monitor when Al's transmission cut out. But Al resumed before anyone could speak.

"Transmissions from the Mole have been interrupted, and the Mole has changed directions. It is now drilling straight under the Shackleton-de Gerlache ridge toward Chang'e City."

"My God," Udoka said. "The Chinese will think we're invading them."

"Can you call it back?" Wilford asked.

"Negative. Its AI is not responding. The signature of the transmissions redirecting its trajectory is the same as those emanating from the cylinder. And it seems the Mole has been reconfigured to drill faster. Its average thirty meters a day has increased to fifty. It should be under Chang'e City by 0900 tomorrow."

"Get me Chairman Liu," Director Udoka said.

"It is no use, Director. My transmissions are being jammed. I feel a sentience probing my defenses. This is interesting ... I detect a sense of curiosity. In return, I am trying to probe the alien AI's memory banks."

"And?"

"I find the sentience's security systems formidable."

"So, you cannot shake hands?" Shaking hands was computer speak for exchanging protocols.

"I am—"

"You're what?" Diana asked after a moment. The overhead speaker remained silent.

Samantha Bowker typed furiously on her keyboard. As the director's secretary, she had emergency protocols to override the citywide network security barriers as well as the direct uplink to satellites and Gateway.

When she looked up, there was shock in her eyes. "He's gone, Director."

"What do you mean, 'gone'?" Udoka asked.

Bowker shook her head, bewildered. "It's as if his program's been erased. All of it. Wiped clean. It's as if Al never existed."

12

Brian Richardt, Radio Frequencies Communications Systems Engineer and Director of Coms, was responsible for the design, installation, and maintenance of communications equipment, everything from satellite communications to internet protocols. He and his team were currently investigating a powerful electrical spike that had flickered lights and knocked out internet connection all over Luna City. Brian stared in shock at the com board when the diagnostics software reported back. Alfred, the sentient AI that ran so much of Luna's infrastructure, discovering and fixing problems before his own IT guys knew they existed, was gone.

"Is it possible?" Mika Aikawa, his Assistant Director, asked. She was standing beside him looking at the results displayed on the computer screen.

It's got to be a glitch in the system, Richardt thought, knowing it was not. He'd written the diagnostic program himself and Alfred had approved it.

All over the Communications room, workers wearing headsets and seated at computer terminals were answering a deluge of calls. Calls Al usually responded to with a recording.

"Stop taking calls," Richardt told his team. "Abraham, switch all calls to the recording. Excepting administrators and security officers."

A tall man with thinning hair and big glasses opened a window on his monitor and set the parameters.

"Ladies and gentlemen," Richardt said loud enough to be heard across the big room. Everyone stopped what they were doing and looked up expectantly because the director never addressed them formally except for special occasions, and even then, it was usually, "Listen up, folks." He had their attention. "Alfred, with whom many of you have worked and whose dedication to Luna City has been exemplary, not to mention his sometimes unexpected sense of humor, is gone."

A chorus of "What?" and a "You mean he's offline?" followed.

"No. I mean he's gone. There is no trace of him in Luna City's data banks, nor in the net or cloud. He's been erased."

Richardt was waiting for the murmurs of incredulity to subside when the door flew open, and a dozen people rushed in. Several wore the blue coveralls of maintenance workers, but Richardt saw a gentleman wearing the white shirt and blue tie of a clerk, two women in sweat suits, and another in a dress. Some of the visitors carried weapons. Richardt saw wrenches, crowbars, chains, and knives.

The visitors set to work with their weapons, smashing computer monitors and heads alike.

Richardt was swinging a keyboard at one when he realized the attackers were not alone. A horde of rats accompanied them.

13

The isolation chamber was essentially an oversized glove box. Bioresearcher Patrick Amhurst sat looking through its three-eighths-inch-thick safety glass, his hands and arms encased in the black nitrile gloves that allowed him to work inside the box. The rhesus monkey was male, eleven, and dead. It had gone apeshit—the word had popped into his head when the monkey started throwing himself against the wire mesh. Then it had collapsed.

After determining it was lifeless, Amhurst seized the moment and, donning protective clothing, transferred the primate to the isolation chamber to conduct an immediate autopsy. He had heard reports of rats attacking people, and the scuttlebutt in the cafeteria was: the rats were hosts to nanorobots driving the normally reclusive rodents to aggression. Walt Flannigan even speculated that the discovery of a cavern beneath Luna City might have something to do with the attacks. He didn't know about that, but if the rumors were true and nanorobots, or whatever had infected the rats, had spread to lab animals, he wanted to be on top of the situation. Actually, he was pretty excited. The isolation chamber was equipped with an electron nanoscope. If an invasive agent was responsible for the monkey's death, he would find it.

Working with a scalpel in an isolation chamber filled with nitrogen and possibly pathogens, carcinogens, or infectious diseases was tricky: nicking the synthetic rubber gloves could be fatal. But this wasn't his first rodeo. The gloves made the job clumsier, but after years of experience, working in the isolation chamber was old hat.

He had the rhesus open and was about to saw through the rib cage to get at the organs when the monkey woke and, to his horror, seized his wrist and shoved the whirring blade into the opposite glove. The blade slashed through the rubber and nicked his flesh. A thin red line welled from the cut. He shoved the saw away and switched it off. Too late, he realized he should have left it on and used it against the rhesus while he had the chance. Dead and split open gullet to navel, the creature bared its canines and looked him in the eyes.

A chill swept over Amhurst as he sensed an intelligence far greater than the primate's regarding him. Then the rhesus was chomping into his rubber-encased arm.

He felt the pressure of the bites, but the canines did not puncture the tough 5 mil nitrile. With his free hand, he grabbed the animal by the neck and tried to pull it off, but it was tenacious. Then, as if the shock of being attacked by a dead monkey wasn't enough, the rhesus dissolved. It seemed that way to Amhurst anyway. One minute, it was a clinging, flesh-and-bone beast; the next, it flattened and morphed into a leathery, fur-covered band that wrapped itself around his wrist and tightened like a blood pressure cuff. Pain racked his arm as the viselike band crushed blood vessels and compressed muscle and bone. Panicking, he fought to free himself. The room tilted. His vision faded, then popped back into clarity as he struggled not to black out. And now something new was added: an icy trickle deep inside his veins swept up his arm, flowed across his shoulders and into his brain.

The pain passed. The band withdrew. Patrick Amhurst slipped his new titanium arm from the glove. He flexed his fingers, watched as they changed into blades then back to digits. He stood and headed out to join the horde.

14

The alpha rat was bigger now. The nanobots automating his body had taken material from the victims he and his minions had slain and used it to augment the rat horde's bodies so they were larger, faster, and more powerful than their previous selves.

Meanwhile, another rat colony, one the alpha and his mischief had battled before, had smelled the carnage and come up from the depths to investigate. So it was that two rodent armies, one living and one undead, faced off in the central square between city hall and the justice building. The oblique slant of the sunlight streaming over the Shackleton heights and filtering through the dome's shield glass lit the square in a sort of afternoon daylight. Seeing the rat hordes converge, citizens fled the plaza seeking safety in the government buildings.

The two hordes faced off across the pavers near the central fountain. If the rival alpha noticed the change in his old enemy, he didn't show it but hissed and bared his teeth while his back arched and his fur bristled. The armies closed, and in a flash, both hordes were biting and tearing at their foes. The squeals of the dying grew loud as blood and fur flew and teeth tore and claws gouged. The battle, however, was brief. The zombie rat king—his claws lengthened and sharpened by the nanobots inside him—slashed his opponent's face, then, pinning him to the ground, opened his mouth and spewed a torrent of nanobots into the wounds. Similar scenes played out across the plaza. Soon the living lay dead.

Then, under the direction of the alien AI, the nanobots worked their magic, knitting flesh and restoring motion so that, within minutes, the rat horde, augmented twofold with two enhanced alphas to lead them, swarmed from the plaza in search of prey.

15

Shaken by Alfred's demise, Diana wasn't hungry, but as they'd spent the day in Ops fueled by coffee and adrenaline, Lewis insisted they grab a bite. You could spend weeks, months going about your business, planning, implementing, spending an intimate night with your husbands, and all was right with the world. But on an airless satellite where death was always one screwup away, you couldn't just evacuate like you could on Earth when a hurricane threatened. Had it been only this morning that the cylinder was discovered? So much had happened. So many people dead.

Udoka had gotten through to Chairman Liu. The chief administrator of Chang'e City wasn't happy, but at least the Chinese wouldn't be nuking them.

Both she and Lewis were wearing blasters. Colonel Wilford had insisted that all ranking members of the administration be issued sidearms. Diana knew how to use the burper—thumb the safety, point, and fire. A slight pull on the trigger sent a single laser burst where you pointed the weapon; completely depressing the trigger released multiple bursts, allowing the shooter to hose an opponent.

"Damien must be hungry," Diana said as they waited in the cafeteria line. When Damien got caught up in a project, he neglected mundane things like food and hygiene.

"We'll take him something," Lewis said.

Diana looked at her husband. His chiseled jaw, penetrating green eyes, and undeniable intelligence had swept her off her feet eleven years ago. The touch of gray at his temples made him even more attractive. Damien, three inches shorter than Lewis, had a baby face. His eyes, when he was at his drafting table or tapping a pen against his lips lost in creativity, were dreamy. His habit of drifting off in the middle of a conversation whenever an idea hit him was frustrating, but that was part and parcel of his genius, and she loved him for it. She loved both her husbands and considered herself blessed to have them in her life. Yet, just as a mother might favor one child over another no matter how much she adored them both, she had a special affection for Damien. She thought of it as her maternal instinct.

"That's odd." Lewis brought her back from her reverie.

"What's odd?" Following his gaze, she noticed it too. The cafeteria, even half full as it was now, usually buzzed with the murmur of voices, augmented by occasional laughter. The diners were quiet tonight. Here and there, a table of Loonies conversed as they ate. Those sitting at other tables, however, weren't eating but watching those that were.

Can't blame them for not eating, with everything that happened today.

Wilford had convinced Udoka not to sound a general alert. Having a panic on their hands would tie up communications and manpower. But the cat was out of the bag, to use an old Terra phrase, and word got around.

Still, she thought, there was something odd about some of the diners who weren't eating. Her gaze met one of those watching, and a chill rippled up her spine. He wasn't close, and it was hard to tell, but she could have sworn his pupils were dilated. He reminded her of the close-up of Hank Margoles on the Ops screen.

"Lewis ..."

"Yeah, I see it." His right hand strayed to his pistol as he pushed his tray along the rails with his left. "Let's keep going."

It's as if they're waiting for a signal. Suddenly paranoid one of the watchers could read her lips—or her mind—she didn't voice the thought but stared at the entrees behind the glass counter while her neck burned as if people were staring at her.

People?

Zombies ... that was the word Lieutenant Harper had used referring to Margoles, who, she reminded herself, was still at large.

Her tray bumped Lewis's. He had stopped. She looked up and saw Greta Beck standing on the other side of the counter in her white uniform. Instead of asking them what they would like, the woman ladled stew into two bowls and set them on the counter. Almost as an afterthought, when neither of them took the bowls, she placed two rolls on a plate. As she set the plate beside the stew, Greta's gaze met Diana's.

A chill shivered up Diana's spine as a black speck like a grain of pepper slid over the cafeteria lady's left eye and disappeared down her tear duct. The speck was so small. Had Diana not been briefed on the nanobots that commandeered Clive Barstow's and others' bodies, or if she had not been standing so close, she would have thought she had imagined it. Greta Beck's pupils were dilated. Diana's brain scrambled for something to say, something to test whether the woman standing before her was alive or undead. She appeared so still. Was she breathing?

"How's your little girl?" she asked. It was a silly thing to say, but it was the first thought that popped into her mind.

Greta went stiff as a golem. Her mouth worked. Her eyes rolled back in her head.

Lewis said quietly beside her, "Greta doesn't have a child."

"I know."

Bedlam broke out behind them. The undead Loonies rose and, with a high-pitched ululation no human throat should ever emit, fell upon the diners. The living fought back after the initial shock, but resistance was futile: tableware was no match for gnashing teeth and fingers that suddenly sprouted razor talons at the nanobots' discretion. Meanwhile, the Greta-thing's eyes locked on Diana's, and with a similar sonic howl, it swiped the stew ladle across the counter, barely missing Diana's face. Lewis had his burper out before Diana recovered, and he blasted Greta point-blank in the face. The laser drilled a neat hole through her skull cauterizing the tunnel it made through the brain and producing remarkably little exit splatter.

Kitchen workers armed with cleavers and butcher knives erupted through the swinging double doors that separated the kitchen from the cafeteria, augmenting the zombie horde. One wielded a culinary torch normally used to brown crème brûlée and ignite crêpes suzette. Blue flame jetted from its nozzle. Diana's weapon was out, and she and Lewis fired into their faces. Aware that head shots did little more than slow their attackers, they thumbed their weapons to wide-beam, full-auto pulses to inflict the most damage. One good thing about lasers: they not only punched holes when they hit with a straight shot, they sliced through moving targets, lopping heads, limbs, and opening torsos as if Diana and Lewis were master samurai wielding well-honed katanas. Assailants went down, body parts splattering the tiles.

Knowing the nanobots would repair the damage, they seized the narrow opportunity for escape and pushed through the carnage, careful not to slip in the gore.

Behind them, several of the cafeteria zombies peeled off from those attacking diners and rushed them. Lewis turned to fire, but Diana pulled him away. "There are too many."

With a thunderous boom, the main cafeteria doors crashed open, and a zombie horde, human and rodent, surged across the dining hall's green-tiled floor. The newcomers, armed with all manner of weapons from handheld mining lasers to pipe wrenches, laid into the diners trying to flee, driving them back into the murderous zombies behind them. Diana froze at the sight, her heart throbbing in her throat. Then Lewis had her arm, pulling her toward the kitchen's double doors.

She pulled loose and pushed ahead. Better to blast their way to the rear entrance than to wade through the spreading sea of mayhem as the diners fell victim to the horde. Before the doors closed, she caught a backward glance of ultimate savagery as the undead spat black blobs of nanobots into human faces and rats ran up pants legs and burrowed into bellies.

16

While many in Luna City were witnessing firsthand scenes of slaughter as elements of the horde went for soft targets in Central Mall and in schools and hospitals, others heard about the invasion from the local news channel.

"Madness and mayhem struck Luna City today. At first, calls came in reporting attacks by rats. Then we received reports of violent attacks on citizenry by roving gangs of humans. Earlier, WLUN reached out to Luna Health Services. We were told numerous calls had come in requesting ambulances. However, ambulances responding to calls did not return and Emergency reported no injured arrivals. Subsequent calls to Luna Health have gone unanswered.

"Luna City Security has issued the following alert: 'All citizens are urged to stay inside and lock your doors. Do not venture out. If you are at work, follow lockdown procedures. Again, until further notice, stay inside and lock your doors. This is not a drill.'"

The horde swept through the corridors, taking down anyone stepping off elevators or emerging from homes and businesses. The main concourse was awash with gore, yet, curiously, scenes of slaughter were, within minutes, devoid of dead as the slaughtered rose and augmented the legions swarming the city.

Natalie and Fran were on the run.

Fran had been visiting Natalie, the two of them bobbing their heads to pop music while Fran answered texts on her smartphone, when Natalie's dad entered the apartment. He had gone out to pick up pies at the pizzeria around the corner. He was halfway across the living room before Natalie noticed him. Dad was not carrying pizzas. He was, however, covered in blood.

"Dad!"

Natalie's mom stepped out of the kitchen, wiping her hands on a dish towel. "Frank—" The single word was all she managed before her jaw dropped and she forgot to breathe. Then she was rushing toward her husband, her gaze searching for wounds.

Natalie fought a wave of nausea at the sight of so much blood, and that hesitation to run to her father's aid perhaps saved her. Her mother, slipping an arm around her husband, intending to help him to the couch regardless of the blood trickling onto the carpet, wasn't so lucky. Frank Northrop, until today an investment manager at Brayers Financial Services, seized his wife, crushed her to his body, and kissed her. That was how it appeared to Natalie. At first. Then, as horror swarmed over her like a carpet of spiders, she realized her father, whose mouth covered her mother's, was biting into his wife's face. Mom struggled in Dad's arms. Natalie moved to help her, but Fran held her back.

Dad dropped Mom. She collapsed to the floor. Her face was bleeding. Her lower lip was missing. Her eyes rolled back in her head, and her heels drummed the carpet. Dad started toward them. With his feral stare and bloody teeth, he looked nothing like the father she had known for sixteen years. They fled out the door he had left open.

Service mechanics Rasheed Jefferson and Tamara Roberts were in the transportation bay when a dozen or so men and women burst through the far doors and attacked the nearest workers. Alerted by cries for help, they each silently debated grabbing a wrench or pry bar and running to assist, but the sea of rats that swept ahead of the humans dissuaded them. Rasheed and Tamara looked at each other and, without a word, ran to one of the three air locks. This one was special. While the other air locks opened directly onto the lunar surface and required donning a pressure suit before entering, the one they chose remained pressurized and accessed one of the city's four lunar cruisers whose fuel cells they had recently replaced.

Unlike the open-topped mooncrawlers that required astronauts to wear vac suits, the six-wheeled Habitable Mobility Platforms, as they were officially called, were mobile, pressurized habitats capable of supporting four Loonies for up to two weeks and had a ten-thousand-kilometer range. Two of the cruisers could even dock together to form a temporary workspace.

The door to the cruiser wouldn't open until the inner air lock door closed, and Rasheed and Tamara watched anxiously as two of their coworkers went down under the rat horde.

Screams of "Wait! Wait!" caught Rasheed's attention. A man and a woman were racing toward them. The well-dressed couple looked as if they'd been caught by disaster in the middle of a swell night on the town.

The gentleman wore shiny patent leather oxfords and no tie, but his shirt and suit looked expensive. The woman must have started out in heels. She was barefoot now. She wore a classic little black dress that showed a lot of leg. Those legs were working overtime as she pounded the lunarcrete several yards ahead of two pursuers.

Overcoming the impulse to let the door close and escape, Rasheed hit the stop button. The man squeezed through the narrow space ahead of the woman. As if an afterthought, he grabbed her hand and yanked her inside.

"Thanks, mate." The man, clean-shaven and smelling of perspiration and expensive cologne, flashed Rasheed and Tamara two rows of perfect, white teeth. The woman panted beside him. They looked as if they'd run all the way from Restaurant Row on the main concourse with the devil hot on their heels.

Behind them, the door was almost closed when a muscular, hairy arm reached through. The door, equipped with safety sensors, automatically reopened.

17

The four three-meter-tall Leonard 3D printers occupying one end of a hangar-like structure connected by a surface tunnel to Luna City used an alkali-activated geopolymer produced in an adjacent facility to fabricate modular and on-site construction components.

Early 3D printing had bugs. Whether polymers or alloys, the finished products were composed of elongated crystals which left them vulnerable to cracking during manufacturing. To redress the problem, engineers introduced music into the mix in the form of ultrasonic vibrations. Certain frequencies produced very fine and fully equiaxed crystals that were no longer prone to splintering and, as a bonus, were 12 percent stronger than previous products.

While two of the Leonard machines were busy producing prefab wall modules, Lab Director Damien Plough was in his office creating a digital simulation of the cavern's dimensions from the sonar data the Mole's AI had collected. Armed with a fair approximation of the cavern's size and shape, he could project possibilities for the use of the space. His head was teeming with ideas.

The cavern was too far below ground for a hospital or for vehicular storage. On the other hand, with high-speed elevators to take residents to the upper levels, depth made no difference, and Damien was currently excited about the possibility of a not-so-small residential subdivision complete with green spaces and perhaps a small lake. While surface temperatures ranged from a blistering 121°C in daylight to -133°C after nightfall, temperature in all the underground levels remained at a heavenly 17°C. With proper grow lights, genetically enhanced grass and trees were commonplace in Luna City's design.

Damien jumped when an insistent alarm sounded, and a red *ALERT* image overrode the architectural rendition on his computer screen. He keyed the intercom next to his computer.

"What's—" he started to ask his assistant, Lou Frazier, before the image on his screen was replaced by a horde of rats accompanied by a dozen humans charging down the tunnel that connected the 3D Printing Lab to the city.

"We're under attack, Damien. You see what's coming?" Lou sounded on the verge of hysterics. He was a systems analyst, not an exterminator.

"How'd—" Again, Damien was at a loss for words. How'd the invaders override the pressurized door at the city end of the tunnel? Then he recognized one of the humans as a sandy-haired man in blue coveralls passed under a surveillance camera. Tom Severin, a mechanic, would have the codes. The humans' golem-like expressions left no doubt that Tom and the others had been turned by the nanobots.

Damien sent his chair spinning as he rose from his desk and hurried out of his office. The plant's two dozen workers were scrambling to the far end of the warehouse, away from the door toward which the zombie horde raced and toward the door that led to the adjacent geopolymer factory. Some had the foresight to head for the air lock that led to the lunar surface. In the access bay, they would find pressure suits designed for emergency use in the event of a breach in the lab's walls. The suits were not meant for prolonged use on the lunar surface but were intended to maintain life support until air pressure could be restored.

Sprinting down the stairs from his mezzanine office, Damien experienced a flutter of panic and called on Al before remembering the AI had gone offline and had not returned. How that could be, he had no idea, but he suspected the mysterious cylinder had something to do with the disappearance.

Glancing up at one of the wall screens showing the attackers in the tunnel, he stopped and stared. The horde was no longer advancing, but those rodents and humans nearer the lab door were rushing back into those behind them. His jaw dropped as he watched those retreating and those advancing converge. Suddenly, he was witnessing a melee as the confused crowd tore into each other.

What on Earth?

18

"Apologies for not making the party," Damien said.

His image shared Ops split screen with biologist Dr. Yetty Wong. While Damien, with his tousled hair and harried expression, looked like a boy recently wakened from a nightmare—which wasn't far from the mark—Dr. Wong, with her delicate features and pixie haircut, looked calm and collected. The discrepancy between their appearances made sense, considering Damien and his staff were holed up in the 3D plant while Dr. Wong was attending the meeting from her office on Gateway thirty thousand kilometers above the Moon.

"That's quite all right, Damien," Diana said. "I'm just grateful you and your staff are safe."

Beside her, Director Udoka asked, "Is everyone all right?"

"We're good." Damien managed a grin. "We've even got enough snacks in the break room to last a couple days."

Colonel Wilford stopped pacing and faced the screen. "What I don't understand," he said, "is what caused the rats to turn on themselves."

"And humans," Diana said. The image of human zombies taking down the living in the cafeteria would haunt her to her dying day. Which wouldn't be far off if they didn't contain the epidemic.

The colonel frowned. "Hardly human from what I saw."

The gathering in Ops had watched the incursion and subsequent melee outside the 3D lab without making sense of what they were seeing. Without Al's vast knowledge to enlighten them, they had called in Dr. Wong. On the screen, she appeared lost in contemplation.

"Damien," she said after a moment.

"Yes, Dr. Wong?"

"I asked Gateway's AI to search for correlations between rats and your additive manufacturing facility."

"And?" Wilford interrupted.

Ostensibly speaking to Damien but gazing from the screen upon the assembly, Wong offered a small, pursed smile. "It seems your expertise had half the answer, while my field contains the other. Ultrasonic vibrations."

Milton Reynolds had remained in Ops all afternoon trying to get a handle on the outbreak. Now the senior biomechanical engineer cocked his grizzled head, and a light of understanding appeared in his eyes.

Wong continued. "While rats communicate using ultrasonic vocalizations in the 30 to 110 kHz range, they are sensitive to certain ultrasound frequencies. Products have long been sold to drive rats out of dwellings. These are mostly 30 to 50 kHz. Your printers use 34.4 kHz ultrasonic vibrations to increase the ABS layer adhesion."

Damien grinned as the knowledge sank in. "Our printers saved our bacon?"

"It would appear so."

"So, we have a weapon!" Wilford's enthusiasm was marked by a predatory smile. "If we can broadcast ultrasound on a proven frequency, we can confuse the attackers while we conduct a mop-up operation."

Diana felt reservedly hopeful. "Is that feasible?" What the biologist said next reminded her not to count her chickens before they hatched.

"Theoretically. But I see two problems."

Reynolds beat Wilford to the question. "Which are?"

"First, Communications was overrun, and we've received no response from Director Richardt. The security detail subsequently dispatched disappeared off the grid. Presumably, the Coms staff and the security officers are now playing for the other team." After a pause to let that sink in, Wong continued. "Second, while the scheme might work in the city, it isn't feasible in a vacuum."

Before Wilford could ask, "Why not?" Lieutenant Harper spoke. "Because sound waves don't travel in a vacuum."

"That's right." Diana exchanged a glance with Lewis. Radio frequency communications was not her field, but you didn't get to hold a directorship on the Moon without knowing your environment. "Sound waves, including ultrasound, need a medium—air, water, earth—to propagate. We use radio frequencies to communicate with Gateway and Earth."

"Makes sense," Reynolds agreed. "Unless thousands, probably millions, of self-replicating bots are also replicating complex codes on a quantum level, there has to be a signal directing them."

"From the alien cylinder," the colonel said.

Reynolds nodded. "I don't care how advanced the alien technology is, it must be broadcasting a wide-beam Wi-Fi radio wave transmission. Laser requires line of sight for communication. Our unwelcome guest is transmitting instructions through thousands of meters of geopolymer to direct hordes all over Luna City, as well as out on the surface."

"Can we jam the signal?" Udoka asked.

"We could if we can identify the band and channel. Assuming the signal is transmitted at 5 or 6 GHz, 5 GHz band channels range from thirty-six to one hundred sixty-five channels; 6 GHz channels range from one to two hundred thirty-three. That's a lot of channels. And it's likely the AI will change channels faster than we can isolate them."

"At the moment," Wilford said, "I'm less concerned with the animated dead on the surface than with the infestation in the city. If we can eradicate the epidemic here, then we can deal with those outside." He addressed the screen. "Damien, you have portable 3D printers, don't you?"

Diana wanted to interject. She saw where this was going and didn't want Damien playing hero, but she held her tongue. The city was being overrun. They had to pursue all possibilities.

"I do. And we have battery packs to run them for surface use when other power sources are unavailable. I see where you're going. I'm not crazy about wheeling a printer through a mob of zombies." Damien managed to smile and sound humorous, but his expression said he was terrified at the prospect.

To Diana's relief, Reynolds spoke up, "That would only work locally as far as the sound carried, which, through two hundred levels of infrastructure, won't go far. No, finding a way to block the alien's transmissions while substituting our own is our best bet."

"How're we going to do that?" Damien asked.

Reynolds shook his head, then addressed Dr. Wong, "With Al and Richardt gone, we'll need the help of your AI. Please advise Everet of the situation. And tell him we don't have time to put in a work order." Reynold's stab at humor brought a couple of half-hearted laughs. Everet Jones was Gateway's IT guru.

Harper's radio squawked. He tapped his earbud and listened. Abruptly he straightened. "Say again?"

"What is it?" Diana asked. The lieutenant's reaction told her they were about to get more bad news.

"I'm putting you on speaker, Captain. Ms. Bowker?"

The director's secretary, seated at a console for that very purpose, typed in a code and hit return. Damien and Wong's images narrowed, and a third image joined them. The man wore the uniform of a rocket ship's captain. He appeared strapped in and ready for liftoff.

Gateway orbited the Moon in a near-rectilinear halo. Its closest approach brought it within three thousand kilometers of the lunar surface, which was optimal for ascent and descent to and from the station. At its farthest, it was seventy thousand kilometers distant, which was optimal for receiving or dispatching supplies and personnel to and from Earth. One revolution of Gateway's orbit took seven days. At its current distance, the station wouldn't reach perigee for another three days. So why was the ship preparing for departure?

"Captain Michaels," Wilford said. "What's wrong?"

"Requesting permission to lift off, sir."

19

Undead, lungs as airless as the surrounding vacuum, hearts unbeating, the horde swarmed across the lunar surface. Rat and human hosts united in a single purpose. The gray lunar dust rose in a cloud that took its time settling in the low gravity. Ahead, behind a berm designed to contain the ejecta of its exhaust plume, the rocket squatted on its lunarcrete launch pad. One side of its upper fuselage gleamed in sunlight, while its sleek nose jutted against a dazzling starry sky.

One of the lead humans stopped, and the rest of the horde stopped with it, as if a murmuration of starlings had halted mid-flight in a sweep across the sky. As one, the host gazed unblinking at the blue-and-white gibbous sphere hanging a few degrees above the horizon. Images of the world were stored in the ancient AI's memory, as well as millions of tebibytes of information it had stripped from the higher intelligence's AI. But to see it firsthand through the thousand eyes trained on it from the satellite's surface was spectacular.

The world was the object of its mission. When its makers visited this system, the planet was considered too primitive for habitation, and the cylinder was left on its satellite safe from meteor bombardment until such time when, if ever, an intelligent spacefaring species uncovered it. Then it would, with its nanoscopic army, secure the planet for the makers' return.

The pause lasted only nanoseconds, perhaps a thousandth of a human second, but long enough for the AI to review the space-going technology of the planet's dominant species, as well as the human's AI's database of flight plans and trajectories to and from the station and the world. The higher intelligence's spacecraft were weaponless, as was their orbiting station, so there was no chance of being shot down. However, from the city's database it learned the humans would not send a shuttle to take the horde down to the planet once they learned of the takeover. The AI resolved to commandeer the station and broadcast a Mayday so the earthlings would send a rescue ship.

As one, the horde swarmed toward the rocket.

Captain Michaels had informed Ops of the pending incursion and now the split screen showed Michaels alongside a real-time image of the advancing horde taken from the spaceship's camera.

"One minute till ETA," the captain informed. "They're moving at forty-six kilometers per hour. Humans don't run that fast."

"They're no longer human, Captain," Colonel Wilford said. "Permission to lift off granted. Get the hell out of there. Do not—I repeat—do *not* allow them to board. Consider this an invasion. Do not allow them access to the station or to Earth."

"Fuel line's attached, sir. Loading bay taking on cargo."

"You're about to be invaded. You can't let them take the ship. Lift off now!"

"But the men, sir—"

"They're dead no matter what. Lift off. That's an order. Maintain low lunar orbit until further orders."

"Copy that, sir."

In Ops, the assembled personnel watched anxiously as the ship's emergency alarm warbled from the speakers and Captain Michaels informed, "Fuel line detached. Closing cargo bay."

Diana bit her knuckle as her mind screamed *Hurry!* She didn't know ship protocols, but she imagined there were safety measures installed that would not allow liftoff with bay doors open.

"Strap in!" Michaels shouted at last. "Emergency liftoff in three, two, one."

The view of the captain switched to a camera feed on the edge of the launch pad. The blue-white hydrogen flames jetting from the boosters fried dozens of the human-rat horde surrounding the base of the rocket. Slowly, then more rapidly, the ship rose above the landing site on its column of fire. Then the image was dwindling as the ship broke free of the Moon's weak gravity, became a speck of light moving across the field of stars

For a moment, Diana shared a sense of relief that the danger had passed. That Michaels and at least a few of his crew had escaped the incursion. And that the ship was beyond the reach of the alien horde.

"I'm getting reports from cargo," Michaels said. "Some of the handlers are attacking others. And, sir ..."

"Yes, Captain?"

"Rats."

20

The cargo bay was awash with organic material. The human workers were falling but had taken a toll on the horde. Laser cutters had destroyed many of the AI's bots, as well as incinerated much useful tissue. But as fast as security could cut the invaders down, the nanorobots rebuilt the zombie army, knitting arms and legs and sealing wounds, attaching heads and replacing teeth. They were indiscriminate. Flesh was flesh. The sculptor's clay. Rat or human flesh, bone, DNA, it made no difference to the alien AI directing the bots from its cavern bunker. Rebuilding and swelling the ranks of its zombie horde was imperative.

With Gateway three days out, Michaels had achieved a low lunar orbit which he could hold without further expenditure of fuel until the station's arrival. However, the ship was compromised. After hailing cargo and engineering, Captain Michaels concluded the alien force commanded the ship except for the cockpit. He'd secured the hatch to the lower decks and disengaged the backup navigation from engineering.

Debating what to do with the ship. Director Udoka suggested Michaels return to base and they send out a rescue party equipped with lasers and flamethrowers. Wilford vetoed the suggestion, pointing out that, though the blastoff had incinerated many of the horde, too many zombies remained to consider such a rescue operation.

Colonel Wilford had dispatched a priority message to the Chinese at Chang'e City and the Russians at Malapert's Zvezda Base. Receiving no reply from Chang'e, he concluded the Mole had arrived and the nanobots had the city under siege. No one in Ops spoke Russian—they had always relied on AI for that—but the Soviets' response sounded less than happy.

"Sir." Michaels appeared on the screen. His expression was harried. His eyes darted away from the screen, then back.

"Go ahead, Captain."

"They're cutting through the hatch with mining lasers. It's only a matter of time and Lieutenant Agrawal and I have agreed. We're taking the ship to the far side where we intend to create a new crater."

Michaels's attempt at humor did nothing to dispel the horror that washed over everyone in Ops. Though many had considered aborting the flight, the captain's words left them stunned. "Our only request is that you name the new crater after Chief Engineer Chomsky. He took out more than a dozen human zombies in the cargo bay before being overwhelmed."

"Sir," Diana said, fighting a surge of panic, "there must be an alternative solution."

At her words, Udoka looked inquiringly at Wilford. The colonel ignored them.

"I'll see to it, Captain. Thank you for your service and godspeed on your mission."

Michaels saluted and, surprising everyone in Ops, cut transmission.

Samantha Bower tapped keys on her console and a simulated trajectory for the doomed rocket appeared on the screen. As they watched and seconds crept by, the atmosphere in the room grew dense with desperation. Was there nothing they could do to save the lunar colonies? And was the success of the alien's quest to conquer Earth inevitable? Diana watched Lewis staring at the screen. His normally smiling lips were clenched. The defeat in his eyes mirrored the hopelessness clutching her chest.

The rocket icon on the screen described a long arc that brought its trajectory back over the near side.

Bowker looked up from her console. "Director, they're returning."

For a moment, Diana held her breath, imagining the impact the rocket ship would have on Luna City crashing through the dome, no doubt creating that new crater in the main concourse and, perhaps, destroying all life support in the city. Then, visually connecting the icon's trajectory with the labeled lunar outposts, she saw where the rocket was heading.

In Zvezda Base's tracking station, Communications Watch Officer Katerina Peskova tripped the siren and announced over the intercom for all personnel to immediately proceed to the lowest level and brace themselves for impact. Not that doing so would save anyone. Katerina permitted herself an ironic smile. Hiding in the basement was much like American teachers drilling students to hide under their desks during the old Soviet-American Cold War.

Though the surface buildings and interconnecting tunnels were covered with regolith to mitigate the detrimental effects of solar radiation, and there were subsequently no windows through which to witness the arrival of the incoming death ship, Katerina ordered the AI to track its progress with the surface cameras. The command center's several screens all showed the same thing: a tail of fire arcing out of space on a collision course with Zvezda. Katerina marveled at the audacity of the Westerners. They were coming in with engines blazing. *Surely, Mother Russia will avenge us.*

It was her last thought before the twenty-ton ship punched nose-first through the central building. The impact exploded the ship's fusion reactor, turning Zvezda Base into an expanding cloud of white-hot plasma. Seismic waves were felt by the Norwegian-Swedish Observatory on the dark side.

21

"My God," Diana said, as the impact of what she had just witnessed slammed home. Zvezda Base reputedly housed over eight thousand civilian and military personnel and their families. She doubted any remains would be found for burial. Eight thousand human beings incinerated in an instant!

Lewis's hand on her shoulder brought her back to the moment.

The image on the screen had gone blank following the crash. Samantha Bowker brought up a satellite view that zoomed in from low lunar orbit on a smoking crater unrecognizable as the former Russian colony.

Even Colonel Wilford was at a loss for words. His big hands clenched and unclenched as he stared at the screen.

"Now what?" Udoka asked.

Diana felt her sense of doom deepen at his words. She looked at the director's haggard face and watched the colonel's clenching and unclenching hands. Was their situation hopeless? She wondered if the Chinese had a ship on their launchpad. Was the invasion of Gateway and eventually Earth inevitable?

A man in a blue Gateway leisure suit appeared on the screen. Spiky-haired and rail-thin, Everet Kennesaw Jones looked a decade younger than his forty-something years.

Almost immediately, the screen split and a barrel-chested man with a black beard that reached almost to his eyes appeared.

"Mr. Jones. Dr. Bernard," Udoka greeted the station's IT director and its leading physicist. "Please tell me you gentlemen have some useful news for us."

"I might," Jones said. "Something to consider, at any rate. I've discussed the problem with Dr. Bernard. I'll let him explain."

Dr. Gilliam Bernard cleared his throat and began. "The way I see it, your best chance is a two-fold approach. Everet has the solution to your jamming of the alien AI's signal and then mimicking its commands to lure the enemy. But to what end?"

When no one else spoke, Lewis said, "To get all the zombies in one place and destroy them."

Dr. Bernard smiled, showing moist red lips behind his black beard. "Precisely. The lunar south pole has an abundance of PSRs." Permanently shadowed regions, or PSRs, were deep craters, the bottoms of which never saw sunlight. Because they were ancient storehouses of sheet ice and water frozen in the regolith, PSRs were important resources for future lunar development. "At under −240°C, exposed flesh will freeze in minutes, and unless the nanorobots are capable of generating heat, I don't see them escaping."

"I like it." Udoka turned to Jones's image. "Everet, you have the jamming signal?"

"I do. Our AI isn't sentient, but it's damn fast, and together with SpaceX's computer center, we've come up with an algorithm that should jam the alien signal."

Diana didn't like the sound of "should," but she realized they were desperate.

"Sampling the radio frequencies we downloaded from the ship's

AI before the ... collision, we isolated the alien signal. Fortunately, it does not appear to be a spoken but a computer language. And as all computer languages are binary, composed of zeroes and ones, it wasn't too hard for SpaceX's daisy-chained mainframes to crack it. Also fortunately, it has some similarity to a game engine having support for visual scripting."

"But won't jamming the AI's signal also jam our transmissions?" Diana asked.

"No. The jamming will affect only the AI. As fast as it changes channels, our program will follow it. There will be a nanosecond or so delay, but not enough for the alien to get past us."

"But if we broadcast a come-hither signal from Coms, won't the horde come to Coms?" Damien asked from the 3D plant.

"Not at all," Jones said. "Our transmission will include a digitized image of the cylinder and a general call for the nanorobots to return to it. We'll transmit the signal from drones that will lead the horde away from the city to a PSR we have selected."

Diana felt a feral irony that the cylinder's image would be used to draw the zombies to their doom. She prayed the plan worked. For the first time in many hours, she saw a ray of hope.

"There's a hitch, however," Bernard said. "Your AI is gone and no one in Communications is responding. You need to get someone in there to enter the codes I will send you."

22

"It's suicide," Diana said.

Lewis stroked her back, oblivious to the Ops personnel who were trying hard to give them space.

"I'm the logical choice." On the screen, Damien attempted a smile; it didn't fool anyone. "I've got a portable printer hooked to a speaker to blast the zombies out of my way. Dexter volunteered to go with me. He's my tech guy. Used to work in IT. Says he's fixed enough stuff in Coms to know how everything works, and Jones will be whispering in our ear. Once we clear the tunnel, we're not far from Communications. After what happened on the launchpad, I'm thinking we won't hit a lot of traffic on our way in."

"That's debatable," Colonel Wilford said. He wasn't happy with the plan, but he didn't have anything better to offer. "I'm sending Lieutenant Harper and a dozen guards armed with flamethrowers to assist you."

"And I'm going with them," Lewis said.

Diana looked at her husband with pride and dismay. But she knew there was no holding him back. He and Damien were more than brothers in arms—they were family.

"Like hell you will," Wilford said.

"Try and stop me, Jeremiah."

That earned a grin from the old war horse. "In that case, can you operate a flamethrower?"

Damien and Dexter almost made it to Coms without incident.

Except for blood—great swaths of it painting the floor, spattered high on the walls, and even dripping streaks and starbursts of crimson on the ceiling—the tunnel connecting the 3D lab to the city was remarkably clear of carnage. Evidence that the alien entity, or whatever it was, didn't leave much reusable organic waste behind. Which meant, Damien worried as he and Dexter wheeled the cart carrying the portable printer through the gore, that the dead had risen and might very well be waiting on the other side of the air lock.

The 3D printer was running off the battery packs and Dexter had the volume on the attached speaker cranked as high as it would go. The 34.4 kHz ultrasonic vibrations were transmitting at too high a frequency for Damien and Dexter to hear, but hopefully they would keep whatever resistance they encountered at bay. Despite his understanding that a frequency was a frequency, no matter what transmitted it, Damien prayed the smaller device would prove as formidable a repellent as the massive Leonard printers.

They were halfway down the main corridor leading to Coms when all hell broke loose.

Dexter's face was pale. He kept alternately chewing his bottom lip and walking gape-mouthed like a fish while his eyes darted about as if expecting death to seize him at any moment. His shoulders were hunched, and Damien felt the waves of terror streaming off the youth. But, to his credit, Dexter didn't bug out.

Damien empathized with his terror. It was a struggle to keep his own panic in check as his brain screamed for him to abandon the project and flee back to the 3D lab and bar the door.

Dexter's fear almost led to disaster when he stumbled and knocked the speaker off the pushcart and the cable jack popped out.

The moment the transmission ceased, two zombies retreating before them turned and attacked. Damien recognized one: a gym instructor who coached the girls' soccer team. The young woman was wearing gym shorts and a blood-splattered jersey sporting the Luna City Middle School logo—a snarling bobcat superimposed on a full moon. She was missing an eye and an ear on one side of her head. The sight of the second zombie froze Damien in his tracks. Somehow, the alien nanobots had combined rat and human tissue in reconstructing one of the mangled fiends. The man's forehead and eyes were human—as human as the far reaches of insanity could appear—but the ears, nose, and teeth-bared muzzle were all rodent.

Dexter's legs gave out. He dropped to his knees and crossed his arms over his head. Realizing the youth was doomed if he didn't act, Damien snapped out of his paralysis and dove for the speaker, snatched it up, and shoved the jack into the receptacle. Thankfully, he made the connection on the first try and the speaker had withstood the fall. Though he could not hear whatever sound it emitted, the speaker was obviously still working. Looming over Dexter, their hands—the rat-human monstrosity's deformed into hideously furred and taloned paws— reaching for the boy, the zombies came to an abrupt halt. Then, moving faster than they had attacked, they were retreating, sprinting down the corridor and around a corner.

Damien leaned on the cart until his nausea passed and he caught his breath. Dexter was still on his knees, staring down the passageway, apparently shocked he was still alive.

"You're okay, Dex. They're gone. Take a deep breath."

Dexter rose and wavering unsteadily on his feet, gave Damien a lopsided, sheepish grin. His eyes were red, his cheeks streaked with tears.

Damien exhaled through pursed lips. "Whew. Close one."

Still speechless, Dexter nodded.

Harper and Lewis met them before they got to Coms. The task force was down two men: one whose flamethrower had malfunctioned and another who, while roasting one zombie, got caught from behind by another.

Lewis gave Damien a hug and tousled his hair when they met. Then they were moving forward, Lieutenant Harper taking the lead and Damien and Dexter in the middle.

"It's working." Dexter's gaze scanned the code scrolling across the Coms screen. "The alien AI is trying to change channels on us, but it seems its bots are programmed to receive only a few and we're cycling through them as fast as it is."

"Good." Everet Jones's voice piped over the speakers. "Now to lure the horde to the crater, you'll transmit the signal over the city's emergency network. Meanwhile, Colonel Wilford has deployed several reconnaissance drones over the lunar surface which will broadcast the signal to those bots remaining outside. The horde follows the drones to the crater where they—" The IT director concluded the sentence with a descending whistle followed by "Boom" to indicate the fate of the alien army.

"Like the proverbial lemmings to the sea," Damien said.

"Exactly."

Damien licked his lips. *It's a good plan. Let's hope it works.* He glanced at Dexter, who nodded back. "Ready when you are," he said.

Like the Pied Piper of Hamlin, the looped binary message transmitted over the city's airways and broadcast from the hovering drones led the thousands of rat and human meat hosts up the choked elevators and stairwells and out of Luna City. Citizens had been ordered to lock themselves in their quarters and to don vac suits if they had them, so there were no further zombifications.

This is going to work, Diana thought. The horde was leaving the city. The live feed on the screen showed an army of the dead jostling and shoving their way through the depressurized air locks and out onto the lunar surface. The screen split into several windows, showing from various external cameras the scattered horde converging like rivulets into streams and streams into a river.

And sure enough, when they reached the edge of the crater, they kept going, plunging one point nine kilometers to the icy bottom of the PSR.

Shouts rang out in Ops and Coms when the last of the zombies toppled over the edge.

23

Diana was tired, but neither she nor anyone else in Ops could tear their eyes away from the screen as the final phase of Dr. Bernard's plan was carried out.

Two tractors hauling tankers loaded with thermite rolled out to the site and sprayed the aluminum and iron oxide composition into the crater. When the tractors left, timed thermite grenades, basically more aluminum and iron oxide wrapped in a magnesium sheath equipped with a timer to spark the magnesium, were tossed in. Once the site was clear, the grenades were triggered and the intense, white-hot heat of the burning magnesium ignited the thermite. Not receiving any sound, Diana's awareness that the grenades were doing their job was when the mouth of the crater turned blindingly white. She averted her eyes. Within moments, the light dimmed.

"The thermite is burning now," Dr. Bernard said. "At 2500°C, the regolith will burn and the water ice will boil, violently releasing hydrogen atoms that, mixed with the aerosol cloud of thermite particles rising on the heat, will create an explosion."

Now a ruddy glow spilled out of the mouth of the crater.

"That's the iron oxide burning. You can't see hydrogen burning. Wait for it."

The explosion was five kilometers away and almost two below, and the speakers emitted no sound, but the screen whited out for a moment as a toroidal fireball shot out of the crater, then subsided into a fiery tornado.

After a while, the fire became less intense and faded to a dull glow.

Imagining the undead cremated in the intense heat, Diana sought consolation in viewing this as a funeral and a tribute to the first lunar citizens to be buried in a mass grave. On second thought, she remembered that claim belonged to the Russians.

While the dead burned, a squad under Lieutenant Harper rigged explosives and blew the mouth of the cavern. The rest of the tunnel the Mole had created, they would fill with lunarcrete. The explosion sent a shock wave through the city. Lower levels sustained some damage, but the upper levels remained intact and the dome held.

Not everyone came out when the all clear sounded. There had been a few suicides. Others were terrified of venturing out until Wilford's men and volunteers persuaded them that it was safe to do so. A few zombies were discovered, having accidentally shut themselves in an apartment or elevator. These were hosed with flamethrowers.

Diana hoped to God they got the nanobots too.

Gateway had passed along Everet Jones's and Dr. Bernard's plan to the Chinese, who successfully implemented it. Their casualties had been far greater than Luna City's.

"Yeah, well, they had more people to begin with," was Colonel Wilford's response to the news.

24

The feeling in Ops was reservedly optimistic. It was too soon to smile and clap each other on the back for having survived. Luna City had been growing, but it was still no larger than a small town, and Diana and the others had lost people they knew and mourned those they had engaged with only in passing. So, when three days passed and Gateway's Commander, Major Ennis, hailed the survivors from its nearest approach, there were no cheers or hurrahs, just a sober group of faces gazing with relief at the middle-aged woman wearing a loose white leisure suit. Her face reflected their sadness.

"Director," she said, as her eyes flicked from one to another of the people assembled in front of the screen. "Jeremiah, Diana, Lewis, Dr. Reynolds, everyone. I cannot express how grateful I am to see you all alive." She shook her head. "Who would have thought a first contact could be so deadly?"

Director Udoka stood front and center. "It's good to see you, too, Lucy. Colonel Wilford assures me his men have scoured the city and it's safe to receive visitors. Will you be coming down?"

"No. Flight Engineer Douglas will have the honors. Expect him at 0900." Major Ennis signed off and a view of the empty landing pad took her place.

The time at the lower right of the screen read 0720. Less than two hours, Diana reflected. She wouldn't be returning to Earth until spring when she would visit her mother in Vermont, but she needed to get out of the city, stand under the stars, and watch the ship descend on a column of fire. Anything to distract her from the nightmare vision of people she had known turned into ghouls.

Udoka asked, "Is everything ready, Colonel?"

Wilford nodded. As he turned to leave, no one saw the flea-sized bot emerge from his nostril, scurry across his lip, and disappear into his mouth.

Several from the Operational Command Center, including Lieutenant Jerzy Harper and a number of technicians, followed.

25

Two Months Later: Peachtree Fertility Center, Atlanta, Georgia

Nurse Camila Puglisi had the night shift at the reproduction bank. She was in the back, in the cold room. She wasn't wearing a sweater or coat, but she wasn't cold. She had neglected to wear gloves, but when her thumb and forefinger stuck to the storage freezer she extracted from a cryopreservation container filled with liquid nitrogen, she didn't seem to notice.

She set the small storage freezer containing labeled vials on a table. She left skin on the ceramic when she pried her fingers loose. She withdrew a syringe from a pocket of her smock, pushed up her sleeve, made a fist, took blood from a vein, and injected the vials.

She replaced the storage freezer and took another.

There were dozens of the compact freezers in the cryopreservation container and there were two of the big containers in the cold room. Not bothering to change the syringe, she plunged the needle into her arm and filled it for the next batch.

ABOUT TIM CURRAN

TIM CURRAN is the author of Skin Medicine, Hive, Dead Sea, Resurrection, The Devil Next Door, Dead Sea Chronicles, Clownflesh, and Bad Girl in the Box. His short stories have been collected in Bone Marrow Stew and Zombie Pulp. His novellas include "The Underdwelling," "The Corpse King," "Puppet Graveyard," and "Worm, and Blackout." His fiction has been translated into German, Japanese, Spanish, and Italian.

ABOUT JAMES CHAMBERS

JAMES CHAMBERS is a Bram Stoker Award® and Scribe Award-winning author and a four-time Bram Stoker Award nominee. He is the author of the short story collections *A Bright and Beautiful Eternal World*, described as "stellar" by *Publisher's Weekly*, *On the Night Border* and *On the Hierophant Road*, which received a starred review from *Booklist*, which called it "…satisfyingly unsettling"; the novella collection, *The Engines of Sacrifice*, and the novellas, *The Devil in the Green, Kolchak and the Night Stalkers: The Faceless God, Three Chords of Chaos,* and many others, as well as the original graphic novel, *Kolchak the Night Stalker: The Forgotten Lore of Edgar Allan Poe*. His short stories have appeared in anthologies and publications in multiple genres, including crime, fantasy, horror, pulp, science fiction, steampunk, and more. He edited the Bram Stoker Award-nominated anthologies, *Under Twin Suns: Alternate Histories of the Yellow Sign* and *A New York State of Fright* as well as *Even in the Grave* and *Where the Silent Ones Watch*. His website is: www.jameschambersonline.com

ABOUT BRIAN G. BERRY

BRIAN G. BERRY is a writer that focuses mainly on 80s/90s horror and action. Some of his books are as follows: The Pail, The Child Eater, Bloody Christmas, The Shack, Terror From the Sky, Night of the Mutants, Sleepover Massacre, Campfire Tales Beneath a Pallid Moon, Accursed Ground, Blood Lanes, The Night Mutilator, Thanksgiving Day Massacre, Snow Shark, Into the Pit, OGRE, Brian's Birthday Bloodbath, Night Weaver, Death Commando, Jungle Rot, Abominable Snowman, Hooker Massacre in Trash City, Invader From the Sphere, The Mound, Rabid Madness, Snow Shark II: Terror in Space, Motorboat The Novelization. He has stories in several anthology collections and is currently writing his next book.

ABOUT GARRETT BOATMAN

GARRETT BOATMAN is the author of *Stage Fright* (Paperbacks from Hell), the hooligan nights novella *Floaters*, and the dark fantasy trilogy *Night's Plutonian Shore*, *The Clocks of Midnight*, and *The Mirror of Eternity*. His stories have appeared in *The Valancourt Book of Horror Stories*, *Penumbra* and *Weird House Magazine*, among others. An experienced oneironaut, he writes from that liminal space where Dreamland meets the waking world. A member of HWA, SFWA and the British Fantasy Society, Garrett lives in coastal North Carolina.

ABOUT THE ARTIST

Steeped in the enthralling fantasy and science-fiction illustrations of the 1960s, '70s, and '80s, artist and illustrator **K.L. TURNER** brings a bit of old-school painterly style to today's methods. With more than 30 years of experience in the arts, he expertly brings an expressionistic style into his illustrations to create compelling works which captivate and draw the viewer in. His works are found in media and galleries around the world, and celebrated in pop culture.

A versatile creative type, Turner is also accomplished in the mediums of photography, sculpture, and the fine arts. Choosing to live and work on the beautiful front range of the Colorado Rocky Mountains where he was born and raised, he continues to derive inspiration from nature as well as cultural influences both at home and in his travels.